NAGUIB MAHFOUZ

THEBES AT WAR

———

Naguib Mahfouz is the most prominent author
of Arabic fiction today. He was born in 1911
in Cairo and began writing at the age of seven-
teen. His first novel was published in 1939.
Since then he has written nearly forty novel-
length works and hundreds of short stories. In
1988 Mr. Mahfouz was awarded the Nobel
Prize in Literature. He lives in the Cairo suburb
of Agouza with his wife and two daughters.

Humphrey Davies (translator) took first class
honors in Arabic at Cambridge University and
holds a doctorate in Near East Studies from the
University of California at Berkeley. His trans-
lations from Egyptian literature range from the
Ottoman period to the present day.

THE FOLLOWING TITLES BY NAGUIB MAHFOUZ
ARE ALSO PUBLISHED BY ANCHOR BOOKS

*The Beggar**
*The Thief and the Dogs**
*Autumn Quail**
The Beginning and the End
Wedding Song†
Respected Sir†
The Time and the Place and Other Stories
The Search†
Midaq Alley
The Journey of Ibn Fattouma
Miramar
Adrift on the Nile
The Harafish
Arabian Nights and Days
Children of the Alley
Echoes of an Autobiography
The Day the Leader Was Killed
Akhenaten, Dweller in Truth
Voices from the Other World
Rhadopis of Nubia
Khufu's Wisdom

The Cairo Trilogy:
Palace Walk
Palace of Desire
Sugar Street

*†published as omnibus editions

THEBES AT WAR

A Novel of Ancient Egypt

THEBES AT WAR

A Novel of Ancient Egypt

———

NAGUIB MAHFOUZ

Translated from the Arabic by
Humphrey Davies

ANCHOR BOOKS
A DIVISION OF RANDOM HOUSE, INC.
NEW YORK

FIRST ANCHOR BOOKS EDITION, OCTOBER 2005

Map courtesy of OasisPhoto.com

The Cataloging-in-Publication Data is on file at the Library of Congress.

ISBN-10: 1-4000-7669-2
ISBN-13: 978-1-4000-7669-7

www.anchorbooks.com

Printed in the United States of America
10 9 8 7 6 5 4 3 2 1

Translator's Introduction

Thebes at War is one of a small number of works by Naguib Mahfouz set in ancient Egypt that have remained little known to readers in the West. Mahfouz's interest in the period during his early years as a writer was, however, intense: his first published work, appearing around 1932, was a translation from English of a young reader's guide to ancient Egypt, while his first three published novels, of which *Thebes at War* is the last, all had pharaonic themes. The first of these, *Khufu's Wisdom* (originally entitled *Hikmat Khufu* but published under the title *'Abath al-Aqdar*, "The Mockery of the Fates") was written between 1935 and 1936 and published in 1939, the second, *Rhadopis of Nubia* (in Arabic, *Radubis*) was written between 1936 and 1937, while *Thebes at War* (*Kifah Tiba*, "Thebes' Struggle") was written between 1937 and 1938.[1] Between the mid-1930s and the mid-1940s, Mahfouz also wrote five short stories set in the pharaonic period.[2]

Though Mahfouz, on completing *Thebes at War*, abandoned his original plan to cover the whole of ancient Egyptian history in a series of forty novels and switched to writing novels with modern settings, these early works, and particularly *Thebes at War*, played an important role in the growth of his recognition as a writer. In 1940, *Rhadopis of Nubia* shared the first prize in a literary contest. Encouraged by this success, Mahfouz entered *Thebes at War* in a competition organized by the Ministry of Education the following year, where it again shared the first prize (with two other novels), leading to the foundation by an admirer of a publishing venture intended, initially, to publicize the works of the young prizewinners. Thus it was that *Rhadopis of Nubia* saw the light of day in 1943, while *Thebes at War* appeared in 1944. A laudatory review of the latter by the young Sayyid Qutb that appeared in the same year launched Mahfouz's reputation among the broader Egyptian reading public. Qutb, who was later to lead the Muslim Brotherhood and was executed by Nasser in 1966 but who at that stage of his life was best known as a literary critic, hailed *Thebes at War* as filling the need for "historical works that can teach young people true love for their country."[3]

Thebes at War treats of what Mahfouz considers "the greatest moment in all of ancient Egypt's three thousand years,"[4] namely, that at which the last pharaohs of the native Seventeenth Dynasty rose up against the domination of the Hyksos, Asiatic foreigners who had dominated northern Egypt from roughly 1640 to 1532 BC (there is debate over whether the Hyksos were an entire people or merely a line of foreign rulers; Mahfouz treats them as the former). This novel is more solidly grounded in historical fact than the two that preceded it, and the novelist bases most of his main characters on real people. Seqenenra, Kamose, and Ahmose, the three pharaohs who succeed one another in *Thebes at War* were, respectively, the two last pharaohs of the Seventeenth Dynasty and the first of the Eighteenth (although recent scholarship would make Ahmose the brother, rather than the son, of Kamose); Tetisheri, the "Sacred Mother" of Seqenenra and, symbolically, of the Egyptian people, existed and was "venerated by later generations as a powerful influence on the fortunes of the dynasty and of the country";[5] Apophis, their foe, was the last king of the Hyksos, and the remains of his citadel of Avaris may be seen at Tell al-Dab'a in the eastern Delta; and Ahmose Ebana, commander of King Ahmose's fleet, takes his name from an Egyptian officer whose autobiography, carved on a pillar of his tomb, is "the only contemporary account extant of the final defeat of the

Hyksos."[6] Seqenenra's mutilated corpse, which may be seen today at the Egyptian Museum in Cairo, is credited with having inspired Mahfouz to write the novel.[7] Similarly, historical events, such as the letter sent by Apophis to Seqenenra that precipitates the outbreak of war, are incorporated into the narrative. Even the green heart pendant that plays a vital role in the romantic sub-plot of *Thebes at War* may well be the "green-stone heart scarab set in gold and inscribed ... for Sobekemsaf [a successor to Ahmose] [that] is now in the British Museum,"[8] spotted by Mahfouz's keen eye and transformed.

Occasional errors do occur. When Kamose says, "In the past, chariots were not instruments of war that the Herdsmen used," (p. 36), he and Mahfouz are mistaken, since it was the Hyksos who introduced the chariot to Egypt. The length of Hyksos rule in Egypt is most often given in the novel as the conventional two hundred years, but in two places as only "a hundred years or more." Queen Tetisheri is said at one point to be sixty years of age; at another, it is stated that she was born in the north before the occupation, in which case she would be anything from "a hundred years or more" to two hundred years in age. These discrepancies have been left as is in this translation. A couple of small errors, however, have been corrected: when an Egyptian border guard is reported as urging villagers to flee north to avoid an expected battle, he would seem to be sending them toward the oncoming Hyksos army; in the translation he advises them to go south (p. 35). Likewise, the sum paid by Isfinis to ransom Lady Ebana is given first as fifty, then elsewhere as fifty thousand, pieces of gold; the translation has made these all fifty.

The general accuracy of Mahfouz's account of the history of the period should not be taken to imply, however, that the work is simply a fictionalized historical narrative. Rather, the author has used the historical elements that suit his purposes as a novelist, while eliminating those that do not. For example, the historical Ahmose, with his commander, Ahmose Ebana, pursued the Hyksos beyond the borders of Egypt and into Palestine. Mahfouz, however, in order no doubt to bring a satisfying closure to the story, gives the impression that the Egyptian campaign ended with the expulsion of the Hyksos from Egyptian soil.

Thebes at War is not just about ancient Egypt. When Mahfouz was writing it, Egypt had been under foreign tutelage, if not outright occupation, for over sixty years. While it is true that the British had unilaterally declared Egypt's independence in 1922, severe restrictions on the country's sovereignty, including the occupation of Egyptian territory (the Suez Canal zone), remained. At another level, as political discourse had evolved from the pan-nationalism of the Ottoman Empire to that of single-state nationalism during the nineteenth century, so Egypt's own largely Turkish-speaking upper class had come to be seen by many as foreigners. Which of the two groups Mahfouz intended the reader to identify with the Hyksos (if indeed either group was more specifically his target than the other) may remain a moot point. What is clear is that this is a profoundly political novel whose ringing patriotism and passionate call to Egyptians to defend their country against any outsider who would seek to dominate it continues to resonate today. Unsurprisingly, *Thebes at War* is a set text in modern Egypt's elementary and intermediate school curricula (thus fulfilling the hope Sayyid Qutb expressed in his review that "the ministry of education should place [the work] in the hands of every student").[9] It has also been turned into a play by Abd al-Rahman al-Abnudi, one of Egypt's leading poets, and is slated to be made into the first Egyptian full-length animated film for children.[10]

The novel's political character is not limited, moreover, to the struggle to regain lost territory and expel the aggressor: other politically charged themes emerge, though not all of these are so explicit or consciously acknowledged by the author. Nubia, the land to the south to which the Egyptian leadership flees to escape the Hyksos' onslaught, clearly does service for modern Sudan, a country that, when Mahfouz was writing, was ruled by Egypt and Britain together in a "condominium" in which Egypt was, humiliatingly, the junior partner. King Ahmose's departing words to the governor of Nubia—"From this day on let us not deny to southern Egypt anything that we desire for ourselves and let us shield it from whatever we would not wish for ourselves" (p. 235)—constitute a clear reference to the importance of the unity of the Nile Valley for the country as a whole. The Nubians themselves, however—and this in no way clashes with the preceding—appear in the novel in a minimal role, as loyal, unspeaking, extras. (Ironically, recent discoveries show that, far from applauding the Seventeenth Dynasty's attempts to drive out the Hyksos, the Nubians in fact seized the opportunity to attack Egypt, in what has been described as "a pincer movement."[11])

At a less explicit level, the novel manifests a clear stratification of races by color. The Egyptians, who are "golden-brown," or "coppery," are clearly and unsurprisingly the ideal of beauty and wholesomeness. They are flanked, as it were, by the "long-bearded Herdsmen with their white skins that the sun will never cleanse," as Kamose puts it (p. 15), and the pygmies, "intensely black in color," who live "in the furthest forests of Nubia, where the divine Nile has its source" (p. 76); the first are grotesque and evil, the second grotesque and comic. Not all that is other, however, is ugly: the Hyksos princess, Amenridis, whose "golden hair stray[s] over her shining forehead" (p. 128), has a disorienting effect on the young Ahmose, and the dynamism of their relationship propels the novel into realms beyond those of national myth and politics alone.

The biggest challenge the text poses the translator may be its highly consistent formality of register; in *Thebes at War*, there is none of the underlying colloquiality that is said to characterize the dialogue, at least, of Mahfouz's later novels, even among the jolly drunks of the scene at the inn, and the work is peppered with the equivalents of words such as "doughty" and "stalwart." While the modern ear may be unaccustomed to these, it should become obvious that, through his masterful use of such language, Mahfouz is able to forge both fine heroic passages appropriate to his message of national glory and tender, lyrical scenes appropriate to his story of love and self-denial.

In representing the names of persons and places, Mahfouz has followed the conventions obtaining among European-language Egyptologists of the time as reproduced in Arabic. However, given the limitations of hieroglyphs (vowels are not represented, and the order in which the syllables were pronounced is not fixed beyond doubt), and given that the scholarly consensus evolves, these conventions have never been either consistent or static. This translation uses the forms most familiar to today's readers (for example, Ahmose for Ahmus), though where more than one form is possible, that which corresponds more closely to the Arabic version has been followed (Amenridis for Amenirdis). I am indebted to Dr. Fayza Haikal and Dr. Salima Ikram, both of the American University in Cairo, for guidance through this tricky field, though any faux pas are of course my own. Mahfouz also tended to follow the Egyptological convention of using the classical forms of place names, even though Greek and Latin did not come into use in Egypt for twelve hundred years or more after the period in which the novel is set. Thus he refers, for example, to Apollonopolis Magna, rather than Edfu.

Not all the places (or people) referred to in the novel can be identified. The map on page 2, on which identifiable places have been plotted, will allow the curious reader to follow the progress of the Egyptian army as described in the narrative.

This translation is dedicated to Phyllis Teresa Mabel Davies, née Corbett.

Notes:

1 I am indebted for these facts, as well as for much of the other information contained in this introduction, to "A Mummy Awakens: The Pharaonic Fiction of Naguib Mahfouz," a doctoral dissertation-in-progress by Raymond Stock of the Department of Asian and Middle Eastern Studies of the University of Pennsylvania (draft dated January 2, 2003). Also useful has been *Nagib Mahfuz – al-Tariq wal-Sada* by Ali Shalash (Cairo: Dar al-Adab, 1990).

2 On these, see *Voices from the Other World: Ancient Egyptian Tales,* translated by Raymond Stock (Cairo: The American University in Cairo Press, 2002).

3 *Arrisalah* [=al-Risala] magazine (Cairo), October 2, 1944, pp. 889–92; the review is reprinted in Shalash, pp. 152–58.

4 Stock, 'A Mummy Awakens,' p. 81.

5 Anthony and Rosalie David, *A Biographical Dictionary of Ancient Egypt* (London: Seaby, 1999), p. 130.

6 Peter A. Clayton, *Chronicles of the Pharaohs* (London: Routledge, 1999), p. 97.

7 Stock, "A Mummy Awakens," p. 83.

8 Clayton, p. 97.

9 Shalash, p. 152.

10 Stock, "A Mummy Awakens," p. 89.

11 Nevine el-Aref, "Elkab's Hidden Treasure," *Al-Ahram Weekly*, 31 July–6 August, 2003.

SEQENENRA

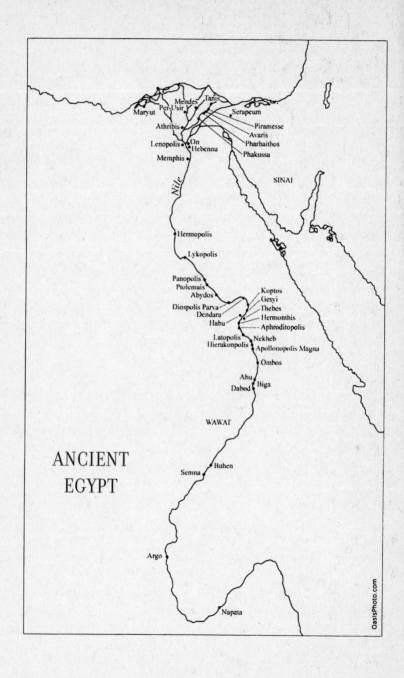

1

The ship made its way up the sacred river, its lotus-crowned prow cleaving the quiet, stately waves that since ancient days had pressed upon each other's heels like episodes in the endless stream of time. On either side, villages dotted the landscape, palms sprouted singly and in clusters, and greenery extended to the east and the west. The sun, high in the sky, sent out beams of light that quivered where they drenched the vegetation and sparkled where they touched the water, whose surface was empty but for a few fishing boats that made way for the big ship, their owners staring questioningly and mistrustfully at the image of the lotus, symbol of the North.

To the front of the cabin on the deck sat a short, stout man with round face, long beard, and white skin, dressed in a flowing robe, a thick stick with a gold handle grasped in his right hand. Before him sat two others as stout as he and dressed in the same fashion—three men united by a single mien. The master gazed fixedly to the south, his dark eyes consumed with boredom and fatigue, and he glared balefully at the fishermen. As though oppressed by the silence, he turned to his men and asked, "I wonder, tomorrow will the trumpet sound and will the heavy silence that now reigns over the southern regions be broken? Will the peace of these tranquil houses be shattered and will the vulture of war hover in these secure skies? Ah, how I wish these people knew what a warning this ship brings them and their master!"

The two men nodded in agreement with their leader's words. "Let it be war, Lord Chamberlain," said one of them, "so long as this man whom our lord has permitted to govern the South insists on placing a king's crown on his head, builds palaces like the pharaohs, and walks cheerfully about Thebes without a care in the world!"

The chamberlain ground his teeth and jabbed with his stick at the deck before him with a movement that betrayed anger and exasperation. "There is no Egyptian governor except for this, of the region of Thebes," he said. "Once rid of him, Egypt will be ours forever and the mind of our lord the king will be set at rest, having no man's rebelliousness left to fear."

The second man, who lived in the hope of one day becoming governor of a great city, fervently replied, "These Egyptians hate us."

The chamberlain uttered an amen to that and said in violent tones, "So they do, so they do. Even the people of Memphis, capital of our lord's kingdom, make a show of obedience while concealing hatred in their hearts. Every stratagem has been tried and nothing now is left but the whip and the sword."

For the first time, the two men smiled and the second said, "May your counsel be blessed, wise chamberlain! The whip is the only thing these Egyptians understand."

The three men relapsed for a while into silence and nothing was to be heard but the slap of the oars on the surface of the water. Then one of them happened to notice a fishing boat in whose waist stood a young man with sinewy forearms, wearing nothing but a kilt at his waist, his skin burned by the sun. In amazement he said, "These southerners look as though they had sprung from their own soil!"

"Wonder not!" the chamberlain responded sarcastically, "Some of their poets even sing the beauties of a dark complexion!"

"Indeed! Next to ours, their coloring is like mud next to the glorious rays of the sun."

The chamberlain replied, "One of our men was telling me about these southerners and he said, 'Despite their color and their nakedness, they are full of conceit and pride. They claim they are descended from the loins of the gods and that their country is the wellspring of the true pharaohs.' Dear God! I know the cure for all that. All it will take is for us to reach out our arm to the borders of their country."

No sooner had the chamberlain ceased speaking than he heard one of his men saying, pointing to the east, "Look! Can that be Thebes? It is Thebes!"

They all looked where the man was pointing and beheld a large city surrounded by a great wall, behind which the heads of the obelisks soared like pillars supporting the celestial vault. On its northern side, the towering walls of the temple of Amun, Divine Lord of the South, could be seen, appearing to the eye like a mighty giant climbing toward the sky. The men were shaken and the high chamberlain knitted his brows and muttered, "Yes. That is Thebes. I have been granted a sight of it before and time has only increased my desire that it submit to our lord the king and that I see his victory procession making its way through its streets."

One of the men added, "And that our god Seth be worshipped there."

The ship slowed and proceeded little by little to draw in to the shore, passing luxuriant gardens whose lush terraces descended to drink from the sacred river. Behind them, proud palaces could be seen, while to the west of the farther shore crouched the City of Eternity, where the immortals slept in pyramids, mastabas, and graves, all enveloped in the forlornness of death.

The ship turned toward the port of Thebes, making its way among the fishing smacks and traders' ships, its size and beauty, and the image of the lotus that embellished its prow, attracting all eyes. Finally, it drew up alongside the quay and threw down its huge anchor. Guards approached and an officer, wearing a jacket of white linen above his kilt, was brought out to it. He asked one of the crew, "Where is this ship coming from? And is it carrying goods for trade?"

The man greeted him, said, "Follow me!" and accompanied him to the cabin, where the officer found himself standing before a high chamberlain of the Northern Palace—the palace of the King of the Herdsmen, as they called him in the South. He bowed respectfully and presented a military salute. With patent arrogance, the chamberlain raised his hand to return the salute and said, in condescending tones, "I am the envoy of Our Master Apophis, Pharaoh, King of the North and the South, Son of Lord Seth, and I am sent to the governor of Thebes, Prince Seqenenra, to convey to him the proclamation that I bear."

The officer listened to the envoy attentively, saluted once more, and left.

2

An hour passed. Then a man of great dignity, somewhat short and lean, with a prominent brow, arrived at the ship. Bowing with dignity to the envoy, he said in a quiet voice, "He who has the honor of receiving you is Hur, chamberlain of the Southern Palace."

The other inclined his stately head and said in his rough voice, "And I am Khayan, high chamberlain of the Palace of the Pharaoh."

Hur said, "Our master will be happy to receive you immediately."

The envoy made a move to rise and said, "Let us go." Chamberlain Hur led the way, the man following him with unhurried steps, supporting his obese body on his stick, while the other two bowed to him reverently. Khayan had taken offense and was asking himself, "Should not Seqenenra have come himself to receive the envoy of Apophis?" It annoyed him excessively that the former should receive him as though he were a king. Khayan left the ship between two rows of soldiers and officers, and saw a royal cavalcade awaiting him on the shore headed by a war chariot and with more chariots behind. The soldiers saluted him and he returned their salute haughtily and got into his chariot, Hur at his side. Then the small procession moved off toward the palace of the governor of the South. Khayan's eyes swiveled right and left, observing the temples and obelisks, statues and palaces, the markets and the unending streams of people of all classes: the common people with their almost naked bodies, the officers with their elegant cloaks, the priests with their long robes, the nobles with their flowing mantles, and the beautifully dressed women. Everything seemed to bear witness to the mightiness of the city and to its rivalry of Memphis, the capital of Apophis. From the first instant, Khayan was aware that his procession was attracting looks everywhere, and that the people were gathering along the way to watch, though coldly and stolidly, their black eyes examining his white face and long beard with surprise, distaste, and resentment. He boiled with anger that the mighty Apophis should be subjected to such a cold welcome in the person of his envoy and it vexed him that he should appear as a stranger in Thebes two hundred years after his people had descended on the land of Egypt and seated themselves on its throne. It angered and exasperated him that his people should have ruled for two hundred years, during which the south of Egypt had preserved its identity, character, and independence—for not a single man of the Hyksos resided there.

The procession reached the square in front of the palace. It was broad, with far-flung corners, government buildings, ministries, and the army headquarters lining its sides. In its center stood the venerable palace, its imposing sight dazzling the eyes—a mighty palace, like that of Memphis itself, with guardsmen topping its walls and lined up in two rows at the main gate. The band struck up a salutatory anthem as the envoy's procession passed, and as the procession crossed the courtyard Khayan wondered to himself, "Will Seqenenra meet me with the White Crown on his head? He lives as a king and observes their etiquette and he governs as kings govern. Will he then wear the crown of the South in front of me? Will he do what his forebears and his own father, Seneqnenra, refrained from doing?" He dismounted at the entrance to the long colonnade and found the palace chamberlain, the head of the royal guard, and the higher officers waiting to receive him. All saluted and they proceeded before him to the royal reception hall. The antechamber leading to the doorway of the hall was decorated on both sides with sphinxes, and in its corners stood giant officers chosen from among the mighty men of Habu. The men bowed to the envoy, making way for him, and Chamberlain Hur walked ahead of him into the interior of the hall. Following, Khayan beheld, at some distance from the entrance and dominating the space, a royal throne on which sat a man crowned with the crown of the South, the scepter and the crook in his hand, while two men sat to the right of his throne and two to the left. Hur, followed by the envoy, reached the throne and bowed to his lord in veneration, saying in his gentle voice, "My lord, I present to Your Highness High Chamberlain Khayan, envoy of King Apophis."

At this the envoy bowed in greeting and the king returned his greeting, gesturing to him to sit on a chair in front of the throne, while Hur stood to the right of the throne. The king desired to present his courtiers to the envoy, so he pointed with his scepter to the man closest to him on his right and said, "This is User-Amun, chief minister." Then he pointed to the man next to him and said, "Nofer-Amun, high priest of Amun." Next he turned to his left and indicated the man next to him. "Kaf, commander of the fleet." He pointed to the man next to him and said, "Pepi, commander of the army." With the introductions completed, the king turned his gaze on the envoy and said in a voice whose tones indicated natural nobility and rank, "You have come to a place that welcomes both you and him who has entrusted you with his confidence."

The envoy replied, "May the Lord preserve you, respected governor. I am indeed happy to have been chosen for this embassy to your beautiful country, of historic repute."

The king's ears did not fail to note the words "respected governor" or their significance, but no sign of his inner perturbation showed on his face. At the same moment, Khayan shot a quick scrutinizing glance from his bulging eyes and found the Egyptian governor to be a truly impressive man, tall of stature, with an oval, beautiful face, extremely dark, his features distinguished by the protrusion of his upper teeth. He judged him to be in his fourth decade. The king imagined that the envoy of Apophis had come for the same reason that had brought earlier missions from the North, namely, to ask for stone and grain, which the kings of the Herdsmen considered tribute, while the kings of Thebes saw them as a bribe with which they protected themselves against the evil of the invaders.

The king said quietly and with dignity, "It is my pleasure to listen to you, envoy of mighty Apophis."

The envoy moved in his seat as though about to jump up and fight. In his rough voice he said, "For two hundred years, the envoys of the North have never ceased to visit the South, each time returning satisfied."

The king said, "I hope that this beautiful custom may continue."

Khayan said, "Governor, I bring you three requests from Pharaoh. The first concerns the person of my lord Pharaoh; the second, his god, Seth; and the third, the ties of affection between North and South."

The king now gave him his full attention and concern showed on his face. The man went on to say, "In recent days, my lord the king has complained of terrible pains that have wracked his nerves by night and of abominable noises that have assaulted his noble ears, rendering him prey to sleeplessness and ill health. He summoned his physicians and described to them his nocturnal sufferings and they examined him with care, but all went away again puzzled and none the wiser. In the opinion of them all, the king was in good health and well. When my lord despaired, he finally consulted the prophet of the temple of Seth and this wise man grasped the nature of his sickness and said, 'The source of all his pains is the roaring of the hippopotami penned up in the South, which has infiltrated his heart.' And he assured him that there could be no cure for him unless they were killed."

The envoy knew that the hippopotami kept in the lake of Thebes were sacred, so he stole a glance at the governor's face to gauge the effect of his words, but found it stony and hard, though it had reddened. He waited for him to make some comment but the man uttered not a word and appeared to be listening and waiting. So, the envoy said, "While my lord was sick, he dreamed he saw our god Seth in all his dazzling majesty visit him and rebuke him, saying, 'Is it right that there should not be a single temple in the whole of the South in which my name is mentioned?' So my lord swore that he would ask of his friend, the governor of the South, that he build a temple to Seth in Thebes, next to the temple of Amun."

The envoy fell silent, but Seqenenra continued to say nothing, though he now appeared as one taken aback and surprised by something that had never before occurred to him. Khayan, however, was unconcerned by the king's darkening mood and may even have been driven by a desire to provoke him. Chamberlain Hur, grasping the danger of the demands, bent over his lord's ear, whispering, "It would be better if my lord did not engage the envoy in discussion now."

The king nodded in agreement, well aware what the chamberlain was driving at. Khayan imagined that the chamberlain was notifying his lord of what he had said, so he waited a little. However, the king merely said, "Have you any other message to convey?"

Khayan replied, "Respected governor, it has reached my lord's notice that you crown yourself with the White Crown of Egypt. This surprises him and he finds it out of keeping with the ties of affection and traditional friendship that bind the family of Pharaoh to your own time-honored family."

Seqenenra exclaimed in astonishment, "But the White Crown is the headdress of the governors of the South!"

The envoy replied with assurance and insistence, "On the contrary, it was the crown of those of them who were kings, and for that reason, your glorious father never thought of wearing it, for he knew that there is only one king in this valley who has the right to wear a crown. I hope, respected governor, that my lord's reference to his sincere desire to strengthen the good relations between the dynasties of Thebes and Memphis will not be lost on you."

Khayan ceased speaking and silence fell once more. Seqenenra was plunged in melancholy reflection, his heart weighed down by the king of the Herdsmen's harsh demands, which attacked the very wellsprings of faith in his heart and of pride in his soul. The impact of these things reflected itself in his pallor and in the stony faces of the courtiers around him. Appreciative of Hur's advice, he volunteered no reply but said in a voice that retained, despite everything, its calm, "Your message, Envoy, involves a delicate matter that touches on our beliefs and traditions. This being so, it seems to me best that I inform you of my opinion on it tomorrow."

Khayan responded, "The best opinion is that on which counsel is taken first."

Seqenenra turned then to Chamberlain Hur and said, "Conduct the envoy to the wing that has been made ready for him."

The envoy raised his huge, short body, bowed and then departed, with a conceited and haughty gait.

3

───────

The king sent for his crown prince, Kamose, who arrived with a speed that indicated how anxious he was to know what message the chamberlain of Apophis had brought. After he had greeted his father reverently and taken his place on his right, the king turned to him and said, "I have sent for you, Prince, to acquaint you with the communication of the envoy of the North, that you may give us your opinion on it. The matter is indeed serious, so listen to me well."

The king related in clear detail to his crown prince what the envoy Khayan had said, the prince listening to his father with a depth of concern that showed on his handsome countenance, which resembled that of his father in its color and features and the projection of the upper teeth. Then the king turned his eyes to those present and said, "So now you see, gentlemen, that to please Apophis we must take off this crown, slaughter the sacred hippopotami, and erect a temple in which Seth is worshipped next to the temple of Amun. Counsel me as to what must be done!"

The indignation that showed on all their faces revealed the anxiety that churned in their breasts. Chamberlain Hur was the first to speak and he said, "My lord, even more than these demands I reject the spirit that dictated them. It is the spirit of a master dictating to his slave, of a king incriminating his own people. To me, it is simply the ancient conflict between Thebes and Memphis in a new shape. The latter strives to enslave the former, while the former struggles to hold on to its independence by all the means at its disposal. There is no doubt that the Herdsmen and their king resent the survival of a Thebes whose doors are locked against their governors. Perhaps they themselves are unconvinced by their claim that this kingdom is merely an autonomous province, subject to their crown, and they have therefore decided to put an end to the manifestations of its independence and to control its beliefs. Once they have done that, it will be easy for them to destroy it."

Hur was strong and forthright in his speech and the king remembered the Herdsmen's kings' history of meddling with the rulers of Thebes, and how the latter would deflect their evil with a fair reply, and with gifts and the appearance of submission, in order to preserve the South from their interference and their evil. His family had played a great role in this, so much so that his father, Seneqnenra, had managed to train mighty forces in secret to maintain the independence of his kingdom should stratagems and a show of loyalty in his voice not suffice. Then Commander Kaf spoke, "My lord, I believe we should yield to none of these demands. How can we agree that our lord should remove his crown from his head? Or that we should kill the sacred hippopotami to please one who is an enemy to even the least of our people? And how can we build a temple to that Lord of Evil whom these Herdsmen worship?"

The high priest Nofer-Amun then spoke, "My king, the Lord Amun will not consent that a temple for Seth, the Lord of Evil, be erected next to His, or that His pure land be watered with the blood of the sacred hippopotami, or that the protector of His kingdom forgo his crown, when he is the first governor of the South to crown himself with it, at His command! No, my lord! Amun will never accept that! Indeed, He waits for the one who will lead an army of His sons to liberate the North and unify the nation! Then it will be once more as it was in the days of the first kings."

Ardor now flowed like blood in the veins of Commander Pepi. Standing and revealing his alarming height and broad shoulders, he said in his deep voice, "My lord, our great men have spoken truly. I am certain that these demands are meant as nothing but a test of our mettle and a way of forcing us into humiliation and submission. What does it tell us that this savage who has descended on our valley from the furthest reaches of the barren deserts should demand of our king that he remove his crown and worship the Lord of Evil and slaughter the sacred hippopotami? In the past, the Herdsmen would ask for wealth and we were not stingy to them with our wealth. But now they are greedy for our freedom and our honor. Faced with that, death would seem easy and delightful to us. Our people in the North are slaves who plough the land and writhe in agony under the tongues of the lash. We hope to free them one day from the torture they suffer, not pass of our own free will into the same wretched state as theirs!"

The king kept silent. He was listening keenly, holding his emotions in check by looking downward. Prince Kamose had tried to explore his face but failed. His inclinations were with Commander Pepi and he said violently, "My lord, Apophis greedily eyes our national pride and wants nothing but to reduce the South to submission as he reduced the North. But the South that would not accept humiliation when its enemy was at the height of his powers will never accept it now. Who now would say that we should squander what our forefathers struggled to maintain and care for?"

User-Amun, the chief minister, was of all the people the most moderate and his policy was ever directed to avoiding the anger of the Herdsmen and exposure to their savage forces, so that he might devote himself to developing the wealth of the South, exploiting the resources of Nubia and the Eastern Desert, and training a strong, invincible army. He was frightened of the consequences to which the impetuousness of the crown prince and the commander of the army might lead. Directing his words to the courtiers, he said, "Remember, gentlemen, that the Herdsmen are a people of plunder and pillage. Though they have ruled Egypt for two hundred years, their eyes are still drawn by gold, for which they will do anything and which distracts their attention from nobler goals."

But Commander Pepi shook his head with its shining helmet and said, "Your Excellency, we have lived with these people long enough to know them. They are people who, if they desire something, ask for it frankly, without seeking to use stratagems and concealment. In the past they asked for gold and it was carried to them. But now they are asking for our freedom."

The chief minister said, "We must temporize until our army is complete."

The commander replied, "Our army is capable of repelling the enemy in its present state."

Prince Kamose looked at his father and found that his eyes were still downcast. Passionately, he said, "What is the use of talk? Our army may need some men and equipment, but Apophis will not wait while we ready our gear. He has presented us with demands which, if we concede them, will condemn us to collapse and obliteration. There is not a man in the South who prefers surrender to death, so let us refuse these demands with disdain and raise our heads before those long-bearded Herdsmen with their white skins that the sun will never cleanse!"

The enthusiasm of the young prince had its impact on the people. Determination and anger showed in their faces and it seemed as though they had had enough of talk and were wanting to take a resolute decision, when the king raised his head and, gazing intently at his crown prince, asked, in his sublimely noble voice, "Do you think that we should reject the demands of Apophis, Prince?"

Kamose replied confidently and vehemently, "Resolutely and disdainfully, my lord!"

"And what if this rejection drags us into war?"

Kamose replied, "Then let us fight, my lord."

Commander Pepi said with enthusiasm no less than that of the prince, "Let us fight until we have pushed the enemy back from our borders and, if my lord so wills, let us fight till we have liberated the North and driven the last of the white

Herdsmen with their long, dirty beards from the land of the Nile!"

Next the king turned to Nofer-Amun, the high priest, and asked him, "And you, Your Holiness, what do you think?"

The venerable old man replied, "I think, my lord, that whoever tries to extinguish this holy burning brand is an infidel!"

Then King Seqenenra smiled in consent and turning to his chief minister, User-Amun, said to him, "You are the only one left, Minister."

The man hurriedly said, "My lord, I do not counsel delay out of dislike for war or fear of it. But let us complete the equipment of the army, which I hope will realize the goal of my lord's glorious family, which is the liberation of the Nile Valley from the Herdsmen's iron grip. Yet if Apophis truly should have his sights set on our freedom, then I will be the first to call for war."

Seqenenra looked into the faces of his men and said in a voice that spoke of resolve and strength, "Men of the South, I share your emotions and I believe that Apophis is picking a quarrel with us and seeks to rule us, either by fear or by war. But we are a people that do not surrender to fear and welcome war. The North has been the Herdsmen's prey for two hundred years. They have sucked up the wealth of its soil and humiliated its men. As for the South, for two hundred years it has struggled, never losing sight of its higher goal, which is the liberation of the whole of the valley. Is it to back down at the first threat, squander its right, and throw its freedom at the feet of that insatiable glutton for him to look after? No, men of the South! I shall refuse Apophis's demeaning demands and await his answer, however he may respond. If it be peace, then let it be peace, and if it be war, then let it be war!"

The king rose to his feet and the men stood as one and bowed in respect. Then he slowly left the hall, Prince Kamose and the high chamberlain behind him.

4

The king made his way to Queen Ahotep's wing. As soon as the woman saw him coming toward her in his ceremonial dress, she realized that the envoy of the North had brought weighty business. Concern sketched itself upon her lovely, dark-complexioned face and she arose so that she might meet him with her tall, slender body, raising questioning eyes to him. Quietly he told her, "Ahotep, it seems to me that war is on the horizon."

Her black eyes showed consternation and she muttered in astonishment, "War, my lord?"

He inclined his head to indicate assent, and related to her what the envoy Khayan had said, the opinion of his men, and what he had resolved to do. As he spoke, his eyes never left her face, in whose surface he read the pity, hope, and submission to the inevitable that burned within her.

She told him, "You have chosen the only path that one such as yourself could choose."

He smiled and patted her shoulder. Then he said to her, "Let us go to our sacred mother."

They walked together side by side to the wing belonging to the queen mother, Tetisheri, wife of the former king, Seneqnenra, and found her in her retiring chamber reading, as was her wont.

Queen Tetisheri was in her sixties. Nobility, grandeur, and dignity distinguished her countenance. Her vivacity was irrepressible and her energy overcame her age, from whose effects she had suffered nothing but a few white hairs that wreathed her temples and a slight fading of her cheeks. Her eyes were as bright as ever and her body as charming and as slender. She shared with all members of the family of Thebes the protrusion of her upper teeth, that protrusion that the people of the South found so attractive and which they all adored. On the death of her husband, the queen had abandoned any role in governing, as the law required, leaving the reins of Thebes in the hands of her son and his spouse. Hers, however, was still the opinion to which recourse was had in times of difficulty, and the heart that inspired hope and struggle. In her retirement she had turned to reading, and constantly perused the Books of Khufu and Kagemni, the Books of the Dead, and the history of the glorious ages as immortalized in the proverbs of Mina, Khufu, and Amenhotep. The queen mother was famed throughout the South, where there was not a man or a woman who did not know her and love her and swear by her dear name, for she had instilled in those around her, and foremost among them her son Seqenenra and her grandson Kamose, a love of Egypt both South and North and a hatred of the rapacious Herdsmen who had brought the days of glory to so evil an end. She had taught them all that the sublime goal to whose realization they must dedicate themselves was the liberation of the Nile Valley from the grip of the tyrannous Herdsmen, and she urged the priests of all classes, whether keepers of temples or teachers in the schools, to constantly remind the people of the ravaged North and their rapacious foe, and of the crimes by which they humiliated and enslaved the people and plundered their land, enriching themselves with their wealth and reducing them to the level of the animals that labored in the fields. If there was in the South a single ember of the sacred fire burning in their hearts and keeping hope alive, then hers was the credit for fanning it with her patriotism and her wisdom. Thus, the whole South thought of her as hallowed, calling her "Sacred Mother Tetisheri," just as believers did Isis, and seeking refuge in her name from the evil of despair and defeat.

Such was the woman to whom Seqenenra and Ahotep made their way. She was expecting their visit, for she had learned of the coming of the envoy of the king of the Herdsmen and she remembered the envoys that these had sent to her late husband, seeking gold, grain, and stone, which they demanded as tribute to be paid by the subject to his overlord. Her husband would send well-loaded ships to escape the power of those savage people and double his secret activities in forming the army that was his most precious bequest to his son Seqenenra and his descendants. She thought of these things as she waited for the king and when he arrived with his spouse, she opened her thin arms to them. They kissed her hands and the king seated himself on her right and the queen on her left. Then she asked her son, with a gentle smile, "What does Apophis want?"

He answered her in accents full of rage, "He wants Thebes, Mother, and all that is of it. Nay, more than that, he would bargain with us this time for our honor."

She turned her head from one to the other, alarmed, and said in a voice that retained its calm despite everything, "His predecessors, for all their greed, were satisfied with granite and gold."

Queen Ahotep said, "But he, Mother, wants us to kill the sacred hippopotami, whose voices disturb his slumbers, and to erect a temple to his god Seth next to the temple of Amun, and that our lord take off the White Crown."

Seqenenra confirmed what Ahotep had said, and told his mother all the news of the envoy and his message. Disgust appeared on her venerable face and the twisting of her lips revealed her exasperation and annoyance. She asked the king, "What answer did you give, my son?"

"I have yet to inform him of my answer."

"Have you come to a conclusion?"

"Yes. To reject his demands completely."

"He who makes these demands will not take no for an answer!"

"And he who is able to refuse them completely should not fear the consequences of his refusal."

"What if he declares war on you?"

"I shall give him war for war."

The mention of war rang strangely in her ears, awakening ancient memories in her heart. She remembered times like these when her husband would not know which way to turn in his distress and he would complain to her of his sorrow and anxiety, yearning to own a strong army with which to repel his enemy's covetousness. Now her son could speak of war with courage, resolution, and confidence, for times had changed and hope had revived. She stole a glance at the queen's face and found it drawn, and she realized that she was confused, the hope of a queen and the apprehension of a wife pulling her mercilessly back and forth. She too was a queen, and a mother, but she could not find it within herself to say anything other than what the teacher of the people and their Sacred Mother must say. She asked him, "Are you ready for war, my lord?"

Firmly he replied, "Yes, Mother. I have a valiant army."

"Can this army free Egypt from its shackles?"

"At the least, it can drive back the aggression of the Herdsmen from the South."

Then he shrugged his shoulders contemptuously and said furiously, "Mother, we have humored these Herdsmen year after year, but this has not succeeded in putting an end to their greed and still they eye our kingdom covetously. Now destiny has intervened and I believe that courage has a better claim on us than delaying tactics and appeasement. I shall take this step and see what follows."

At this Tetisheri smiled and said proudly, "Amun bless this high and lofty-minded soul!"

"So what say you, Mother?"

"I say, my son, 'Follow your chosen path, and may the Lord protect you and my prayers bring you blessing!' That is our

goal, and that is what the youth whom Amun has chosen to realize Thebes' immortal hopes must do!"

Seqenenra was filled with joy and his face shone. He bent
over the head of Tetisheri to kiss her brow and she kissed his
left cheek and Ahotep's right and blessed them both and they
returned, happy and rejoicing.

5

It was announced to the envoy Khayan that Seqenenra would
receive him on the morning of the following day, and at the appointed time the king went to the reception hall followed by his
senior chamberlains. There he found the chief minister, the
high priest, and the commanders of the army and navy waiting
for him about the throne. They rose to receive him and bowed
before him and he took his seat upon the throne and gave them
permission to sit. Then the chamberlain of the door shouted to
announce the arrival of the envoy Khayan, who entered with
his fat, short body and long beard, walking haughtily and asking himself, "What lies, I wonder, behind this council? Peace or
war?" When he reached the throne, he bowed in greeting to the
one seated there and the king returned the greeting and gave
him permission to be seated, saying, "I hope you passed a
pleasant night?"

"It was a pleasant night, thanks to your generous hospitality."

He glanced quickly at the king's head and, seeing upon it the
White Crown of Egypt, his heart sank and he blazed with fury,
feeling that it was intolerable for the governor of the South to
challenge him thus. The king, for his part, went to no lengths
to be polite to the envoy, for he was not unaware of what his
refusal of the demands meant. Wishing to state his opinion

baldly, decisively, and straightforwardly, he said, "Envoy Khayan, I have studied the demands that you have so faithfully conveyed to us and I have consulted the men of my kingdom about them. It is the opinion of us all that we should refuse them."

Khayan had not been expecting this abrupt, frank refusal. He was struck dumb and overcome with astonishment. He looked at Seqenenra in amazement and disbelief, and his face turned as red as coral. The king went on, "I find that these demands violate our beliefs and our honor, and we will permit no one to violate even a single belief of ours, or our honor."

Khayan recovered from his astonishment and said quietly and haughtily, as though he had not heard what the king had said, "If my lord asks me, 'Why does the governor of the South refuse to construct a temple to Seth?' what shall I say to him?"

"Say to him that the people of the South worship Amun alone."

"And if he asks me, 'Why do they not kill the hippopotami that rob me of my sleep?'"

"Tell him that the people of the South hold them sacred."

"Amazing! Is not Pharaoh more sacred than the hippopotami?"

Seqenenra hung his head for a moment, as though thinking of a reply. Then he said in resolute tones, "Apophis is sacred to you. These hippopotami are sacred to us."

A wave of relief passed through the courtiers at this vehement reply. Khayan, on the other hand, was furious, though he did not allow his anger to get the better of him and held himself back, saying quietly, "Respected Governor, your father was governor of the South and did not wear this crown. Do you think that you have greater rights than your father claimed for himself?"

"I inherited from him the South and this has been its crown from ancient times. It is my right to wear it as such."

"Yet in Memphis there is another man who wears the double crown of Egypt and calls himself Pharaoh of Egypt. What do you think of his claims?"

"I think that he and his forebears have usurped the kingdom."

Khayan's patience was exhausted now and he said furiously and with contempt, "Governor, do not think that by wearing the crown you are raised to the rank of king. For a king is first and foremost strength and power. I find nothing in your words but contempt for the good relations that tied your fathers and your ancestors to our kings and a striving for a challenge whose results you cannot guarantee."

Anger appeared on the faces of the retinue but the king preserved his calm and said affably, "Envoy, we do not run officiously after evil. But should any man impugn our honor, we shall neither concede nor favor the safe course. It is one of our virtues that we do not exaggerate in evaluating our strength, so do not expect to hear me boast and vaunt. But know that my fathers and my forefathers preserved what they could of the independence of this kingdom and that I will never squander what the Lord and the people have undertaken to preserve."

A sarcastic smile spread over Khayan's thin lips, concealing his bitter hatred. In an insinuating tone he said, "As you wish, Governor. My role is merely that of messenger and it is you that shall bear the consequences of your words."

The king bowed his head and said nothing. Then he stood, signaling the end of the audience. All rose to do him honor and remained standing until he was hidden from their eyes by the door.

6

The king, aware of the danger of the situation, wished to visit the temple of Amun to pray to the Lord and to announce the struggle in its sacred courtyard. He made his wish known to his minister and courtiers, and these set off in their groups, minis-

ters, commanders, chamberlains, and high officials, to the temple
of Amun to be ready to receive the king. Thebes, unknowing,
took note of what was going on behind its proud palace walls,
many whispering to one another that the envoy of the North
had arrived in high state and departed in anger. Word spread
among the Thebans that Seqenenra was to visit the temple of
Amun to seek His guidance and ask Him for help. Large crowds
of men, women, and children went to the temple, where they
were joined by yet more, who surrounded it and spilled out
into the streets that led to it. With solemn, worried, and curious faces they questioned one another in eager tones, each in-
terpreting the matter as he saw fit. The royal escort arrived,
preceded by a squadron of guards and followed by the king's
chariot and by others bearing the queen and the princes and
princesses of the royal house. As a wave of excitement and joy
swept over the people, they waved to their sovereign, cheering
and exulting. Seqenenra smiled at them and waved to them
with his scepter. It escaped no one's notice that the king was
wearing his battle dress with its shining shield, and the people's
eagerness to hear the news grew. The king entered the courtyard of the temple, the men and women of his family walking
behind him. The priests of the temple, the ministers, and the
commanders received them prostrate, while Nofer-Amun cried
out in a loud voice, "God keep the king's life forever and preserve the kingdom of Thebes!" the people enthusiastically repeating his cry over and over and the king greeting them with a
gesture of his hand to his head and a smile from his broad
mouth. Then the whole group moved into the Hall of the Altar,
where the soldiers immediately offered an ox as a sacrifice to
the Lord. All then circumambulated the altar and the Hall of
the Columns, where they formed two lines and the king gave
his scepter to crown prince Kamose and proceeded to the sacred stairway, which he ascended to the Holy of Holies, cross-
ing the sacred threshold with submissive steps and closing the
door behind him. Twilight seemed to envelope him and he

bowed his head, removed his crown out of reverence for the purity of the place, and advanced, on legs trembling in awe, toward the niche in which resided the Lord God. There he prostrated himself at His feet, kissed them, and was silent for a while until his agitated breathing could quiet itself. Then he said in a low voice, as though in intimate conversation, "Lord God, Lord of glorious Thebes, Lord of the lords of the Nile, grant me your mercy and strength, for today I face a grave responsibility, before which, without your aid, I shall find myself helpless! It is the defense of Thebes and the fight against your enemy and ours, that enemy who fell upon us from the deserts of the north in savage bands that laid waste to our houses, humiliated our people, closed the doors of your temples, and usurped our throne. Grant me your aid in re-pelling their armies, driving out their divisions, and cleansing the valley of their brutal power, so that none may rule there but your brown-skinned sons and no name be mentioned there but yours!"

The king fell silent, waited for a moment, then plunged once more into an ardent and lengthy prayer, his brow resting upon the statue's feet. Then he raised his head in holy dread until he was looking at the god's noble face, enshrouded in majesty and silence, as though it were the curtain of the future behind which Fate lay hidden.

———

The king, who had replaced the White Crown on his sweat-banded forehead, emerged before his people, who prostrated themselves to him as one. Prince Kamose presented him with his scepter and, taking it in his right hand, he said in a stento-rian voice: "Men of glorious Thebes! It may be that our enemy is assembling his army on the borders of our kingdom as I speak, to invade our lands. Prepare yourselves then for the struggle! Let each one's battle cry be to expend his greatest efforts in his work, that our army be strengthened for steadfastness and combat. I have prayed to the Lord and sought His aid and the Lord will not forget His country and His people!"

With a voice that shook the walls of the temple, all cried out, "God aid our king Seqenenra!" and the king turned to leave. However, the high priest of Amun approached and said, "Can my lord wait a little so that I may present him with a small gift?"

The king replied, smiling, "As Your Holiness wishes."

The high priest made a sign to two other priests, who went to the treasure chamber and returned carrying a small box of gold, to which all eyes turned. Nofer-Amun approached them and opened the box carefully and gently. The watchers beheld inside a royal crown—the double crown of Egypt. Eyes widened in astonishment and glances were exchanged. Nofer-Amun bowed his head to his lord and said in a voice that shook, "This, my lord, is the crown of King Timayus!"

Some of those present cried out to one another, "The crown of King Timayus!" and Nofer-Amun said with ardor and in a strong voice, "Indeed, my lord! This is the crown of King Timayus, the last pharaoh to rule united Egypt and Nubia before the Herdsmen's invasion of our land. The Lord in His wisdom took retribution on our country during his era and this noble crown fell from his head, after he had suffered greatly in defending it. Thus, it lost the throne and its master, but kept its honor. For this reason, our ancestors removed it to this temple, to take its place among our sacred heirlooms. Its owner died a hero and martyr, so it is worthy of a mighty head. I crown you with it, King Seqenenra, son of Sacred Mother Tetisheri, and proclaim you king of Upper and Lower Egypt and of Nubia, and I call on you, in the name of Lord Amun, the memory of Timayus, and the people of the South, to rise up, combat your enemy, and liberate the pure, beloved valley of the Nile!"

The high priest approached the king and removed the White Crown of Egypt from his head and handed it to one of the priests. Then he raised Egypt's double crown amidst shouts of joy and praise to God, placed it on his curly hair, and shouted aloud: "Long live Seqenenra, Pharaoh of Egypt!"

The people took up the call and a priest hurried outside the temple and acclaimed Seqenenra as pharaoh of Egypt, the Thebans repeating the call with wild enthusiasm. Then he called for men to fight the Herdsmen, and the people responded with voices like thunder, certain now of what they had suspected before.

Pharaoh saluted the priests, then made his way toward the door of the temple, followed by his family, the men of his palace, and the great ones of the southern kingdom.

7
___

As soon as Pharaoh returned to his palace, he called his chief minister, high priest, chief palace chamberlain, and the commanders of the army and navy to a meeting and told them, "Khayan's ship is bearing him swiftly northwards. We shall be invaded as soon as he crosses the southern borders, so we must not lose an hour of our time."

Turning to Kaf, commander of the fleet, he said, "I hope that you will find your task on the water easy, for the Herdsmen are our pupils in naval combat. Prepare your ships for war and set sail for the north!"

Commander Kaf saluted his lord and quickly left the palace. The king then turned to Commander Pepi and said, "Commander Pepi, the main force of our army is encamped at Thebes. Move with it to the north and I will catch up with you with a force of my stalwart guard. I pray the Lord that my troops prove themselves worthy of the task that has been placed upon their shoulders. Do not forget, Commander, to send a messenger to Panopolis, on our northern borders, to alert the garrison there to the danger that surrounds it, so that it is not taken by surprise."

The commander saluted his lord and departed. The king looked in the faces of the chief minister, the high priest, and the head chamberlain and then said to them, "Gentlemen, the duty of defending our army's rear will be thrown on your shoulders. Let each of you do his duty with the efficiency and dedication that I know are yours!"

They replied with one voice, "We stand ready to lay down our lives for the king and for Thebes!"

Seqenenra said, "Nofer-Amun, send your men to the villages and the towns to urge my people to fight! And you, User-Amun, summon the governors of the provinces and instruct them to conscript the strong and the able among my people; while to you, Hur, I entrust the people of my house. Be to my son Kamose as you are to me."

The king saluted his men and left the place, making his way to his private wing to bid farewell to his family before setting off. He sent for them all, and Queen Ahotep came and Queen Tetisheri, and Prince Kamose, and his wife Setkimus with their son Ahmose and their little daughter, Princess Nefertari. He received them lovingly and sat them around him. Tenderness filled his breast as he looked into the eyes of the faces dearest to his heart, seeing, it seemed to him, but one face repeated with no differences but those of age. Tetisheri was in her sixties and Ahotep, like her husband, in her forties, while Kamose and Setkimus were twenty-five. Ahmose was not yet ten and his sister Nefertari was two years younger. In every one of their faces, however, shone the same black eyes, in every one was the same mouth with its slight upper protrusion, and the same golden-brown complexion that lent the countenance health and good looks. A smile played on the king's broad mouth and he said, "Come. Let us sit together for a while before I go."

Tetisheri said, "I pray the Lord, my son, that you go forth to decisive victory!"

Seqenenra said, "I have great hope of victory, Mother."

The king saw that the crown prince was dressed for war and realized that he imagined that he was going with him. Feigning ignorance he asked him, "Why are you dressed like that?"

Astonishment appeared on the youth's face, as though he was not expecting the question and he said in surprise, "For the same reason that you are so dressed, Father."

"Did you receive an order from me to do this?"

"I didn't think that there was any need, Father."

"You were wrong, my son."

Alarm appeared on the youth's face and he said, "Am I to be forbidden the honor of taking part in the battle of Thebes, my lord?"

"Fields of battle are no more honorable than any other. You will remain in my place, Kamose, to look after the happiness of our kingdom and supply our army with men and provisions."

The youth's face turned pale and he bowed his head as though the king's command weighed heavily upon him. Tetisheri, wishing to make it easier for him, said, "Kamose, it is no mean task to take on the burdens of government, nor one to shame a person. It is a work worthy of such as you."

Then the king placed his hand on the crown prince's shoulder and said, "Listen, Kamose. We are approaching a murderous war from which we hope, with the Lord's help, to emerge the victors and liberate our beloved land from its shackles. But it is only wise to consider all possible outcomes. As our sage Kagemni has said, 'Do not put all your arrows in one quiver!'"

The king ceased speaking, silence reigned, and no one uttered a word until the king resumed by saying, "If the Lord, in His wisdom, wills that our struggle for the right should meet with failure, it must not come to an end. Listen to me, all of you. If Seqenenra falls, do not despair. Kamose will succeed his father, and if Kamose falls, little Ahmose will follow him. And if this army of ours is wiped out, Egypt is full of men. If Ptolemais falls, let Koptos fight! If Thebes is invaded, let Ombos and

Sayin and Biga leap to its defense! If the whole South falls into the hands of the Herdsmen, then there is Nubia, where we have strong and loyal men. Tetisheri will pass on to our sons what our fathers and forefathers passed on to us, and I warn you against no enemy but one—despair."

The king's words had a great impact on all their hearts. Even little Ahmose and Nefertari were downcast and disconcerted and wondered at their grandfather's speaking to them in these serious tones for the first time. Queen Ahotep's eyes filled with tears, at which Seqenenra showed displeasure, telling her in a tone not without reproach, "Do you weep, Ahotep? Observe the courage of our mother, Tetisheri!"

Then he looked at young Ahmose, to whom he was greatly attached and who was a true copy of his grandfather, and he pulled him to him and asked him, smiling, "Which is the enemy of which we must beware, Ahmose?"

The boy replied, not understanding fully the meaning of what he said, "Despair."

The king laughed and kissed him again. Then he stood and said gently, "Come, let us embrace!"

He embraced them all, starting with Tetisheri, his wife Ahotep, and Setkimus, his son's wife, then Ahmose and Nefertari. Then he turned away from them toward Kamose, who was standing rigid and dejected, and he extended his hand to him and squeezed it hard, then bent over it and kissed it and said in a low voice, "Safety be with you, my dear son!"

The king waved to them with his hand and left the place with firm steps, his face filled with courage and resolve.

———

The king set forth at the head of a force of his guards and encountered in the palace square throngs of Thebans, men and women, who had come to salute their king and cheer those who set off in hopes of liberating the valley. Seqenenra made his way through their surging waves in the direction of Thebes' northern gate and there he found the priests, ministers, chamberlains, notables, and higher officials gathered to bid him farewell. They prostrated themselves to his cavalcade and long called his name, and the last voice that the king heard was that of Nofer-Amun telling him, "Soon I shall receive you, my lord, your head wreathed in laurels! God hear my prayer!"

The king passed through the Great Gate of Thebes on his way to the north and left the mighty walls of the city behind him, much affected by what he had seen and heard, sensible of the gravity of the great work that lay before him and preoccupied with how it might redound to the happiness or misery of his people for years to come. The destiny of Egypt had been placed in his hands and he faced head-on the fearful dangers that his father had dealt with by tarrying and delaying. Seqenenra was no pampered ruler, but steadfast, courageous, rough-hewn, and pious by nature; he had great hope and was full of confidence in his people. He caught up with his army before evening, at the camp in the town of Shanhur, to the north of Thebes, and Commander Pepi received him at the head of the division commanders. Exhaustion and hardship had lowered his spirits and his condition did not escape the notice of the king, who said to him, "I see you are tired, Commander."

The commander, pleased to see his lord, said, "We have managed, my lord, to gather the garrisons of Hermonthis, Habu, and Thebes. Altogether, they compose an army of close to twenty thousand warriors."

As the king proceeded in his chariot between the soldiers' tents, a wave of enthusiasm and joy overcame them and his name resounded through the camp.

Then he turned back and returned to the royal tent, Commander Pepi at his side. The king was reassured as to his army, to whose training he had devoted the best years of his youth, and he said, "Our army is valiant. How do you find the morale of the commanders?"

"All are optimistic, my lord, and eager for war. There is none that does not express his admiration for the archers' division, of historic fame."

The king said, "I share with you in this admiration. Now listen to me. We must lose no time beyond that necessary to rest this number of soldiers. We must meet our foe—if he really attacks us—in the sloping valley between Panopolis and Batlus. It is very rugged, with narrow entry points. The military advantage there belongs to him who holds its heights. Also, the Nile's stream there is narrow and this may help our fleet during its engagement with the enemy."

"We shall start marching, my lord, just before dawn."

The king nodded his head in assent and said, "We must reach Panopolis and be camped in its valley before Khayan returns to Memphis."

Then the king summoned his commanders to meet with him.

8

The army moved just before dawn, preceded to its objectives by a force of scouts. The chariot division, formed of two hundred chariots and with Pharaoh at their head, went first, followed by the lancers; then came the archers' division, then the small arms division and the carts for the supplies, weapons, and tents. At the same time, the fleet set sail for the north. The darkness was intense, its blackness alleviated only by the rays of the watching stars and the lights of the torches. When they reached the city of Gesyi, everyone awoke to welcome Pharaoh and his army. The peasants hurried from the furthest fields carrying palm fronds, sweet-smelling herbs, and jugs of beer and they walked alongside cheering and presenting the soldiers with flowers and cups of the delicious beer, and did not leave them until they had gone some distance and the darkness of the night had faded and the calm blue light of dawn had poured into the eastern horizon, announcing the coming of day. Day broke, light bathed the world, and the army marched quickly on until, just before midafternoon, it reached Katut where it rested for a while among the people of the place, who received them warmly. The king decided that the army should camp for the night at Dendara, issuing an order to resume the march, and the army proceeded until it reached Dendara as night was falling, surrendering there to a deep sleep.

Day after day the army rose before dawn and marched on till dark, until it found itself encamped at Abydos. Scouts were patrolling to the north of the city when one of their officers saw, at great distance, groups of people moving over the earth. At the head of a troop of his men, he made toward the approaching people, things becoming clearer the further he went down the valley. He saw crooked lines of peasants moving in bands carrying whatever of their belongings they could and some driving flocks or cattle, their appearance indicating misery and dispossession. Wondering, the man rode up to those at the front and was about to question them when one of them shouted to him, "Save us, soldier! They surprised us and destroyed us!"

Alarmed, the officer shouted back, "Save you? What has alarmed you?"

Many of them answered with one voice, "The Herdsmen, the Herdsmen!"

And the first man said, "We are the people of Panopolis and Ptolemais. One of the border guards came to us and told us that the Herdsmen's army was attacking the borders with huge forces that soon would burst through to our village. He advised us to flee to the south. Terror seized the village and the fields and we all hurried to our homes to call our women and children and carry away whatever we could. Then we fled and left the villages behind us and we haven't rested for an instant since yesterday morning."

Faintness and fatigue were visible in the faces and the officer told them, "Rest a little, then be quickly on your way. Shortly this quiet valley will be turned into a field of combat!"

Then the man gathered the reins of his horse and galloped off to the commander's tent at Abydos and informed him. Pepi went immediately to Pharaoh and told him the news, which he received with astonishment and distress, shouting, "How can that be? Could Khayan have informed Memphis in so short a time?"

Pepi replied in fury, "There can be no doubt, my lord, that the enemy assembled its army on our borders before sending us its envoy. They set a trap for us and only presented their demands in the hope that we would reject them. When Khayan crossed our border on his way back, he gave the order to the assembled armies to attack. This is the only reasonable explanation for such a violent and rapid assault."

King Seqenenra's face turned pale with anger and fury and he said, "So Panopolis and Ptolemais have fallen?"

"Alas, yes, my lord. The valor of our small garrison alone was not sufficient to defend them."

The king shook his head in sorrow and said, "We have lost our best fighting ground."

"That will have no effect on the courage of our magnificent fighting men."

The king thought for a moment, then said to the commander of his armies, "We must evacuate Abydos and Dendara completely."

Pepi looked questioningly at the king, who said, "We cannot defend these cities."

Pepi grasped what his lord meant. He asked, "Does my lord wish to meet the enemy in the valley of Koptos?"

"That is want I want. There, the enemy can be attacked from many directions. There are natural forts in the sides of the valley. I shall leave bands behind in the cities that we evacuate to harry them without engaging them in combat. This will hold up their advance until we have strengthened our positions. Come, Pepi. Send your messengers to the cities to evacuate them and order the commanders to retreat at once. Lose no time, for the end of one of the ropes of the swing in which the destiny of our people is balanced is now in the hand of Apophis!"

9

The crier called out to the peoples of Abydos, Barfa, and Dendara, "Take your belongings and your money and go south! Your homes have become a battle ground that will know no mercy." The people knew the Herdsmen and their ways. Fear seized them and they rushed to get their money and possessions, which they piled onto carts pulled by oxen, and to gather their cattle and flocks, driving them fast. They sorted themselves out and hastened southward, leaving their lands and homes, brokenhearted. The further they went, the more they threw dark looks behind them, their hearts tugging them toward their homes. Then fear would seize them and they would hasten on toward the unknown that awaited them. On their way, they would pass divisions of the army and their hearts would feel easier in their breasts. Hope would toy with their painful dreams and their lips would part in a smile of joy that would shine in the sky of their woes as the sun's rays light up a gap in the clouds revealed for a second on an overcast day. They would wave to them and many would call out, "The lands entrusted to our keeping have been wrested from us. Restore them to us, brave soldiers!"

While this was happening, Pharaoh was overseeing the distribution of his forces in the valley of Koptos, watching with sad eyes the bands of fugitives whose stream surged endlessly past. He felt their sorrows as though he were one of them, his pain redoubling every time the wind brought their acclamations of his name and their prayers for him to his ears.

Commander Pepi was in constant contact with the scouts, receiving news from them and then passing it on to his lord. Thus it was that news of the enemy's attack on Abydos and the obstinate resistance of its small garrison reached him, brought by their last survivor. On the morning of the following day, the messenger brought news of the Hyksos attack on the city of Barfa and of the stratagems and dogged maneuvers to which its defenders had resorted in order to delay the enemy's advance as much as they could. At Dendara, the garrison had stood firm against the advancing enemy for many long hours, forcing it to use large numbers of troops against them, as though it were attacking an army fully manned and equipped. The scouts and some officers who had escaped from the garrisons of the invested cities put the enemy's forces at between fifty and seventy thousand, with a chariot division of not less than a thousand vehicles. The king received this last intelligence with surprise and dismay, as neither he nor any other member of his army had expected the army of Apophis to possess so many. He said to his commander, "How can our chariot division overcome this terrible number?"

Pepi was at a loss as he asked himself this same question and he said to his lord, "The archers' division will take on the task, my lord."

The king shook his head in astonishment and said, "In the past, chariots were not instruments of war that the Herdsmen used, so how is it that their army has many times more of them than ours?"

"What pains me, my lord, is that the hands that made them are Egyptian."

"That, indeed, is a painful thought. But can the archers resist a flood of chariots?"

"Our men, my lord, do not miss their marks. Tomorrow Apophis will see that their forearms are more powerful than his chariots, however many they may be!"

That evening Pharaoh withdrew on his own, feeling helpless and oppressed. He prayed long and ardently to the Lord, imploring Him to send him cheer, steady his heart, and make victory his and his army's lot.

Everyone could feel the closeness of the enemy. They raised their level of alertness and passed the night anxiously, longing for the morning so that they might throw themselves into the battle of death.

10

The army roused itself a good while before daybreak. The doughty bowmen took their fortified places in the field with a small force of chariots to assist each. Seqenenra stood before his tent with his commander Pepi in the middle of a ring of the men of his stalwart guard. He was saying to them, "It would be unwise for us to fling a division of chariots into a confrontation with forces it cannot overcome. However, these scattered chariots will help our fortified archers to wound the enemy's horsemen and their horses. Apophis will doubtless begin his attack with the chariots, because the other divisions of the army cannot engage until the outcome of the chariot battle is clear. So let us direct our attention to disabling the Herdsmen's chariots, to allow the invincible divisions of our army to enter the battle and destroy the enemy."

Destruction of the enemy's chariots was the dream in which he dwelt. With all his heart he pleaded with his Lord Amun in prayer, "O God, decree that we may overcome this obstacle!

Take the part of your faithful sons, for if you forsake us today your name will go unspoken in your noble sanctuary and the doors of your pure temple will close!"

The king and Commander Pepi mounted their chariots and the royal guard surrounded them, while two hundred war chariots stood behind them. Then the javelin division advanced and formed two lines, to the king's right and left. All were waiting for him to give the call to battle, once the archers and the chariots that supported them had carried out their first task.

As first light began to appear, a scout came and informed the king that the Egyptian fleet had engaged with the Herdsmen's in the battle for the garrison to the north of Koptos. The king said to the commander of his army, "Apophis has realized no doubt that he will face fierce resistance. This is why he has ordered his fleet to attack, so that he can drop troops behind our positions."

Pepi replied, "The Herdsmen, my lord, have not mastered the art of fighting on board ship. The sacred Nile will swallow the corpses of their soldiers and with them Apophis's hopes of besieging us."

Seqenenra had great confidence in the men of the Theban fleet, yet he recommended to the commander of the scouts that he stay in constant contact with the naval battle. The darkness started to dissipate and morning to come and the battlefield started to reveal itself to the watching eyes. Seqenenra beheld his archers, bows in hand, with the few chariots readying themselves to fight beside them. And on the other side he saw the Herdsmen's army spreading like churned dust. The enemy was waiting for the morning to appear and as soon as it did so, the chariots moved in readiness for the battle. Then some of them swooped down on some of the forward fortified positions and arrows flew, horses neighed, and warriors screamed. Other forces leapt forward, then engaged with the Egyptian archers and some of the Egyptian chariots in violent combat. Seqenenra shouted, "Now the battle for Thebes is joined!"

Pepi said in vibrant tones, "Indeed, my lord. And a fine beginning our soldiers have made!"

All eyes were trained on the field, watching the progress of the battle. They saw the Herdsmen's chariots attack a line, then split into separate groups and charge the archers rapidly and violently, pouncing on any Egyptian chariots that barred their way. The dead fell quickly on either side, with death-defying courage. The archers showed their mettle, standing firm against their attackers, picking off their horsemen and steeds and decimating them, leading Pepi to shout out, "If the fighting goes on this way, we shall get the better of their chariots in a few days!"

Meanwhile, the Herdsmen's forces would charge and fight, then retire to their camp, while others swooped down, so as to not exhaust their strength. At the same time, the Egyptians defended themselves without let or rest, solidly established in their positions. Whenever Seqenenra saw one of his horsemen or chariots disabled, he would angrily cry "Alas!" keeping an exact tally of how many of his army had been lost. The numbers of units used by the Herdsmen for the attack started to increase and they started to charge first in threes, then in sixes, then in tens. The fighting grew fiercer and fiercer and the number of the Hyksos's chariots multiplied until Seqenenra was overwhelmed with anxiety and said to Pepi, "We somehow have to counter the increase in enemy numbers to restore balance to the field."

"But, my lord, we must keep our reserve chariots till the final stages of the fight."

"Don't you see how the enemy comes back at us every little while with new troops fresh for the fight?"

"I see their plan, my lord, but we cannot keep pace with them, so many are their chariots and so few are ours."

The king gritted his teeth and said, "We never expected that they would have this superiority in chariots. Whatever happens, I cannot leave my archers without relief, for they are the only archers in my army."

The king ordered twenty chariots to charge in five units. They swooped down like predatory eagles and brought new life to the field, but Apophis, hoping to repel Seqenenra's new onslaught once and for all, sent twenty units into the field, each composed of five chariots. The earth shook with their clatter, the air was filled with clouds of flying dust, the battle reached fever pitch, and blood flowed like a river. Time passed and the battle's violence neither abated nor diminished, until the sun was at the center of the sky. Then scouts came and announced to the king that the Herdsmen's fleet had pulled back after having two of its ships taken captive and another sunk. The news of the victory came at just the right time to strengthen the Egyptians' resolve and steady their hearts. The officers broadcast it among the battling divisions and to those waiting their turn to enter the fray and it called forth an echo of joy in their breasts and an upsurge of energy in their hearts. However, the same news rang in Apophis's ears too, and, overcome with anger, he immediately changed his deliberately paced plan and issued an order to the whole chariot force to charge and exact revenge. Seqenenra saw a vast flood of chariots swooping down on his valiant archers from every side and clutching them in its sharp talons. The king was greatly alarmed and shouted out in rage, "Our troops, exhausted by constant struggle, cannot withstand this flood of chariots alone!"

He turned to the commander of his army and said in decisive tones that brooked no discussion, "We shall enter a decisive battle with the forces that we have. Order our brave officers to lead our divisions to the attack and inform them of my desire that each perform his duty as a soldier of immortal Thebes!"

Seqenenra knew the horror that awaited him and his army but he was brave and possessed of great faith and, not hesitating for even a moment, he looked to the sky and said in a clear voice, "Lord Amun, do not forget your faithful sons!" then issued the order to the chariot force surrounding him to charge and sprang forward at their head to meet the enemy.

Now began a battle of the greatest horror, in which the screams of man and horse rang loud, helmets flew, heads rolled, and blood flowed. The bravery of the Egyptians, however, was of no avail against the swift armored chariots, which decimated their ranks and harvested them like chaff. Seqenenra fought magnificently, never despairing or flagging, appearing at times as though he were the angel of death, choosing whomever he wished from the enemy. The battle went on until the late afternoon, at which point victory appeared to favor the Herdsmen, who gathered themselves to deliver the final stroke, and a large chariot, guarded by a mighty force led by an intrepid horseman with a long, shining white beard, charged at Seqenenra's chariot and forced its way through the ranks with extraordinary bravery. The king grasped the objective of the daring horseman and hastened toward him till they met face to face. They exchanged two terrible thrusts with their javelins, each deflecting the thrust aimed at him with his shield as he readied himself for the fight. Seqenenra saw his opponent unsheathe his sword and realized that his first attempt had not satisfied him. He unsheathed, therefore, his own and rushed toward him, but, at that critical moment, an arrow lodged in his arm, his hand was seized by a spasm, and the sword fell from it. Many of the king's guard cried out, "Beware, my lord, beware!" but the foe reached him faster than the warning and with all his strength aimed a terrible blow at his neck. It found its mark and, an expression of excruciating pain upon his dark-complexioned face, he came to a halt, incapable of further resistance. His foe seized a javelin with his right hand and flung it hard and it lodged in the king's left side. He staggered as though stupefied and fell to the ground. Shouts arose all around and the Egyptians said, "Dear God! The king is fallen! Defend the king!" while the enemy commander, with a triumphant smile, cried out, "Finish the impudent rebel off, and spare not one of his men!" The fighting intensified around the king's fallen body, and a horseman, consumed with malice, swooped down upon it, raised his sharp axe, and brought it down on his head. The double crown of Egypt was dislodged and fell and the blood spurted like a spring, at which the man dealt him another blow, above his right eye, smashing the bones and hideously scattering the brains. Many were those who wanted to snatch from that bloody feast some morsel to satisfy their rancor and they rushed in upon the corpse, aiming at it cruel, insane jabs that struck the eyes, mouth, nose, cheeks, and chest, and ripped the body to pieces, bathing it in a sea of blood.

Pepi fought at the head of those of his soldiers that remained, pushing back the enemy forces surging toward the spot where his lord had fallen. Once they had despaired of gaining anything further by continuing the battle, life lost its meaning for the soldiers, who determined to seek martyrdom on the spot that their brave sovereign had watered with his blood. One by one they fell, until night overtook them and the world put on mourning, and the two sides ceased fighting, exhausted by their efforts, weakened by their wounds.

11

The soldiers came out with torches to look for their dead and wounded. Commander Pepi stood next to his chariot, utterly exhausted, his heart preoccupied with thoughts of the corpse whose guiltless blood had stained the field. He heard the voice of a commander saying, "What a wonder! How could the fighting have come to an end so fast? Who would believe that we lost the bulk of our forces in a single day? How could Thebes' courageous soldiers have been overcome?"

Another voice, so exhausted as to sound like a death rattle, responded, "It was the chariots that could not be resisted. They destroyed all Thebes' hopes."

Commander Pepi called out to them, "Soldiers, have you performed your duty to the corpse of Seqenenra? Let us search for it among the corpses!"

A shudder passed through their drooping bodies and each took a torch and followed Pepi in silence, tongue-tied by the depth of their sorrow. At the spot where the king fell they split up, the moans of the wounded and the raving of the feverish ringing in their ears. Pepi could barely see what was before him for sorrow and pain, and could not believe that he was indeed searching for the body of Seqenenra. It was too much for him to grant that the fight for Thebes had ended on that sorrowful day. With tears streaming from his eyes, he said, "Bear witness and wonder, land of Koptos! We search for the body of Seqenenra among your dunes. Be gentle with it and make a soft bed for its injured ribs! Did it not sacrifice itself for you and for Thebes? Alas, my lord, who will stand up for Thebes now that you are gone? Who do we have but you?" He remained thus distressed until he heard a voice call out, "Companions, come! Here is the body of our lord." He ran toward him, torch in hand, his eyes wide with terror at the awful sight that he was about to see. When he reached the corpse, an echoing scream of anger mixed with pain escaped his lips. He found the king of Thebes a disfigured lump of torn flesh, bones protruding, blood everywhere, and the crown thrown aside. In anger he shouted, "Vile foreigners! They have treated the body as hyenas would the corpse of the ravening lion. But it can never harm you that they have torn your pure body, for you lived as a king of Thebes must live and died the death of a valiant hero!" Then he shouted to those around him who were struck motionless by sorrow, "Bring the royal litter! Off with you, you sleepers!" Some officers brought the litter and all helped to lift the body and place it upon it, while Pepi lifted up the double crown of Egypt and placed it beside the king's head, then wrapped the corpse in a winding sheet. They raised the litter in painful silence and proceeded with it toward the broken camp and placed it in the tent that had lost its protector and master forever. All the commanders and officers who had escaped with their lives stood around the litter with heads bent, worn out with misery, their looks filled with a deep sadness. Pepi turned to them and said in a strong voice, "Arouse yourselves, companions! Do not surrender to sorrow! Sorrow will not bring Seqenenra back to us, yet it may make us forget our duty toward his corpse, his family, and our country, for whose sake he was killed. What has happened has happened, but the remaining chapters of the tragedy are still to be acted out. We must be steadfast at our posts so that we may perform our duty to the full."

The men raised their heads and gritted their teeth as do those who are filled with resolve and strength and looked at their commander as though thereby to offer him their pledge of death. Pepi said, "The truly courageous do not let disasters make them forget their duty. It may be true that we must admit that we have lost the battle for Thebes but our duty is not yet over. We must prove that we are worthy of a noble death, as we were of a noble life!"

All then shouted, "Our king has set us his example. We shall follow in his footsteps!"

Pepi's face rejoiced, and he said with pleasure, "You are the offspring of brave soldiers! Now listen to me! Few of our army remain, but tomorrow we shall lead them into battle to the last man and by fighting delay the advance of Apophis long enough for Seqenenra's family to find a means of escape, for as long as the members of this family are alive, the war between us and the Herdsmen is not over, though the battlefields may fall silent for a while. I shall leave you for a few hours to carry out my duty toward this corpse and its valiant offspring, but shall return to you before dawn, that we may die together on the field of battle."

He asked them to pray together before the body of Seqe-nenra and they knelt together and immersed themselves in ardent prayer, Pepi completing his with the words: "Merciful God, enfold our valiant sovereign with your mercy in Osiris's abode, and grant our destiny be a death as happy as his, so that we may meet him in the Western World with heads held high!"

Then he called some soldiers and ordered them to carry the litter to the royal ship, and he turned toward his companions and said, "I commend you to the Lord's safekeeping! Till we meet again soon."

He walked behind the litter till they placed it in the deck cabin, then said to them, "When the ship has brought you to Thebes, proceed to the temple of Amun and place it in the sacred hall and do not answer any who question you about him until I come to you."

Then the commander returned to his chariot and ordered the driver to proceed to Thebes and the chariot dashed off with them at tremendous speed.

————

Thebes had surrendered its eyelids to sleep under a curtain of darkness that enveloped its temples, obelisks, and palaces, unaware of the weighty events taking place outside its walls. Pepi made his way straight to the royal palace and announced his arrival to the guards. The head chamberlain came quickly, returned his greeting, and asked anxiously, "What news, Commander?"

In accents heavy with sadness, Pepi replied, "You will know everything in due time, Head Chamberlain. Now I seek your permission for an audience with the crown prince."

The chamberlain left the room ill at ease, returning after a short while to say, "His Highness awaits you in his private wing." The commander went to the crown prince's wing and entered, finding him in the reception hall. He prostrated himself before the prince, who was astonished at the unexpected visit. When Pepi raised his head and the prince saw his haggard face, tired eyes, and pallid lips, anxiety seized him and he asked, as the chamberlain had done, "What news, Commander Pepi? It must be an important matter that calls you to leave the field at this time."

The commander replied in a voice heavy with sorrow and gloom, "My lord, the gods—for reasons whose wisdom is hidden from me—are still angry with Egypt and its people!"

The words seized the prince's soul like a stranglehold about his neck and he fathomed what grievous news they indicated. Anxious and fearful, he asked, "Has our army met with a disaster? Is my father asking for aid?"

Pepi hung his head and said in a low voice, "Alas, my lord, Egypt lost its shepherd on the evening of this ill-fated day."

Prince Kamose leapt up in terror and shouted at him, "Is my father really injured?"

Pepi said in a sad, heavy voice, "Our sovereign Seqenenra fell fighting at the head of his troops like a mighty hero. That noble, undying page in the annals of your mighty family has been turned."

Raising his head, Kamose said, "Dear God, how could you let your enemy overcome your faithful son? Dear God, what is this catastrophe that falls on Egypt? But what use is it to complain? This is not the time to weep. My father has fallen, so I must take his place. Wait, Commander, till I return to you in my battle dress!"

However, Commander Pepi said quickly, "I did not come here, my lord, to summon you to the fight. That matter, alas, is decided."

Kamose gave him a sharp hard look and asked, "What do you mean?"

"There is no point in fighting."

"Has our brave army been destroyed?"

Pepi hung his head and said with extreme sorrow, "We lost the decisive battle by which we had hoped to liberate Egypt, and the main force of our army was destroyed. There is no real advantage to be gained from fighting and we will fight only to provide the family of our martyred sovereign time to escape."

"You want to fight so that we can flee like cowards, leaving our soldiers and our country prey to the enemy?"

"No. I want you to flee as do the wise who weigh the consequences of their actions and look to the distant future, submitting to defeat should it occur, and withdrawing from the combat for a time, then losing no time in gathering their scattered forces and starting anew. Please, my lord, summon the queens of Egypt and let the matter be decided by counsel."

Prince Kamose summoned a chamberlain and sent him to look for the queens, while he kept pacing to and fro, alternately seized by sorrow and anger, the commander standing before him uttering not a word. The queens came hurrying, Tetisheri and Ahotep, then Setkimus, and when their eyes fell on Commander Pepi and he had bowed to them in greeting, and they had seen the anguish written on Kamose's face despite his apparent calm, they felt fear and agitation and looked away. Impatiently, Kamose and he asked them to sit and said, "Ladies, I called you to give you sad news."

He paused a moment so that they would not be taken unawares, but they were alarmed and Tetisheri asked anxiously, "What news, Pepi? How is our lord Seqenenra?"

Kamose replied in a trembling voice, "Grandmother, your heart is perceptive, your intuition speaks true. God strengthen your hearts and help you bear the painful news. My father Seqenenra was killed in the field and we have lost the battle."

He turned his head from them so that he would not see their grief and said, as though to his own despairing soul, "My father has been killed, our armies defeated, and our people condemned to suffer every woe, from the near south to the distant north."

Tetisheri, unable to restrain herself, let out a sigh so anguished she seemed to be vomiting up the fragments of her heart, and said, hand on heart, "How sharp a wound for this aged heart to bear!"

Ahotep and Setkimus sat with lowered heads, hot tears oozed from their eyes, and, were it not for the commander's presence, they would have sobbed out loud.

Surrounded by all this sorrow, Pepi stood silent, his heart heavy, every sense shattered. He hated to waste time futilely and, fearing that the opportunity for his lord's family to escape would be lost, he said, "Queens of the family of my lord Kamose, be patient and strong! Though the matter is too grave for composure, yet the moment calls for wisdom and not for a surrender to sorrow. I entreat you, by the memory of my lord Seqenenra, staunch your tears with patience and pack your belongings, for tomorrow Thebes will be no safe refuge."

Tetisheri asked him, "And Seqenenra's body?"

"Put your mind at rest, My lady. I shall fulfill my duty to it in full."

Once more she posed a question, "And where do you want us to go?"

"My lady, the kingdom of Thebes will fall into the hands of the invaders for a while but we have another safe home in Nubia. The Herdsmen will never covet Nubia, for life there is a struggle they are too pampered to bear. Take it as a secure refuge. There you have supporters from our own people and followers among our neighbors, and there you will be able to take stock in peace, foster hope for a new future, and work for that with patience and courage, until such time as the Lord grants that glorious light pierce the shadows of this dark night."

Kamose was listening to him calmly and tranquilly and he said, "Let the family flee to Nubia. For myself, I prefer to be at the head of my army and share its fortunes, in life and in death."

Seized by anxiety, the commander looked pleadingly at his lord and said, "My lord, I can never turn you aside from something that you have decided, so I entrust the matter to your wisdom. All I ask is that you listen to me a little.

"My lord, to fight today is to waste oneself wantonly and destruction will be the unavoidable outcome. Egypt will not benefit by your death, nor will your death alleviate any of her sufferings. However, there is no doubt that if she lose you, she will lose something that cannot be replaced. All hopes of salvation depend on your life, so do not deny Egypt hope after she has been denied happiness. Make Napata your goal and set off! There you will find space to think and plan and prepare means of defense and struggle. This war will not end as Apophis wants, for a people such as ours that has lived a sovereign nation cannot tolerate humiliation for long. Thebes will be liberated within a short time, my lord. Your determination will never flag and you will pursue the filthy Herdsmen until you have driven them from your country. The glory of that wonderful day hovers before my eyes in the darkness of the melancholy present. So do not hesitate, but be resolute in your wisdom. Now that I have shown you the proper path, decide as you see fit."

Pepi stopped speaking but his eyes continued to plead and hope and Tetisheri turned to Kamose and said in a low voice, "What the commander says is true, so follow his advice."

The unhappy commander felt a ray of hope and joy sprang again in his heart, but Kamose frowned and said nothing. Lying for the first time in his life, Pepi said, "I myself will join you there in a short while. I have two sacred duties to perform: to take care of my lord's corpse, and to oversee the reinforcement of the walls of Thebes. Perhaps that way, by successful resistance, it will be able to bargain for surrender on the best terms."

The queens were unable to contain themselves any longer and burst out weeping, and Pepi himself was overcome and said, "We must be brave in the face of this adversity. Let us take Seqenenra as our model and remember always, my lord, that the cause of our defeat was the war chariots. If one day you turn against the enemy anew, make chariots your weapon.

Now I must go to summon the slaves to load up the golden valuables and weapons that are in the palace that cannot be dispensed with."

With these words, Commander Pepi left.

12

The palace was filled with sudden activity. All the rooms were lit and the slaves set about loading up the clothes, arms, and caskets of gold and silver, taking them to the royal ship in mournful silence under the supervision of the head chamberlain. The royal family waited the while in King Kamose's room, plunged in melancholy silence, heads bent, eyes darkened with despair and grief. They remained thus for a while, until Chamberlain Hur came in to them and said in a low voice, "It is finished, my lord."

The chamberlain's words entered their ears as an arrow does the flesh. Their hearts beat fast and they raised their heads distractedly, exchanging looks of despair and grief. Was everything truly finished? Had the hour of farewell come? Was this the end of the era of the palace of the pharaohs, of Thebes the Glorious, and of immortal Egypt? Would they be denied henceforth the sight of the obelisk of Amenhotep, the temple of Amun, and the hundred-gated walls? Would Thebes reject them today only to open its gates tomorrow to Apophis so that he might ascend the throne and hold the power of life and death in his hands? How could the guides become the lost, the lords the fugitives, the masters of the house the dispossessed?

Kamose saw that they had not moved, so he rose lethargically and muttered in a low voice, "Let us bid farewell to my father's room." They stood as he had, and the family proceeded with heavy, listless steps to the room of the departed king and stood before its closed door, intimidated, not know-ing how they could intrude without his permission or face its emptiness. Hur moved forward a step and opened the door. They entered, their labored breaths and ardent sighs preceding them, and their looks hung with tenderness and love on the mighty hall, the luxurious seats, and elegant tables, their atten-tion coming to rest on the king's oratory, with its beautiful, sanctified niche, in which had been sculpted his image, making obeisance before the Lord Amun. All of them could see him sit-ting on his divan, supporting himself on his cushion, smiling his sweet smile at them, and inviting them to sit. They all felt his soul enfold them and surround them and their sorrowful spirits hovered in the heaven of their memories—memories of a mother, a wife, and a son, memories whose traces mingled with their deep sighs and freely flowing tears.

Kamose awoke to the hearts dissolving about him, and, ap-proaching the image of his father, bent reverently before it, gave its brow a kiss, and then turned aside. Next Tetisheri came forward and bent over the beloved image, planting on its brow a kiss into which she put all the pains of her bereaved and mourning heart. All the family bade farewell to the image of their lost lord and then they left as they had entered, in sorrow-ing silence.

Kamose found Chamberlain Hur waiting for him and asked, "And you, Hur?"

"My duty, my lord, is to follow you like a faithful dog."

The king put his hand on his shoulder in thanks and they all advanced through the pillared halls, Commander Pepi going before them and Kamose walking at the head of his family, fol-lowed by the little prince and princess, Ahmose and Nefertari, then Tetisheri, then Queen Ahotep, and then Queen Setkimus, with Chamberlain Hur bringing up the rear. They descended the stairs to the colonnade, arriving finally in the garden, where slaves accompanied them on either side, carrying torches and lighting the way before them. They reached the ship and were taken out to it one by one, until it had gathered them all. Now came the moment of departure and they took there a farewell look, their eyes losing themselves in the darkness that reigned over Thebes as though enfolding it in garments of mourning. Their stricken hearts broke, wrung by the pain of their tender longing, silence engulfing them so that they seemed almost to have melted into the darkness. Pepi stood before them not saying a word and not daring to break that sad silence, until the king noticed his presence and, sighing, said to him, "The time to say farewell has come."

Pepi said, in a sad and trembling voice, fighting hard to master his emotions, "My lord, would that I had died before I found myself in this position. Let my consolation be that you travel in the path of the Lord Amun and of glorious Thebes. I see that the time to say farewell has truly come, as you say, my lord. So go, and may the Lord protect you with His mercy and watch over you with the eye of His concern. I hope that I may live long enough to witness the day of your return as I have the day of your departure, so that my eye may be gladdened once more by the sight of dear Thebes. Farewell, my lord! Farewell, my lord!"

"Say, till we meet again!"

"Indeed! Till we meet again, my lord!"

He approached his lord and kissed his hand, still controlling his emotions lest he wet that noble hand with his tears. Then he kissed the hands of Tetisheri, Queen Ahotep, Queen Setkimus, the crown prince Ahmose, and his sister Nefertari. He took the hand of Chamberlain Hur affectionately, bowed his head to them all, and left the ship, dazed and silent.

At the garden steps, he stood and watched as the ship started to move with the touch of the oars on the water and drew away from the shore, slowly and deliberately, as though feeling the weight of the sadness of those on board, who had all gathered at the rail, their throbbing spirits bidding farewell to Thebes. Then he let himself go and wept, surrendering himself till his body shook. He continued to look after the precious ship as it slipped into the darkness until it was swallowed by the night. Then he sighed from the depths of his heart and remained where he was, unable to leave the shore and as lonely as if he had fallen live into a deep grave. Finally, he turned slowly away and returned to the palace with slow, sluggish steps, muttering "My Lord, my Lord, where are you? Where are you, my Masters? People of Thebes, how can you sleep in peace when death hovers over your heads? Arise! Seqenenra is dead and his family has fled to the ends of the earth, yet you sleep. Arise! The palace is empty of its masters. Thebes has bid farewell to its kings and tomorrow an enemy will occupy your throne. How can you sleep? Outside the walls, humiliation lies waiting!"

Taking a torch, the commander walked dejectedly through the halls of the palace, moving from wing to wing until he found himself before the throne room, and turned toward it and crossed its threshold, saying, "Forgive me, my lord, for entering without your permission!" To the light of the torch he advanced with faltering steps between the two rows of chairs on which the affairs of state had been settled until he ended at the throne of Thebes and knelt, then prostrated himself and kissed the ground. Then he stood sadly in front before it, the light of the torch flickering with a reddish glow upon his face, and said in a loud voice: "Truly a beautiful and immortal page has turned! We, the dead tomorrow, shall be the happiest people in this valley that never before knew night. Throne, it saddens me to tell you that your master will never return to you and that his heir has gone to a distant land. As for me, I shall never allow you to be the site where the words that tomorrow will consign Egypt to misery take form. Apophis shall never sit upon you. May you disappear as your master disappeared!"

Pepi had resolved to summon soldiers from the palace guard and carry the throne off to wherever he might decide.

13

The soldiers picked up the throne as he commanded and set it on a large carriage. The commander walked before it to the temple of Amun and there they picked up the throne a second time and proceeded behind their commander, preceded by priests, to the sacred hall. In the sacred dwelling, close to the Holy of Holies, they beheld the royal litter, surrounded by soldiers and priests. They placed the throne at its side, astonishment registering on the faces of the priests, who had no forewarning of the matter. Pepi ordered the soldiers to depart and asked for the chief priest. The priest disappeared for a short while, then returned following the priest of Amun, who, understanding well the gravity of such a nocturnal visit, came hurrying, his hand extended to the commander, and saying in his quiet voice, "Good evening, Commander."

Pepi answered in accents that betrayed his concern and anguish, "And to you too, Your Holiness. May I speak with Your Holiness alone?"

The priests heard what he said and quickly withdrew despite their curiosity and disquiet, leaving the place empty. When the chief priest noticed the litter and the throne, dismay appeared on his face and he said to the commander, "What has brought the carriage here? What is this litter and how comes it that you have left the field at this time of night?"

Pepi replied, "Listen to me, Your Holiness. There is nothing to be gained by delay or by making light of our situation. But you must hear me out so that I may inform Your Holiness of everything I know and then go to perform my duty. A battle that will be remembered forever has taken place, in which pain and glory alike took part. No wonder, for we have lost the battle for Egypt, our sovereign has been slain defending his country, treacherous hands have ripped apart his pure body, our royal family has fled Thebes, and, when the people of Thebes awake, they will find no trace of their kings or their glory. Gently, Your Holiness, gently! It is midnight, or almost so, and my duty calls out to me to make haste. This litter bears the corpse of our sovereign Seqenenra and his crown and here is his throne. This is our national heritage that I entrust to you, Priest of Amun, that you may preserve the body and keep it safe and keep these relics in a secure resting place. Now I commend you to the Lord's safekeeping, priest of that Thebes that will never die, though it reel under its wounds!"

The priest would have interrupted the commander, so agitated was he, but the commander did not allow him and he maintained a wooden silence, holding himself unmoving as though lost to all feeling. Pepi grasped the stupefaction and pain that the man must be feeling and said, "I commend you to the Lord's keeping, Your Holiness, confident that you will carry out your duties toward these sacred, precious relics in full."

The commander turned away from him toward the litter, bowed his head reverently to kiss its covering, and gave it a military salute. Then he walked backward away from it, the litter hidden from his eyes by his tears. When he reached the stairs leading to the Hall of the Columns, he turned his back and walked quickly out of the temple, sparing glances for nothing. He knew that the time had come for him to rejoin his officers and men, so that he might make the last attack with them, as he had promised.

His preoccupation with his duties did not, however, make him forget something which, as soon as he thought of it, weighed unceasingly on his heart: his family—Ebana his wife, his little son Ahmose, and all the kin who lived together on his farm on the outskirts of Thebes. He could not cover the distance to his farm by night and were he to do so he would not be able to fulfill his promise to his soldiers and they would think he had fled. He would meet his end without casting a farewell glance at the faces of Ebana and Ahmose. Yet there was something that weighed even more on his heart. He asked himself sorrowfully, "Will the Herdsmen leave the landowner on his land or leave those who have wealth their wealth? Tomorrow, the masters will be driven into the streets or murdered in their houses and Ebana and Ahmose will be left with no one to take their part." The man grew dejected and for a long while his heart tugged toward his house and family, but his heart was on one course and his will of steel on another. He sighed in sorrow and said, "Let me then write her a letter," and, having spread out a sheet on his chariot, wrote to Ebana, extending his greetings, commending her to the Lord's keeping, and praying for his son's safety and happiness. Then he narrated to her the events that had occurred and what had happened to the army and its sovereign. And he told her of the royal family's flight to a place unknown (omitting, for reasons of his own, to mention Nubia) and advised her to collect as much of her wealth as she could and flee with her son and those of the family and their neighbors who were dependent on her to the country outside Thebes, or to one of the quarters of the poor, where she could mix with the common folk and share with them a common fate. Finally, he gave her and his son his blessings and ended the letter by saying, "We shall meet for certain, Ebana, here or in the Netherworld." He gave the letter to his driver and charged him to take it to his country villa and deliver it to his wife, then jumped into his chariot, cast a last look at the temple of Amun and the peacefully sleeping city as it lay plunged in darkness and cried out from the depths of his heart, "Lord God, keep your city safe! Thebes, farewell!"

Then he gave his horses their heads and they galloped off with him along the road to the north.

14

The commander reached camp after midnight. The injured army slept, so he went to his tent and threw himself on his bed exhausted, saying, "Let us rest a little, so that we may die a death worthy of the commander of the army of Seqenenra" and closed his eyes. Unbidden thoughts, however, interposed a thick veil between him and sleep. Phantoms of the horrors with which he had been afflicted during the preceding day and night appeared before him. He saw the archers facing the chariots that poured down upon them like a flashflood; his lord Seqenenra falling smitten, the javelin in his side; Kamose raging with anger, then submitting in sorrow, while Tetisheri moaned from the wound inflicted on her ancient heart; the farewell to Ebana and little Ahmose; and the lowering clouds gathering on the southern horizon. These thoughts seemed to come together into a single wave that rose and then broke, unbeknownst to him, for sleep had slipped between his eyelids.

He awoke at dawn to the sound of a trumpet and rose, feeling a strange energy at odds with the exhaustion, weakness, and lack of sleep that he had suffered. He left his tent and in the quietness of morning heard movement stirring throughout the camp and saw the wraiths of his men coming toward him, recognizing his faithful, valiant officers from their voices and greeting them warmly. They had done much during his absence. One of them said, "We sent the wounded in boats to Thebes and those who were lightly injured too, so that they could join the defenders of the walls of Thebes. Thebes will certainly defend itself well, to obtain the best conditions."

Another officer told him with great ardor, "We people of the South pay little heed to life at times of trial. There isn't a man among us whose patience has not run out waiting for the final battle."

A third said, "How we long to find martyrdom in this sacred spot, watered by the pure blood of our sovereign!"

Pepi praised them warmly and related to them what had taken place in Thebes by way of the flight of the royal family but did not tell anyone where they were headed. This news affected the officers deeply and they cheered for King Kamose, for Ahmose the crown prince, and for the Sacred Mother, Tetisheri.

The shadows of night dissolved and a brilliant light was reflected on the sky of the horizon. The soldiers formed their ranks in preparation for the battle of death. The king of the Herdsmen understood well what had come over the army of the Egyptians after the death of their sovereign and he wanted to strike a lightning blow with such forces as would paralyze any resistance on their part. Thus, chariots and archers readied themselves at the head of his troops, in order to put paid with one stroke to the small army that barred their way. When the two hordes caught sight of one another, the fighting started, the raging sea joined up with the quiet stream, the army of Apophis closed in on the Egyptian army, and the wheel of death started to turn. The Egyptians gave everything men can give by way of bravery and heroism, but they fell fast, hero after hero, and the horses' hooves trampled them cruelly. It seemed to Pepi that the battle would be over quickly, especially when he saw how many commanders and officers were meeting their ends. Seeing his right wing rapidly reduced to nothing and the enemy on the verge of surrounding them, he decided to end his life as nobly as possible. He surveyed the army of his enemy and set his sights on the place where the flag of the Hyksos fluttered above Apophis and his higher commanders, among whom, no doubt, stood the killer of Seqenenra, and he made that his target, ordering his guard to follow him and protect his back; then he ordered his driver to dash forward. It was a sudden move, unexpected by the enemy, which was ever cautious of its own safety. His chariot avoided all those that sought to bar its path and, firing its arrows into the hearts of the lancers, drew closer and closer to Apophis, till most had divined its goal. Then they cried out in fear and anger, and Pepi and those with him fought as though crazed by love of death. Death pampered them long enough for them to burst through the ranks to the line of Apophis and his commanders, where Pepi found himself surrounded on all sides by enemy horsemen and saw hundreds of foot soldiers interpose themselves between his chariot and the king. He fought fiercely, blood flowing from his face, neck, and legs, until it seemed to the enemy that he must be immortal, and the arrows and javelins, the swords and daggers, tore at him like ravenous dogs and he fell as Seqenenra fell, surrounded closely by his valiant guards, the army shaken by his terrible attack. The combat, in the field, was at its end and the Egyptians were breathing their last. Apophis ordered his men to draw back from the corpse of the man who had swooped down upon him through the serried ranks. He descended from his chariot and approached it on foot till he was standing at its head and contemplated the arrows that were planted in every part of it like the quills of a hedgehog. Then he shook his big head and smiled and said to those around him, "He died a death worthy of our bravest men!"

15

Thebes awoke as on any other day, knowing nothing of what was written for it on Fate's tablet. Then villagers appeared, carrying the wounded from the field of battle. The people gathered around them and started asking them question after question. The peasants told them the truth of what had happened, telling them that the army had been defeated and Pharaoh killed, and that his family had fled to an unknown place. The people were stupefied and exchanged looks of denial and alarm. As the news spread in the city, it filled with disturbance and commotion, the people leaving their houses, hastening to the highways and markets, and gathering in the government offices and the temple of Amun to take comfort from the crowd and listen to their leaders. The nobles and the rich who owned estates and villas fled them in terror and groups escaped to the south or hid themselves in the poor quarters.

More sad news arrived, of the fall of Gesyi and Shanhur, and of the Herdsmen's advance toward Thebes to besiege it and force it to surrender. The ministers, the priests, and the thirty judges met in the Hall of the Columns at the temple of Amun and consulted with one another, all aware of the gravity of the situation and feeling that the end was near and resistance futile. Nevertheless, they did not favor surrender without conditions or restrictions, believing that they could stay behind their impenetrable walls till they had obtained a promise to spare the blood of the citizens—all but User-Amun, who was greatly agitated and unable to contain his anger. He told them, "Never surrender Thebes! Let us resist to the death like our sovereign Seqenenra. The walls of Thebes cannot be breached and if they are really threatened, then let us lay waste to the city and set fire to it! Let us leave nothing to Apophis from which he might benefit!"

User-Amun raged and gestured with his hands as though he were preaching, but the men were not enthusiastic about his idea. Nofer-Amun said, "We are responsible for the lives of the people of Thebes and its destruction will expose thousands of them to the loss of their houses and to hunger and misery. Though we have lost the battle, let our goal be to minimize the damage and limit the destruction."

Meanwhile, the Herdsmen were pitilessly attacking the northern wall, the guards resisting them steadfastly and courageously, the dead falling on both sides. The ministers had made an inspection of the wall and were reassured as to the resistance, but the enemy's fleet assaulted that of the Egyptian's after receiving reinforcements, and a fierce battle took place that ended with the smashing of the Egyptian navy. The Herdsmen's fleet then laid siege to western Thebes and many soldiers disembarked to the south of the city, making the siege of the city complete. They followed with a fierce attack from the north, south, and east, threatening it with famine and thirst. The leaders thus saw no alternative but to surrender in order to avoid a catastrophe and they sent an officer to announce a halt to the fighting and seek permission for an envoy from the city to approach in order to discuss the conditions for a final surrender. The officer returned having secured this agreement and the fighting on all the walls came to a halt. The leaders chose Nofer-Amun, the High Priest of Amun, to be their envoy.

The priest accepted reluctantly and mounted his carriage, which took him, eyes downcast, heart broken, toward the Herdsmen's camp. On his way, he passed the various divisions drawn up in rows in all their strength, arrogance, and vainglory. He found some officers waiting for him, at their head a man of short stature, stout, with a thick beard, whom he recognized from the first glance as the envoy Khayan, the herald of ill-fortune who had brought ruin with him to the kingdom of Thebes. The gloating nature of his reception was not lost on Nofer-Amun—the man appeared arrogant, haughty, and puffed up with pride. Looking at Nofer-Amun out of the corner of his eye, he said without greeting, "You see, Priest, the pass to which your prince's views have brought you? You get very excited and make beautiful speeches, but you cannot fight a war and your kingdom has been condemned to disappear forever!"

The chamberlain did not wait for a reply but proceeded in front of him toward the king's tent. Nofer-Amun saw that the tent was like a pavilion, hung with curtains, before it the white, gross guardsmen with their long beards. Permission was granted and he entered and saw in the foreground King Apophis, dressed as a pharaoh, and with the double crown of Egypt on his head. He was terrifying in appearance, with penetrating gaze, white-complexioned with a reddish cast, and a beautiful, flowing beard. He was seated in the midst of a circle of his commanders, chamberlains, and advisers, and the priest bowed to him respectfully and stood silently waiting his command. The king said in sarcastic tones, "Welcome to the priest of Amun, who after today will never again be worshipped in the land of Egypt!"

The priest did not acknowledge these words and remained silent. Then the king laughed loudly and asked him contemptuously, "Are you come to us to dictate to us your conditions?"

Nofer-Amun replied, "Nay, I have come, King, to listen to your conditions, as must the leader of a people who have lost their battle and their sovereign. I have but one request, that you spare the blood of a people who took up arms only to defend its existence."

The king shook his large head and said, "It would be better for you, Priest, to listen carefully to me. The law of the Hyksos does not change over the days and the generations. It is the way of war and power forever. We are white and you are dark. We are masters and you are peasants. Throne, government, and command are ours. So say to your people, 'He who works on our land as a slave will be paid and he who cannot bring himself to do so, let him flee wherever he please in some other land.' And tell them, 'I shall spill the blood of a whole town if any harm comes to one of my men. And if you wish me to spare the people's blood, other than that of Seqenenra's family, have your lords come to me on their knees, the keys of Thebes in their hands. As for you, Priest, go back to your temple and close its doors upon yourselves forever!"

Apophis did not wish to extend the meeting further and he rose to show that it was over, so the priest bowed again and departed the place.

Thebes drank its cup to the dregs. The ministers and judges took its keys and went to Apophis and knelt before him. Thebes opened its gates and Apophis entered at the head of his victorious, conquering armies.

On that day, Apophis made the blood of the family of the ruler of Thebes free for any man to take and ordered all the borders between Egypt and Nubia closed. Then he celebrated his victory with a mighty celebration in which all his armies took part and he divided the land and the wealth among his men. And the South, land and people, fell into his hands.

TEN YEARS LATER

1

The clouds of darkness parted, revealing the sleepy blue of dawn. The surface of the Nile appeared, breathing the breezes of first light. A convoy of ships was descending the river, its head pointing toward the border of Egypt, to the north. The sailors were Nubians, while their two commanders, who were seated in the ship's forward deck cabin, were Egyptians, as their brown complexion and clear features showed. The first was a youth barely twenty years old, endowed by nature with great height, a slender, graceful figure, and a firm, broad chest. His oval face was radiant with the bloom of youth and an exquisite beauty, his black eyes with purity and goodness, and his fine, straight nose with strength and symmetry. It was one of those faces to which nature lends its own majesty and beauty in equal portion. He was wearing the clothes of a rich merchant and had wrapped his lissome body in a costly cloak that perfectly fitted his form. His companion was a man in his sixties, somewhat lean and short, with a prominent, high, straight forehead. His posture manifested the tranquility that often accompanies old age, while his eyes were penetrating. His interest appeared to center more on the youth than on the merchandise carried by the ship and when the convoy approached the region of the border, they left the cabin and went to the prow, gazing with tender, longing eyes. With excitement and apprehension, the youth asked, "Do you think we will set foot on the soil of Egypt? Tell me what we are going to do now."

The old man replied, "We shall anchor the convoy on this shore and send an envoy in a boat up to the border to find a way ahead, which he will pave with pieces of gold."

"Everything depends on their reputation for acquiescence to bribery and responsiveness to the lure of gold. But if our expectations are disappointed . . ."

The youth stopped talking, anxiety in his eyes. The old man said, "So long as one expects nothing but evil from these people, his expectations will not be disappointed!"

The ship turned toward the shore, the rest of the convoy following, and dropped anchor. The youth chose himself to be the convoy's representative. He was so excited and determined that the old man did not stop him and the youth transferred to a boat and rowed with his sinewy arms, leaving the convoy and heading for the border. The old man followed him with his eyes, pleading earnestly, "Lord God Amun, this little son of yours seeks entry to your country for a noble purpose: to strengthen your authority, elevate your name, and liberate your sons. Help him, Lord! Grant him victory, and keep him safe!"

The youth left, pulling strongly on the oars, his back to his goal, turning every now and then to look behind him, his breast burning with longing. As he approached, the very air of his country seemed to acquire a new deliciousness, to which his heart responded with violent pounding. Then, at one of his backward glances, he saw a small war ship moving upstream toward him to cut him off. He realized that the border guards had noticed him and were coming to investigate and brought his boat toward the ship until he heard the voice of the officer standing in the bow shouting at him, "What are you doing, fellow, approaching the prohibited area?"

The youth kept silent until the boat was in the lee of the ship, then respectfully and humbly greeted the bearded officer and, feigning stupidity, said, "The Lord Seth bless you, brave officer! I am bound for your glorious country with costly merchandise!"

The officer scowled and said roughly, "Be off with you, fool! Don't you know that this route has been closed for ten years?"

The handsome youth made a show of astonishment and said, "Then what must one like me, who has collected together costly goods to bring to the divine pharaoh of Egypt and the men of his kingdom, do? Will you allow me to meet the noble governor of Biga Island?"

The officer responded brutally, "You would do better to go back to where you came from while still alive, if you don't want to be buried where you stand prattling."

The youth pulled out from under his cloak a purse, full of gold pieces, and threw it at the officer's feet, saying, "In our country, we greet our gods by offering them presents. Accept my greetings and my request!"

The officer picked up the purse and opened it and his finger-tips played with the pieces of gold. His eyelids blinked and he looked back and forth in stupefaction from the gold to the youth. Then he shook his head as though unable to hide his ex-asperation at this young man who had forced him to go back on his decision and he said in a quiet voice, "Entering Egypt is for-bidden. However, your honorable intentions may merit your ex-emption from the ban. Follow me to the governor of the island."

The youth was delighted, and took his seat once more in the boat and pulling strongly and energetically on the oars contin-ued downstream in the wake of the ship, heading for the shore of Biga. The ship anchored, and then the boat, and the youth put his feet on the ground with care and affection, as though treading on something pure and holy. The officer said to him again, "Follow me!" and he followed in his footsteps. In spite of his effort to maintain control of his emotions, he let himself go; intoxication filled his senses and sublime tenderness seized his heart, which would not stop beating wildly. His feelings be-came so agitated that he fast became overwhelmed. He was in the land of Egypt! The Egypt of which he retained the most beautiful recollections, the most charming images, and the happiest memories! He would have loved to be left alone to fill his breast with its soft breeze and rub its dust into his cheeks! He was in the land of Egypt!

He awoke from his reverie to the unfamiliar voice of the officer telling him for the third time, "Follow me!" and he looked and he saw the palace of the governor of the island. The officer went in and he followed, paying no attention to the piercing looks directed toward him from all sides.

2

He was given permission to enter the reception hall, the officer preceding him. It was the place where the governor received those whose complaints could be settled simply with gold. The youth cast a look at the governor as he went by, taking in his thick, long beard, his piercing, almond-shaped eyes, and his prominent nose, so hooked as to look like the sail of a boat. The man regarded the newcomer minutely, with a cautious and dubious look. The youth bowed before him with great reverence and said with extreme politeness, "The Lord bless your morning, noble governor!"

The officer had spoken to him of the strange arrival who carelessly threw down purses full of gleaming gold pieces and led a convoy loaded with gifts with which to acquire the acquaintance of Egypt's masters. He returned the greeting with a wave of his hand and asked in a gruff, deep voice, "Who are you, and of what country?"

"My lord, I am called Isfinis and my country is Napata, of the land of Nubia."

The man shook his head doubtingly and said, "But I see that you are not Nubian and, if my eyes are not mistaken, you are a peasant."

Isfinis's heart beat hard at this description, which the governor uttered in a tone that was not without contempt. He replied, "Your knowledge of men has not betrayed you, my lord. I am indeed a . . . peasant, of an Egyptian family that migrated to Nubia many generations ago and worked in trade for a long period before the borders between Egypt and Nubia were closed, putting an end to our livelihood."

"And what do you want?"

"With me is a convoy laden with the good things of the country from which it comes. I wish to make it my vehicle to make the acquaintance of Egypt's masters and win their patronage."

The governor played with his beard and looked sharply and doubtfully at him. He said, "Are you saying that you underwent the hardships of the voyage just to 'make the acquaintance of the masters and win their patronage'?"

"Noble governor, we live in a land of wild beasts and treasures, where life is extremely harsh, and hunger and drought have sunk their talons into men's necks. We are skilled at working gold, but exhaust ourselves to obtain a bowl of grain. If your lordships accept my gifts and give me permission to trade between the south and the north, your markets will fill with precious stones and animals and I will have transformed the misery of my people into blessing."

The governor laughed loudly and said, "I see your head is full of dreams! Oughtn't you to start by pleading and begging? But no, you want your efforts to be crowned with royal commands to your benefit! So be it. The stupid are many. Tell me, though, fellow, what 'treasures' does your convoy bring?"

Isfinis bowed his head respectfully and said with the seductiveness of the clever merchant, "Would my lord not prefer to visit my ships to see their treasures himself and choose some precious stone that pleases him?"

Greed and covetousness stirred in the governor's soul. The idea struck him as excellent and he told Isfinis, as he got up to go with him, "I will grant you that honor."

Isfinis preceded him to the warship and thence to the convoy and displayed for the onlookers the bangles, jewelry, and marvelous animals. The governor looked over these treasures with an eye gleaming with rapacious greed and Isfinis presented him with an ivory scepter with a knob of pure gold decorated with emeralds and rubies, which the governor accepted without a word of thanks. Uninvited, he took costly bracelets, rings, and earrings and started to say to himself, "Why shouldn't I let this merchant enter Egypt? This isn't trade. These are captivating gifts that Pharaoh will certainly welcome. If he then grant their owner his wish, he will have got what he came for, and if he refuses, it is nothing to do with me. I have a wonderful opportunity that I must seize. Khanzar, governor of the South, loves all such precious things. Why don't I send him the merchant? He will remember me for my action in presenting him with such treasure and creating an opportunity for him to increase his dealings with his lord. If one day he should want to appoint a governor for one of the larger provinces, he will certainly think of me."

Turning to Isfinis, he said, "I shall give you an opportunity to try your luck. Go straight to Thebes. Here is a letter to the governor of the South. Take it to him so that you can display your treasures and ask for his intercession on behalf of your request."

Isfinis was overjoyed and bowed to the governor in thanks and relief.

3

The first thing that Isfinis did the moment the governor had departed from the ship was to tell the old man who accompanied him, "From this moment on there is no Ahmose here and no Hur. Instead there are Isfinis the trader and his agent Latu."

The old man smiled and said, "You speak wisely, Isfinis the Trader!"

The convoy spread its sails, its oars moved, and it set off downstream with the current toward the borders of Egypt, which it crossed without incident. Isfinis and Latu were standing at the front of the ship enduring the same longing, their eyes almost overflowing with tears. Isfinis said, "A good start!"

Latu replied, "Indeed, so let us pray to the Lord Amun in thanks and ask Him to guide our steps and crown our efforts with an outright victory!"

They knelt down on the deck of the ship and prayed together, then stood as they were before. Isfinis said, "If we succeed in restoring the ties with Nubia to what they were in the past, we shall have won half the battle. We shall give them gold and take men!"

"Don't worry—they are incapable of resisting the lure of gold. Haven't the borders that have been closed for ten years been opened to us? The Herdsman is very arrogant, conceited, and extremely brave, but he is lazy and prefers to employ others, thinking himself above trade, and he cannot tolerate life in Nubia. Thus, his only path to its gold is through someone like Isfinis the Trader who volunteers to bring it to him."

They went on together, casting looks toward the unknown that awaited them beyond the distant horizon that disappeared into the valley of the Nile, turning their gaze on the brilliant green that clothed the villages and hamlets, the birds circling above and the oxen and cattle grazing contentedly below. Here and there, peasants were working, naked, not raising their heads from the land, and the sight of them stirred in the youth's breast both love and anger, while his heart burned with affection and frustration. He said, "See how the soldiers of Amenhotep work as slaves for the stupid, conceited whites with their dirty beards!"

The convoy continued its progress, passing Ombos, Salsalis, Magana, Nekheb, and Tirt, till Thebes was only an hour away and Isfinis asked, "Where should the ship anchor?"

Latu replied, smiling, "To the south of Thebes, where the quarters of the poor and the fishermen are. All of them are purebred Egyptians."

The youth was reassured by his words and, glancing ahead, saw at a distance a ship proceeding toward them. He stared as it slowly approached till he was able to make out its features. He beheld a huge, beautifully-made vessel of outstanding elegance, with, in the middle, a high, handsome deck cabin, its sides glittering with exquisite artwork. It seemed to him that he had seen something like it before. Latu nudged his arm and murmured, "Look."

The young man looked and said quickly, "My God, it's a royal ship!" Then he went on, "It is traveling without guards, so maybe its passenger is a palace official, or a prince seeking solitude."

The ship drew close and almost caught up with the convoy, the unaccustomed sight of which had piqued the curiosity of those onboard. A woman emerged from the deck cabin followed by a bevy of slave girls, whom she preceded unhurriedly like a ray of radiant light dazzling the eyes—blond, the breeze playing with the hem of her white robe, her fine golden tresses dancing. They felt sure she must be a princess from the palace of Thebes, seeking the solace of the breeze.

They saw her point her finger at one of the ships behind them, her mouth open in amazement, while wonder likewise sketched itself on the comely faces of the slave girls. Isfinis looked backward and saw one of the pygmies that he had brought walking on the deck of the ship and realized why the beautiful princess was amazed. He looked at Latu, saying smilingly that one of the gifts had found the appreciation it deserved, but Latu was gazing at the woman, his eyes hard and face dark. The woman called a sailor, who made his way to the side of the ship and shouted, directing his call to Latu in accents that brooked no refusal, "Halt, Nubian, and drop anchor!"

Isfinis acceded to the order and issued a command to the convoy to halt. The royal vessel then drew near to the ship carrying the pygmy and the sailor asked Isfinis, "What is this convoy?"

"A trade convoy, sir."

He gestured with his hand at the pygmy, who was fleeing to the bowels of the ship, and said, "Is the creature dangerous?"

"Not at all, sir!"

"Her Pharaonic Highness wishes to look at the creature close up."

Latu whispered, "That is the title of Pharaoh's daughter."

Isfinis for his part lowered his head in respect and said, "It is my pleasure to obey!"

He quickly left the ship in a boat with which he crossed to the other ship, where he climbed onto the deck to receive the princess, who, with her entourage, was approaching in a boat from her ship. They mounted the deck, preceded by the princess, and the youth bowed before her with a show of reverence, resisting his feeling of humiliation, and pretending to be embarrassed and confused. He stammered, "You do our convoy great honor, Your Highness!"

Then he lifted his head and observed her from close up with a quick glance. He beheld a face that embodied both beauty and pride, for there was in it as much to provoke fascination as there was to invoke respect, and he beheld blue eyes in whose clear gaze shone haughtiness and boldness. She paid no attention to his greeting but looked around the place, no doubt seeking the pygmy. She asked him in a melodious voice that gave all who heard it the impression of thrilling music, "Where is the wonderful creature that was here?"

The youth said, "He will present himself."

He went to a hatch that opened into the interior of the ship and called, "Zolo!"

Soon, the head of the pygmy appeared through the hatch, followed by his body. Then he approached his master, who took him by the hand to where the princess and her slave girls stood, the pygmy walking with his chest thrust forward and his head tilted backward in an absurd display of pride. He was no more than four hand spans in height, intensely black in color, and his legs were bowed. Isfinis said to him, "Greet your mistress, Zolo!"

The pygmy bowed till his frizzy hair touched the ground. The princess was reassured and asked, her eyes never leaving the pygmy, "Is he animal or human?"

"Human, Your Highness."

"Why should he not be considered an animal?"

"He has his own language and his own religion."

"Amazing! Are there many like him?"

"Indeed, my lady. He belongs to a numerous people, composed of men, women, and children. They have a king and poisoned arrows that they shoot at wild animals and raiders. Yet Zolo's folk quickly take a liking to people. They give sincere affection to those they take as friends and will follow them like faithful dogs."

Wondering, she shook her head with its crown of golden tresses and her lips parted to reveal pearly, regular teeth as she asked, "Where do Zolo's people live?"

"In the furthest forests of Nubia, where the divine Nile has its source."

"Make him talk to me if you can."

"He cannot speak our language. At most he can understand a few commands. But he will greet my lady in his own language."

Isfinis said to the pygmy, "Call down a nice blessing on our lady's head!"

The pygmy's large head shook as though he were trembling, then he uttered strange words in a voice that was more like the lowing of cattle and the princess could not suppress a sweet laugh. She said, "Truly, he is strange. But he is ugly; it would give me no pleasure to acquire him."

The youth looked crestfallen and said, with the glibness of the cunning merchant, "Zolo, my lady, is not the best thing in my convoy. I have treasures to captivate the soul and steal the heart!"

She turned contemptuously from Zolo to the boastful salesman and for the first time cast him a scrutinizing glance. Finding before her his towering height and youthful bloom, she was amazed that a common trader should appear thus. She asked him, "Do you really have something likely to please me?"

"Indeed, my lady."

"Then show me a specimen . . . some examples of your wares."

Isfinis clapped his hands and a slave came to him and he directed a few words to him in a low voice. The man absented himself for a while, then returned carrying, with the help of another, an ivory box. This they placed in front of the princess and opened. Then they moved aside. The princess looked inside the box, while the slave girls craned their necks, and saw a dazzling array of gleaming pearls, earrings, and bracelets. She examined these with a practiced eye, then stretched out her soft, supple hand to take a necklace of incomparable simplicity and perfection: an emerald heart on a chain of pure gold. She took the heart in her fingers and murmured, "Where did you get this gem? There is nothing like it in Egypt!"

The youth said proudly, "It is the greatest of Nubia's treasures!"

She murmured, "Nubia . . . Zolo's country. How beautiful it is!"

Isfinis smiled and looking attentively at her fingers he said, "Now that it has attracted your highness's admiration, it would not do for it to be returned to its box."

Without embarrassment she replied, "Indeed. But I do not have the money to pay for it with me. Are you going to Thebes?"

He said, "Yes, my lady."

She said, "You will have to come to the palace and take the money."

The youth bowed respectfully and the princess cast a farewell look at Zolo, then turned away, moving past with her supple, slender form, followed by the slave girls. The youth's eyes hung on her until the ship's side hid her. Then he recalled himself and returned to his ship where Latu awaited him impatiently, asking him before the youth could say anything, "What news?"

He gave him a summary of what the princess had said, then asked smilingly, "Do you think she's really the daughter of Apophis?"

Latu replied angrily, "She is a devil, daughter of a devil!"

Latu's rough words and angry looks awakened the youth from his reverie. It came to him that the person who had aroused his admiration was the daughter of the humiliator of his people, and his grandfather's killer, and that he had not felt in her presence the resentment and hatred that he should. He was angry with himself, fearing that the tone in which he had related her words might have had its source in an admiration that would hurt the honest old man. He said to himself, "I must be worthy of the duty that I came here to perform!" So it was that he did not look after the princess's boat but instead stared long at the horizon and tried to feel hatred for her, sensing that she was a power that must be resisted in every way. She had passed out of his life forever, but . . . dear God, her beauty had enchanted him, and no one who had the misfortune to see her could close his eyes to the power of its light.

At that moment he thought of his young wife Nefertari, with her straight body, golden-brown face, and enchanting black eyes, and all he could do was to stammer, "How different from each other these two lovely images are!"

4

Thebes' southern wall with its splendid gates appeared, the temples and obelisks rising up behind, magnificence incarnate and terrifying to behold. The two men stared at the city, their eyes filled with tenderness and sorrow.

Latu said, "The Lord grant you life, glorious Thebes!"

And Isfinis responded, "At last, Thebes, after long years of exile!"

The ship turned toward the shore, the others of the convoy following in its wake, sails furled and oars raised. It made its way among a great number of fishing boats full of fish, some still pulsing with life, the sailors standing in the waists of the vessels with their naked, copper bodies and muscle-bound arms. An intoxicating joy diffused throughout Isfinis's body as he looked at them and he said to his companion, "Let's hurry! I'm longing to talk to any Egyptian!"

The weather was moderate and gentle and the sky a clear blue, the rising sun bathing in its rays the Nile, the banks, the fields, and the towns. They went on shore wrapped in their cloaks and placing Egyptian caps, like those of the great merchants, on their heads. They took a few steps in the direction of the quarter of the fishermen, groups of whom were standing on the shore, their hands holding the ropes of the nets that the boats cast into the depths of the Nile, singing songs and hymns. Others were filling the carts with fish and thrashing the backs of the oxen harnessed to them toward the marketplaces. A few minutes' walk from the shore, small or middling mud-brick huts roofed with palm trunks had been set up, giving an appearance of homeliness and indigence.

Isfinis moved from place to place, senses alert, eyes open, watching the fishermen closely, following their movements, and listening to their hymns. He felt toward them an affection and a sorrow that were accompanied by admiration and respect. As he moved among them, familiarity, confidence, and love blended in his heart and he wished that he could stop them and hug them to his breast and kiss their dark faces marked by hardship and poverty. He remembered what Tetisheri had told him about them when she said, "What strong, long-suffering men they are!"

Latu, sharing the youth's emotions, said, "Don't forget that these fishermen are better off than the peasants. The Herdsmen consider themselves too good to go down to their quarter, so they spare them, without meaning to, their arrogant manners and evil acts."

The youth frowned in anger and pain and said nothing. They strode on, attracting looks with the dignity of their bearing and the magnificence of their dress. Isfinis noticed close by them a youth in his teens coming toward them carrying a basket. Around his waist he wore a short kilt, but the rest of his body was bare. He was tall and slender and his face was handsome. Isfinis said, "Look at that boy, Latu. Wouldn't he make a good warrior in the chariot division if he weren't so young?"

The youth was passing close by them, and, wanting to speak with him, Isfinis greeted him with a wave and said, "Lord grant you life, young man! Could you kindly direct us to a place where we can rest?"

The youth stopped and was about to reply but, when his eyes took them in, he closed his mouth and cast at them a strange look, expressive of anger and contempt, and he turned his back on them and went on. The two men exchanged a look of astonishment and distaste and Isfinis followed the youth and said, barring his path, "Brother, what makes you deny us an answer and turn your back on us in anger?"

The youth yelled, "Get away from me, Herdsmen's slave!" and walked angrily on, lengthening his steps and leaving Isfinis astonished and perplexed. Latu caught up with him, saying, "He's mad, for sure."

"He's not mad, Latu. But why would he call me a slave of the Herdsmen?"

"A laughable accusation, indeed!"

"Indeed! But given the behavior of the Herdsmen, from where does he get the courage to challenge us? He's a truly daring young man, Latu. His behavior with us proves that ten years of the Herdsmen's stifling rule has not been enough to root out the anger from those of noble spirit."

They resumed their course until a loud clamor attracted their attention. Looking to the right, they saw a large building with a small entranceway and narrow openings in its upper wall, and groups of people entering and leaving. The youth asked his companion, "What is this building?"

Latu replied, "An inn."

"Let's take a look."

Latu smiled and said, "Let us do so."

5

They entered the inn together and found themselves in a large space with high walls from whose ceiling hung a dust-covered lamp, and in the middle of which jars had been placed surrounded by a wall two cubits tall and one thick, on which earthenware cups were arranged in rows and around which sat the drinkers. Inside the enclosure stood the innkeeper, filling cups for those around him, or sending them with a young serving boy to those sitting on the floor in the corners. Every time he raised his head from his jars, one of the drinkers would assail him with some joke or pleasantry, only to be rebuffed with coarse language, insults, and abuse. The two men looked around the place and Isfinis decided to shove his way into the crowd near the server, so he took his companion by the hand and shouldered his way toward the wall until he reached it, amidst stares of astonishment and annoyance. Feeling a little tired, he said to the tavern-keeper affably, "My good man, would you be able to provide us with a couple of chairs?"

The annoyance of those around increased at his tone and the strangeness of his request, while the tavern-keeper replied without bothering to look at them, "Sorry, prince. The patrons of my establishment are drawn exclusively from those who favor Mother Earth as a seat!"

The assembled drunks laughed at Isfinis and his companion and one of them came up to them, a short man with a coarse face and neck and a huge belly. He bowed to them mockingly and said, his speech slurred with drink, "Gentlemen, allow me to offer you my belly to sit on!"

Isfinis realized his mistake and the harm it had done him and his companion, and to make it good said, "We gratefully accept your offer, but how will you drink your vintage wine without your belly?"

The youth's reply pleased the drunks and one of them called out to the fat man, "Answer, Tuna, answer! How can you drink your cups if you give your belly away to the gentlemen?"

The man frowned in thought and scratched his head in bewilderment, his lower lip hanging down like a piece of bloody liver. Then his bloodshot eyes lit up as though he had found a happy solution and he said, "I'll drink it predigested!"

The men laughed and Isfinis, who liked the answer, told him soothingly, "I'll forego the kind offer of your mighty belly, which was created to be a wineskin, and not a seat."

Then Isfinis looked at the tavern-keeper and said to him, "My good man, fill three cups, two for us and one for our witty friend Tuna!"

The man filled the cups and presented them to Isfinis. Tuna seized his and emptied it into his mouth at one go, unable to believe his luck. Then he wiped his mouth with his palm and said to Isfinis, "You're certainly a rich man, noble sir!"

Isfinis replied smilingly, "Praise God for his blessings!"

Tuna said, "But you're Egyptians, from the look of you!"

"You have keen eyes! Is there any contradiction between being Egyptians and being rich?"

"Certainly, unless you're in the rulers' good graces."

Here another interjected, "People like that imitate their masters and don't mix with the likes of us!"

Isfinis's face darkened and the image of the youth who had angrily shouted "Herdsmen's slave!" at him a while before came back to him. He said, "We are Egyptians from Nubia and have only recently arrived in Egypt."

Silence fell, the word "Nubia" ringing strangely in the men's ears. However, they were all drunk and the wine-chatter could not get a purchase on their minds, and they were incapable of pulling their thoughts together. One of the men looked at the men's two cups, which they had not yet touched, and said with a heavy tongue, "Why don't you drink, may the Lord bless you with the wine of Paradise?"

Latu replied, "We drink rarely, and when we drink, we drink slowly."

Tuna said, "That's the way! What's the point in running away from a happy life? Me, on the other hand, I'm fed up with my work, I'm even fed up with my family and children, and I'm sickest of all with myself, so all I want is never to take the cup away from these lips!"

A drunk clapped in pleasure at what Tuna had said and shook his head in delight, saying, "This inn is the refuge of those who have no hope, of those who proffer trays of food while they are hungry, who weave luxurious garments while they are naked, and who play the buffoon at the celebrations of their overlords, though their hearts and spirits are broken."

A third man said, "Listen, men of Nubia! A drinker is never happy until his legs give way, for all he wants to do is lose consciousness. Take me, for example: every night I have to be carried home to my hut!"

Isfinis recollected himself and realized that he was among the most wretched of humanity. "Are you fishermen?" he asked them.

Tuna replied, "All of us are fishermen."

The innkeeper shrugged his shoulders contemptuously and said, without looking up from his work, "Not me—I'm a tavern keeper, sir!"

Tuna guffawed, then pointed with a thick finger at a short, thin, fine-boned man with wide, bright eyes. He said, "If you want to be precise, this man's a thief."

Isfinis looked at the man curiously and the man felt embarrassed and tried to reassure him by saying, "Don't worry, sir! I never steal anything in this quarter!"

Tuna commented, "He means that as there's nothing worth stealing in our quarter, he keeps company with us like anybody else and practices his art in the suburbs of Thebes, where there's money everywhere and everyone's well-off."

The thief himself was drunk and said apologetically, "I'm not a thief, sir. I'm just someone who roams around, east and west, wherever his feet carry him. And if I stumble on a lost goose or chicken in my path, I guide it to a safe place, usually my hut!"

"And do you eat it?"

"God forbid, sir! Good food gives me stomach poisoning! I just sell it to anyone who'll buy."

"Aren't you afraid of the constables?"

"I'm very afraid of them, sir, because the only ones allowed to steal in this country are the rich and the rulers!"

Tuna added his word to that of the thief, saying, "The rule in Egypt is that the rich steal from the poor, but the poor are not allowed to steal from the rich."

As he spoke his eyes were focused greedily on the two full cups and he changed the course of the conversation by saying accusingly, "Why do you leave your cups untouched, just waiting to stir up trouble among the drinkers?"

Isfinis smiled and said affably, "They're yours, Tuna!"

His mouth watered and he seized the cups in his thick hands, directing warning looks at those around him. Then he emptied them into his belly one after the other and sighed contentedly. Isfinis grasped the meaning of the man's threat and ordered as much beer and wine as they wanted for those nearby. Everyone drank and raised a happy clamor and started talking and singing and laughing. Hardship and poverty were written on the faces of all, but at that moment they appeared happy, laughing and giving no thought to the morrow. Isfinis threw himself into the spirit of things gaily enough, though his low spirits would revisit him from time to time. They had been with the men quite some time when a man came into the inn who appeared to be one of them, and greeted them with a wave and ordered a cup of beer. Then he said to those around him in a tone that gave nothing away, "They have arrested the Lady Ebana and taken her to the court."

Most of the men were too befuddled with drink to pay him any attention but others asked, "And why is that?"

"They say that a high-ranking officer of the Herdsmen crossed her path on the Nile shore and wanted to take her as one of his women. She resisted and pushed him away."

Many of the men yelled angrily and Isfinis asked him, "And what will the court do to her?"

The man stared at him unbelievingly and said, "It will sentence her to pay a fine that she cannot afford in order to give her no way out. Then it will order her to be flogged and thrown into prison."

Isfinis's face changed and he turned pale and said to the man, "Can you show us how to get to the court?"

Tuna stammered, "It will do you more good to drink, because whoever defends this woman will anger the high-ranking officer and expose himself to who knows what punishment!"

The man who had spread the news asked him, "Are you a stranger, sir?"

"Yes," Isfinis replied. "And I want to attend this trial."

"I'll be your guide to the court if you wish."

As they left the inn, Latu bent over his ear and whispered, "Take care not to get involved in anything that will spoil our delicate mission!"

Isfinis did not answer, but turned on his heel and followed the man.

6

The court was crammed with petitioners, plaintiffs, and witnesses and the seats in the hall were filled with people of every class. In the place of honor sat judges with flowing beards and white faces, a figurine of Thamy, the goddess of justice, dangling on the chest of their chief. The two colleagues took seats close to one another and Latu whispered to Isfinis, "They imitate the externals of our system."

They scrutinized the faces and realized that most of those present were Hyksos. The judges summoned the accused, interrogated them rapidly, and issued their sentences fast and mercilessly. Cries of complaint and lamentation arose from the naked victims with their copper-colored bodies and brown faces. Lady Ebana's turn came and the usher called, "Lady Ebana!"

The two men looked apprehensively and saw a lady approach the dais with measured steps, her bearing displaying dignity and sorrow, her features full of beauty despite her being close to forty years in age. A Hyksos man, dressed in fine clothes, followed her, bowed respectfully to the judge, and said, "Honorable Lord Judge, I am the agent of Commander Rukh—whom this woman attacked—and I am called Khumm. I shall represent his lordship before the court."

The judge nodded his head in agreement, astonishing Latu and Isfinis. The judge said, "What does your master accuse this woman of?"

The man replied with distaste and irritation, "My master says that he met this woman this morning and wished to add her to his harem, but she refused ungratefully and rejected him with an impudence that he considered an attack on his honor as a soldier."

The man's statement set off a clamor of indignation among those present and people put their heads together, whispering disapprovingly. The judge made a gesture toward the people with his staff of office and they fell silent. Then he said, "What say you, woman?"

The woman had maintained her calm, as though despair of fair treatment had absolved her of any susceptibility to fear. She said quietly, "This man's statement is inaccurate."

The judge angrily rebuked her, saying, "Take care that you do not say anything that might touch the dignity of the honorable complainant, for your crime will then be twice as bad! Tell your story and leave the judgment to us!"

The woman's face reddened in embarrassment and she said, still maintaining her calm, "I was on my way to the fishermen's quarter when a carriage barred my way and an officer got down and told me to get in, without delay and without any previous acquaintance. I was terrified and wanted to get away from him, but he took hold of my hand and told me that he was doing me an honor by adding me to his women. I told him that I refused his offer, but he scoffed at me and told me that when a woman makes a show of refusal she really means, 'Yes.'"

The judge gestured to her to stop speaking, as though it pained him to hear her mention details that might detract from the officer's dignity. Then he asked her, "Answer! Did you assault him or not?"

"Certainly not, sir! I insisted on refusing and tried to slip from his grasp, but I did not attack him either with my hand or my tongue, and any number of people from the quarter can attest to that."

"You mean the fishermen?"

"Yes, sir."

"The testimony of such people is not accepted in this sacred place."

The woman fell silent and a look of perplexity and confusion appeared in her eyes. The judge asked her, "Is that all you have to say?"

"Yes, sir. And I swear that I did not harm him by word or deed."

"The one who brings a complaint against you is a great personage, a commander of Pharaoh's guard, and his words are true until proven otherwise."

"And how am I to prove otherwise, when the court refuses to hear my witnesses?"

The judge said angrily, "Fishermen do not enter this place, unless brought here as suspects!"

The man turned away from her and leant toward his colleagues to discuss their opinions. Then he sat upright once more and said, directing his words to Lady Ebana, "Woman, the commander intended to do you a favor and you rewarded him very badly. The court gives you a choice between paying fifty pieces of gold or prison for three years, with a flogging."

The public listened attentively to the sentence and satisfaction showed on all their faces, except for that of one, who shouted in a voice full of emotion, as though unable to control himself, "Lord Judge! The woman is wronged and innocent. Let her go! Pardon her, for she is wronged!"

The judge, however, grew furious and fixed the owner of the voice with a look that silenced him, while people stared at him from every side. Isfinis recognized him and said to his companion in amazement, "It's the youth who was angry when we spoke to him and accused us of being Herdsmen's slaves."

Isfinis was enraged and full of pain. He went on and said, "I will not let that imbecile of a judge throw that lady in prison!"

Latu said anxiously, "Your mission is more important than taking the part of a wronged woman. Be careful that what you do does not turn against us!"

But Isfinis paid no attention to his companion. He waited until he heard the judge ask the woman, "Will you pay the sum required?"

Then he rose, and said in a beautiful, sweet-toned voice, "Yes, Lord Judge!"

All heads turned toward him to examine the bold and generous man who had come forward to save the woman at the last moment and the woman looked at him in astonishment, as did the youth who had defended her with his tears and plea. The commander's agent flashed a fiery and threatening glance at him but the youth paid no attention and went up to the judges' dais with his tall, slender figure and captivating, comely face and handed the required fine over to the court.

The judge pondered in confusion, asking himself, "Where did this peasant get the gold, and where did he get such courage?" But there was nothing for it and he turned to the woman and said, "Woman, you are free. Let the fate from which you so narrowly escaped be a lesson to you!"

7

They left the court together, Latu, Isfinis, the Lady Ebana, and the unknown youth. As they were leaving, the woman looked at Isfinis and said in a voice he could barely hear, "Sir, your chivalry has saved me from the shades of the dungeon. I must therefore consider myself your slave by virtue of the favor you have done me and you have placed me under an obligation I can never repay."

The youth seized Isfinis's hand and kissed it, his eyes brimming with tears, and said in a trembling voice, "The Lord pardon my earlier poor opinion of you and grant you the best of reward for what you have done for us by saving my mother from the depths of prison and the pain of flogging!"

Isfinis was overcome by emotion and said gently, "You owe me nothing. You suffered the most horrible injustice, my lady, and injustice, though it may affect only one, pains all the just. All I did was to get angry and give vent to my anger—so there is no debt and nothing to repay."

This speech did not convince the Lady Ebana, who continued to be overcome with emotion, stammering in her confusion, and saying, "What a noble deed! How far beyond description and how far above praise!"

Her son was not less affected. Seeing Isfinis looking at him, he said apologetically, "When we met I thought you were creatures of the Herdsmen because of how rich you seemed to be. Now it turns out that you are two generous Egyptians from I know not where. I swear I shall not leave you until you have been kind enough to visit our small hut, so that we can drink a cup of beer together to celebrate our being honored with your acquaintance. What do you say?"

The invitation delighted Isfinis, who wanted to mix with his fellow countrymen, and who was attracted to the youth by his verve and good looks. He said, "We accept your invitation with the greatest of pleasure."

The youth was overjoyed, as was his mother, but she said, "You must excuse us, for you will not find our hut appropriate to your high status."

Latu said deftly, "With hosts such as yourselves we shall

want for nothing, and besides, we are traders, used to the discomforts of life and the hardships of the road."

They continued in their path, united in feelings of affection, as though they had been friends for years. As they walked, Isfinis said to Ebana's son, "What should we call you, my friend? My name is Isfinis, and my companion is called Latu."

The youth bowed his head respectfully and said, "Call me Ahmose."

Isfinis felt as though someone had called to him and he looked curiously at the youth.

After half an hour, they reached the hut. It was plain, like a fisherman's hut, and consisted of an outer courtyard and two small interconnecting rooms. However, despite the plainness of its furnishings and its poverty, it was clean and well arranged. Ahmose and his two guests sat in the courtyard, opening the door wide so that the breeze from the Nile and the sight of the river might be unimpeded. Ebana went off straightaway to prepare the drinks and they remained silent for a while, exchanging glances. Then Ahmose said hesitantly, "It is strange to see Egyptians looking so distinguished. How is it that the Herdsmen have left you to get rich when you are not their creatures?"

Isfinis replied, "We are Egyptians of Nubia, and we entered Thebes today."

The youth clapped his hands in astonishment and delight and said, "Nubia! Many people fled there during the Herdsmen's invasion of our country. Are you some of those who took flight?"

Latu was by nature extremely cautious, so he said quickly, before Isfinis could answer, "No. We migrated there earlier for trade."

"And how did you manage to enter Egypt, when the Herdsmen have closed the borders?"

The two men realized that Ahmose, despite his tender years,

was well informed. Isfinis felt a sense of fondness and ease toward him, so he told him the story of their entry into Egypt. While he was speaking, Ebana returned carrying the cups of beer and grilled fish. She put the drink and the food before them and sat listening to Isfinis's story until he ended by saying, "Gold stupefies these people and captivates their minds. We will go to the governor of the South and show him our best treasures and we hope that he will agree, or obtain an agreement for trade between Egypt and Nubia, so that we can go back to our old work and our trade." She offered them the cups of beer and the fish and said, "If you achieve your goal, you will have to bear the full load of the work yourselves, for the Herdsmen refuse to work in trade and the Egyptians are incapable, in their present conditions of poverty and misery, of taking part."

The traders had their own thoughts on this, but preferred to remain silent. They set to eating the fish and drinking the beer, commending the lady highly and praising her simple table, so that she blushed and launched into profuse thanks to Isfinis for his kind deed. She became quite carried away and said, "You extended me your noble hand at the moment when I most needed it, but how many a wretched Egyptian there is who is crushed by the millstones of oppression, morning and evening, and finds no one to help him!"

Ahmose became excited too, and as soon as his mother had said these words, his face flushed with anger and he said earnestly, "The Egyptians are slaves to whom crumbs are thrown and who are beaten with whips! The king, the ministers, the commanders, the judges, the officials, and the property owners are all Herdsmen. Today, all authority is with the whites with their filthy beards and the Egyptians are slaves on the land that yesterday was theirs."

Isfinis was looking at Ahmose during his outburst with eyes that shone with admiration and sympathy, while Latu kept his eyes down to hide his emotion. Isfinis asked, "Are there many who are angry at these injustices?"

"Indeed! But we all suppress our ire and put up with the ill treatment, as is the way with anyone who is weak and has no alternative. I ask myself, 'Is there no end to this night?' It is ten years since the Lord in His anger at us allowed the crown to fall from the head of our sovereign Seqenenra."

The men's hearts beat hard and Isfinis turned pale. Latu looked at the youth in astonishment and then asked him, "How is it that you know this history despite your young years?"

"My memory retains a few unshakable pictures—clear and unfading—of the first days of suffering. However, I owe my knowledge of the sad story of Thebes to my mother, who never ceased repeating it to me."

Latu gave Ebana a curious look that disturbed the woman. Seeking to reassure her he said, "You are an outstanding woman and your son is a noble young man."

To himself Latu said, "The lady is still cautious in spite of everything." It had been his intention to ask about some matters that concerned him but, setting these aside for the moment, the old man deftly changed the course of the conversation, directing it to trivial matters and making everyone feel at ease once more, in an atmosphere of mutual affection. When the two traders got up to leave the house, Ahmose said to Isfinis, "When will you go, sir, to the governor of the South?"

Isfinis replied, surprised by the question, "Perhaps tomorrow."

"I have a request."

"What is it?"

"That I may go with you to his estate."

Isfinis was pleased and said to the youth, "Do you know the way there?"

"Very well."

Ebana tried to object, but her son silenced her with a nervous gesture of his hand and Isfinis smiled and said, "If you have no objection, he can be our guide."

8

The first half of the following day passed in preparations for the visit to the governor. Isfinis was well aware of the importance of this visit and knew that the future of all his hopes was hostage to its outcome, not to mention the hopes of those whom he had left behind him in Napata, where despair and hope struggled to dominate their mighty souls. He loaded his ship with caskets of finely-wrought objects and pearls, cages holding strange animals, the pygmy Zolo, and a large number of slaves. Ahmose appeared at the end of the afternoon, greeted them joyfully, and said, "From this moment on, I'm your slave!"

Isfinis took his arm under his own and the three of them proceeded to the cabin on deck. Then the ship set sail toward the north under a clear sky and with a favorable wind. The people in the cabin fell silent, each absorbed in his own thoughts, his eyes fixed on the shore of Thebes. The ship passed the quarters of the poor and approached the lofty palaces half-hidden among spreading palms and sycamore figs, among whose branches fluttered birds of every kind and color and which served to divide one estate from another. Behind them, the green fields stretched out, crisscrossed by silver streams, valleys, palm trees, and grapevines, grazed by oxen and cows, the patient, naked peasants bent over them at their labors. On the shore, devices had been constructed that scooped water from the Nile, to the tune of exquisite songs. Breezes played with the trees, bringing with them the susurration of foliage, the twittering of small birds, the lowing of cattle, and the fragrance of flowers and sweet-smelling herbs. Isfinis felt as though memory's fingertips were caressing his feverish brow as he recalled spring days when he would go out into the fields carried in his royal litter, slaves and guards marching before him, and the peasants, overjoyed to see the pure young child, would greet him, scattering roses on his fortunate path.

He was wakened by the voice of Ahmose saying, "There's the governor's palace!"

Isfinis sighed and looked where the youth was pointing. Latu looked too and an expression of amazement and distaste filled the old man's eyes.

The ship turned toward the palace, its oars stilled. A small war craft, bursting with soldiers, barred its way and an officer shouted at them roughly and arrogantly, "Get your filthy ship away from here, peasant!"

Isfinis leapt from the cabin, went to the ship's side, and greeted the officer respectfully, saying, "I have a private letter to His Highness, the governor of the South."

The officer gave him a sharp, brutal stare and said, "Give it to me and wait!"

The youth extracted the letter from the pocket of his cloak and gave it to the officer, who examined it carefully and then gave an order to his men, who turned the craft toward the garden steps. The officer called a guard and handed him the letter. The guard took it and departed in the direction of the palace. He disappeared for a short while then returned in a hurry to the officer and said a few words to him in secret, after which the officer gestured to Isfinis to bring the ship in close. The youth ordered his sailors to row on until the ship anchored at the palace mooring, where the officer said to him, "His Highness awaits you, so unload your goods and take them to him."

The youth issued his orders to the Nubians and these, Ahmose among them, unloaded the caskets, while others removed the cages of animals and Zolo's litter. In parting, Latu said to the youth, "The Lord grant you success!"

Isfinis caught up with the procession and together they crossed the luxuriant garden in total silence.

9

The trader went to meet the governor. A servant led him to the reception hall, his slaves following with their burdens. The youth found himself in an opulent hall of great elegance, on whose floor, walls, and ceiling artwork glittered. In the forefront of the hall sat the governor on a soft couch, wearing a flowing robe, like a block of solid masonry. The features of his large face were strong and clear, while the sharpness of his gaze indicated courage, intrepidness, and candor. Isfinis made a gesture to his men, who put the caskets and cages down in front of them. He took a few steps toward the middle of the hall, then bowed reverently to the governor and said, "God Seth grant you life, mighty governor!"

The governor cast at him one of his strong, piercing looks. The youth's noble appearance and towering height pleased him and his face registered his satisfaction with his appearance as he asked, "Have you really come from the land of Nubia?"

"Indeed, my lord."

"And what do you hope for from this journey of yours?"

"I desire to present to the masters of Egypt some treasures such as are found in the land of Nubia in the hope that these will give them pleasure and they will ask for more."

"And what do you want yourself in return?"

"Some of the grain that is surplus to Egypt's needs."

The governor shook his large head and a mocking look appeared in his eyes as he said frankly, "I see that you are young, but bold and adventurous. Fortunately for you, I like adventurers. Now, show me what treasures you have brought."

Isfinis called to Ahmose, who approached the governor and placed the casket he was carrying at his feet. The trader opened it, revealing rubies worked into jewelry of many forms. The governor examined these, his eyes alight with avarice, greed, and admiration, and he started turning them over in his hands. Then he asked the youth, "Is such jewelry abundant in Nubia?"

Isfinis answered him without hesitation, having prepared his reply before coming to Egypt.

"It is one of the strangest things, my lord, but these precious stones are to be found in the deepest jungles of Nubia, where wild beasts roam and deadly diseases lurk everywhere."

He showed the governor a casket of emeralds, then one of coral, then a third of gold, and a fourth of pearls. The man examined them slowly, breathless to the point that by the time he had finished he seemed like one ecstatic with drink. Next, Isfinis showed him the cages of gazelles, giraffes, and apes, saying, "How beautiful these animals would appear in the gardens of the palace!"

The governor smiled, saying to himself, "What an irresistible devil of a youth!" The governor's astonishment reached its peak when Isfinis raised the curtain of the litter and Zolo's strange person appeared. The governor rose involuntarily and went up to the litter and walked around it, saying questioningly, "Amazing! Is it animal or human?"

Isfinis replied with a smile, "Human, of course, my lord, and one of a numerous people."

"This is the most amazing thing I have ever seen or heard."

The man called a slave and told him, "Call the Princess Amenridis and my wife and brother!"

10

The people whom the governor had summoned arrived. Isfinis thought it best to lower his eyes out of respect, but he heard a thrilling voice that shook him to the core saying, "What makes you disturb our gathering, Governor?"

Isfinis stole a glance at the new arrivals and saw at their head the princess who had visited his convoy the day before and picked out the emerald heart. Her appearance, as he had come to expect, dazzled the eyes. The youth no longer had any doubt that Governor Khanzar and his wife were of the royal family. At the same time, he caught sight of another face not unfamiliar to him, the face of the man who followed the princess and the governor's wife—the judge who had passed sentence on Ebana the day before. The resemblance between the judge and the governor was obvious to him. The princess and the judge clearly recognized him too, for both cast him meaningful glances. The governor, ignorant of the wordless exchange taking place before him, bowed to the princess and said, "Come, Your Highness, and see the most precious things to be found within the bowels of the earth and the strangest to be found on its surface!" He turned to the caskets loaded with precious stones, the cages of animals, and Zolo's litter and they drew close, infatuated, astonished, and admiring, the pygmy receiving his usual portion of repugnance and curiosity. The governor's wife was the most astonished and admiring and approached the ivory caskets with fascination. The judge, however, turned to Isfinis and said to him, "Yesterday I was puzzled as to the source of your wealth, but now I understand everything."

The governor turned toward them and asked his brother,

"What do you mean, Judge Samnut? Have you met this young man before?"

"Indeed I have, my Lord Governor. I saw him yesterday in court. It seems that he is ever ready with himself and his wealth, for he donated fifty pieces of gold to save a peasant woman charged with insulting Commander Rukh from prison and flogging. It appears that the commander was afflicted on one and the same day by a peasant woman who spoke to him cheekily and a peasant who defied his anger!"

Princess Amenridis laughed lightly and sarcastically and said as she cast a glance at the youth's face, "What is so amazing in that, Judge Samnut? Isn't it natural that a peasant should roll up his sleeves to defend a peasant woman?"

"The fact is, my lady, the peasants can do nothing. The whole thing is just a matter of gold and its power. He spoke true who said that if you want to get anything out of a peasant, first make him poor, then beat him with a whip!"

The governor, however, was by nature enamored of any act of daring and bravery and he said, "The trader is a daring young man, and his penetration of our borders is just one sign of his courage. Bravo to him, bravo! Would he were a warrior that I might fight him, for my sword has rusted from resting so long in its scabbard!"

Princess Amenridis said in sarcastic tones, "How could you not show him mercy, Judge Samnut, when I am in his debt?"

"In his debt, Your Highness? What a thing to say!"

She laughed at the governor's astonishment and related to him how she had seen the convoy and how Zolo had attracted her to the ship, where she had picked out the beautiful necklace. She told her story in accents indicative of the freedom and daring she enjoyed and of a love of sarcasm and banter. Governor Khanzar's astonishment vanished and he asked her playfully, "And why did you choose a green heart, Your Highness? We have heard of pure white hearts and wicked black hearts, but what might be the meaning of a green heart?"

The princess replied, laughing, "Direct your question to the one who sold the heart!"

Isfinis, who had been listening keenly but dejectedly, replied, "The green heart, Your Highness, is the symbol of fertility and tenderness."

The princess said, "How I need such a heart, for sometimes I feel that I am so cruel that it even gives me pleasure to be cruel to myself!"

Judge Samnut meanwhile had been taking a long look at Zolo and tried to draw his sister-in-law's attention to him, though she refused to be distracted from the caskets of precious stones. The judge, disgusted at the pygmy's appearance, said, "What an ugly creature!"

Isfinis replied, "He belongs to a pygmy race that finds us unpleasant to look at and believes that the Creator gave us distorted features and hideous extremities."

Governor Khanzar laughed mightily and said, "Your words are more fantastic than Zolo himself and than all the strange animals and treasures that you bring."

Fixing Isfinis with a suspicious look, Samnut said, "It seems to me that this youth has set our minds in a dither with his fancies, for it is certain that such pygmies can have no concept of beauty or ugliness."

Princess Amenridis stared at the pygmy as though in apology and said, "Do you find my face ugly to look at, Zolo?"

Khanzar started roaring with laughter once more, while Isfinis's heart trembled before the splendor of her beauty and her captivating coquetry. At that moment, he wanted to gaze at her forever. After this, silence reigned and the youth understood that it was time to go. Fearing that the governor would dismiss him without his having brought up the subject that he had come for, he said to him, "Great Governor, may I dare to hope to realize my ambitions under the aegis of your generous patronage?"

The governor thought, his hand playing in his thick black beard. Then he said, "Our people have grown tired of war and raiding and turned to luxury and ease. By nature they feel themselves above trading, so the only access to such costly gems is through adventurers such as you. However, I do not want to give you my decision now. Before doing that I must talk to my lord the king. I shall offer his exalted person the most beautiful of these treasures, in the hope that he may approve my opinion."

Isfinis, elated, said, "My Lord Governor, I am keeping aside for our lord Pharaoh a costly gift that was made especially for his exalted person."

The governor scrutinized his face for a moment and an idea that might draw him closer to his master's favor formed in his head. He said, "At the end of this month, Pharaoh celebrates the victory feast, as has been his custom for the last ten years. It may be that I can make a pleasant surprise of you and your pygmies for the sovereign and you might then present him with your gift, which no doubt befits his high standing. Tell me your name and status."

"My lord, I am called Isfinis and I reside where my convoy is moored on the shore at the fishermen's quarters, to the south of Thebes."

"My messengers will come to you soon."

The youth bowed with the greatest respect and left the place followed by his slaves. The princess had been looking at his face as he spoke to the governor about his ambitions, listening to him closely, and she followed him with her gaze as he left. The traits of nobility and burgeoning comeliness in his face and form pleased her and she felt sorry that fate had made trade, and the transport of pygmies, his lot. Alas, how she wished she might come across such stature in the body of one of her own kind, who tended to obesity and shortness. Instead, she had found it in the body of a brown-skinned Egyptian who traded in pygmies. Sensing that the image of this beautiful youth was stirring up some emotion within her, she seemed to grow angry and she turned her back on the governor and his family and quit the hall.

11

Isfinis and the slaves returned in the footsteps of their guide to the garden. The stirring of a breeze from Thebes quieted his burning excitement and he breathed a deep breath that filled his breast, for he considered that the outcome of this journey of his had been a great success. At the same time, though, his mind dwelt on Princess Amenridis and summoned up the memory of her glowing face, golden hair, and scarlet lips, and of the emerald heart that dangled on her swelling bosom. Dear God! He would have to neglect to ask her for the money, so that it would remain forever both his heart and hers. He said to himself, "She is a woman raised in the lap of luxury and love who thinks, no doubt, that the whole world will do her bidding if she but crook her finger. She is bold and merry too, but her laughter is pampered and not without cruelty. She jokes with the governor and makes fun of an unknown trader, though she is not yet eighteen. If tomorrow I were to see her mounted on a steed and setting arrow to bow, I would not be surprised."

He told himself not to surrender to thoughts of her and, to give effect to his own advice, he turned back to thoughts of his success. He thought appreciatively of Governor Khanzar. He was a mighty governor, strong and of great courage, yet kind-hearted, and possibly very stupid too. He was greatly attracted to gold like the majority of his people. He had gobbled up all those gifts of gold, pearls, emeralds, rubies, animals, and poor Zolo without a word of thanks. However, it was this greed that had opened the gates to Egypt for him and brought him to the palace of the governor and would end up by bringing him soon to Pharaoh's palace. Ahmose was walking close to him, and he heard him whisper, in a barely audible voice, "Sharef!" He imagined he must be talking to him, so he turned to him and found that he was looking at an ancient man carrying a basket of flowers and walking about the garden with feeble steps. The old man heard the voice calling him and he looked all around him, searching with his weak eyes for who was calling him. However, Ahmose shunned him and turned his back on him. Isfinis was astonished and threw a questioning look at Ahmose, but the young man lowered his gaze and did not say a word.

They reached the ship and went onboard, and found Latu waiting for them, great concern showing on his pale face. Isfinis smiled and said, "We succeeded, through the kindness of the Lord Amun."

The anchor was raised, the oars moved, and Isfinis had drawn close to Latu and was telling him all that had been said at the interview, when his words were interrupted by the sound of weeping. They turned toward its source and saw Ahmose leaning on the railing of the ship sobbing like a child. His appearance startled them and Isfinis remembered his strange behavior in the garden. He went up to him, followed by Latu, and, putting his hand on his shoulder, he said to him, "Ahmose, why are you crying?"

The boy did not answer, however, or give any sign he had heard a word of what was said. Instead, he surrendered himself to his tears in a transport of sorrow that rendered him oblivious to all else. Disturbed, the two men gathered round him, took him to the cabin, and sat him down between them, while Isfinis brought him a cup of water and said, "Why are you crying, Ahmose? Do you know that old man whom you called Sharef?"

Ahmose replied, shaking with the force of his tears, "How could I not know him? How could I not know him?"

Isfinis asked him in amazement, "Who is he? And why are you crying so?"

Sorrow shook Ahmose out of his silence and he gave vent everything that was inside him, saying, "Ah, Lord Isfinis, this palace that I entered as one of your servants is my father's!"

Isfinis registered astonishment, while Latu peered at the youth's face with keen interest as he resumed his speech, absorbed in the throes of his sorrow, "This palace that Governor Khanzar has usurped is the cradle of my childhood and the playground of my youth. Between its high walls, my poor mother spent the days of her youth and ease in the protective arms of my father, before the disaster befell the land of Egypt and the invaders' feet trod the sacred soil of Thebes."

"Who then was your father, Ahmose?"

"My father was the commander of the army of our martyred sovereign Seqenenra."

Latu said, "Commander Pepi? My God! Indeed, this is the palace of the valiant commander."

Ahmose looked at Latu in astonishment and asked him, "Did you know my father, Lord Latu?"

"Was there any of our generation who did not know him?"

"My heart tells me that you are one of the nobles whom the invaders drove away."

Latu fell silent, not wanting to lie to the son of Commander Pepi. Then he asked him, "And how did the life of the valiant commander end?"

"He was martyred, my lord, in the final defense of Thebes. My mother obeyed his final testament and fled with me amidst a throng of nobles to the quarter of the poor where we live now. The ancient nobility of Thebes dispersed and some of them disguised themselves in tattered clothes and escaped to the fishermen's quarter, while the family of our sovereign took a ship for an unknown destination. The temple of Amun closed its doors on its priests, all ties between them and the rest of the world severed, and it was left to the white foreigners with their beards to stroll about the land without a care, owners of all. Khanzar did the best out of it, for his sister is the king's wife and he gave him my father's estate and palace and appointed him governor of the South in reward for the crime committed at his hands."

Latu asked him, "What crime did the governor commit?"

Ahmose had stopped crying and said in a tone of great anger, "His criminal hand it was that brought down our sovereign Seqenenra!"

Isfinis, recoiling as one touched by a searing flame, was unable to remain seated and leapt up threateningly, anger of a sort to strike terror into men's hearts drawn on his face, while Latu closed his eyes, his face pale, his breath labored. Ahmose looked from the one to the other and found, at last, people who shared his burning emotions. He raised his head to the heavens and murmured, "The Lord bless this sacred anger!"

The ship arrived at its moorings as the sun was sinking into the Nile and the glow of evening stained the horizon. They made for Ebana's house and found the lady lighting her lamp. As soon as she became aware of their approach, she turned toward them with a smile of welcome on her lips. Latu and Isfinis came up to her and bowed to her with respect and the older man said in a solemn voice, "The Lord bless the evening of the widow of our great commander Pepi!"

The smile disappeared from her lips and her eyes widened in amazement and alarm. She fixed a look of reproof and rebuke on her son and tried to speak, but could not, her eyes brimming with tears. Ahmose went up to her, put his hands between hers, and said to her tenderly, "Mother, do not be afraid or sad! You know what kindness these two have shown me. Know too that they are, as I thought, among the ancient nobles of Thebes whom tyranny forced into exile, brought here by their longing to see the face of Egypt once again."

The woman regained her composure and stretched out her hand to them, while they gazed at her, their faces eloquent with candor and sincerity. They all sat down close to one another and Isfinis said, "It is a great source of pride for us to sit with the widow of our brave commander Pepi, who died in defense of Thebes so that he could join his lord by the noblest of routes, and with his zealous son Ahmose."

Ebana said, "I am truly happy that a fortunate coincidence has brought me together with two noble men of the old order. Let us reminisce together over days past and share our common feelings about the present. Ahmose is a youth full of ardor, worthy of his name, which his father gave him in honor of Ahmose, grandson of our sovereign Seqenenra and son of our king Kamose, the two being born on the same day—may the Lord bless him wherever he be!"

Latu spread his hands in support of her words and said honestly and sincerely, "The Lord keep our friend Ahmose, and his mighty namesake, wherever he be!"

12

The affection between the two traders and Ebana's family took firm hold and they lived together as one family, spending only the evenings apart. The men learned that the fishermen's quarter was crowded with people in hiding, merchants of Thebes and former owners of its estates and farms. Happy to learn this, the men desired to make the acquaintance of some of the more prominent among them, a wish that they made known to Ahmose, once they had made sure of the trustworthiness of the people. The youth welcomed the idea and chose four of those closest to his mother: Seneb, Ham, Kom, and Deeb. Having revealed to them the secret of the traders' identity, he invited them one day to his house, where Latu and Isfinis received them. The men were dressed in the garb of the poor—a kilt and

worn linen upper garment. All welcomed the traders and exchanged greetings with a warmth indicative of their honesty
and affection. Ahmose said, "Those you see are, like yourselves, ancient lords of Egypt and all of them live as do the mis-
erable, neglected fishermen, while the accursed Herdsmen have
sole possession of their land."

Ham asked the traders, "Are you from Thebes, gentlemen?"

Latu replied, "No, sir. However, we were once landowners
in Ombos."

Seneb said, "Did many fly, like you, to Nubia?"

Latu replied, "Indeed, sir. At Napata especially there are
hundreds of Egyptians, from Ombos, Sayin, Habu, and Thebes
itself."

The men exchanged glances, none of them doubting the
traders after what Ahmose had told them of what Isfinis had
done for his mother at the court. Ham put the question, "And
how do you live at Napata, Lord Latu?"

"We live a life of hardship like the Nubians themselves, for
the soil of Nubia is generous with gold, miserly with grain."

"You are, however, fortunate, since the hands of the Herdsmen cannot reach you."

"No doubt. That is why we think constantly of Egypt and
its enslaved and captured inhabitants."

"Do we not have a military force in the south?"

"We do, but it is small, and Ra'um, the Egyptian governor
of the south, uses it to keep order in the towns."

"What might be the feelings of the Nubians toward us, following the invasion?"

"The Nubians love us and submit willingly to our rule. That
is why Ra'um finds no difficulty in ruling the towns with an in-
significant force. Were they to rebel, they would find no one to
discipline them."

The men's eyes lit up with dreams. Ahmose had told them
how the two traders had managed to cross the border and visit
the governor, and how Isfinis was going to present Apophis

with a gift at the victory feast. Ham asked with displeasure, "And what do you hope to gain by presenting your gift to Apophis?"

Isfinis said, "To stir his greed, so that he will give me permission to carry on trade between Nubia and Egypt and exchange gold for grain."

The men were silent and Isfinis said nothing for a while, thinking. Finally he decided to take a new step on the road of his mission. He said solemnly, "Listen well, gentlemen. The goal we seek to achieve is not trade and it is not proper that trade should be the goal of people presented to you in the house of the widow of our great commander Pepi. What we do hope is to link Egypt to Nubia by means of our convoy and to employ some of you as workers, in appearance, and transport you to our brothers in the south. We shall carry gold to Egypt and return with grain and men and maybe we shall come back one day, with men only. . . ."

Everyone listened with astonishment mixed with joy and their eyes flashed with a sudden light. Ebana cried, "Lord! What lovely voice is this that revives the dead hopes in our hearts?"

Ham cried, "Dear God! Life stirs again in the graveyard of Thebes."

And Kom exclaimed, "Young man, whose voice resurrects our dead hearts, we were living till now without hope or future, weighed down by the misery of our present and finding no escape from it but in recalling the glorious past and mourning it. Now you have opened the curtain on a splendid future."

Isfinis was overjoyed and hope filled his heart. In his beautiful, stirring voice he said, "Weeping is no use, gentlemen. The past will disappear into ancient times and obliteration so long as you are content to do nothing but mourn it. Its glory will remain close at hand only if you work it energetically. Let it not sadden you that today you are merchants, for soon you will be soldiers with the world in the palms of your hands and its fortresses at your feet. But tell me the truth, do you have trust in all your brethren?"

With one breath they responded, "As we trust ourselves!"

"You are not afraid of spies?"

"The Herdsmen are mindless tyrants. They have been lulled by their ability to keep us slaves for ten years and take no precautions."

Isfinis clapped his hands in delight and said, "Go to your faithful brethren and tell them the good news of fresh hope and bring us together as often as you can so that we may exchange views and advice and pass on to them the message of the south. If the Egyptians of Napata are angry in their safe haven, you have even better reason to be so."

The men eagerly gave their assent to what he had said and Deeb said, "We are angry, noble youth. Our efforts will prove to you that we are angrier than our brethren of Napata."

They bowed to the two traders and departed, overcome by an upsurge of anger and eagerness for battle that would neither quieten nor go away. The two men heard Ebana sigh and say, "Lord! Who will direct us to the family of our martyred sovereign? And where on the face of the earth is he?"

Two weeks passed, during which Isfinis and his older companion did not taste rest. They met with Thebes' hidden men at the house of Ebana and made known to them the hopes of the Egyptians in exile, thus planting hope and life in their hearts and pouring strength and a thirst for battle into their souls till the whole of the fishermen's quarter was waiting impatiently and anxiously for the hour when Isfinis would be summoned to the royal palace.

The days passed until one day one of the chamberlains of the governor of the South came to the fishermen's quarter asking after the convoy of the one named Isfinis, then handed him a letter from the governor permitting him to enter the royal palace at a certain time on the day of the feast. Many saw the messenger and rejoiced, hope dawning in their hearts.

On that evening, as the convoy slept, Isfinis remained alone on deck in the calm and glory of the quiet night, bathed in the moonlight, which poured gemstones and pearls of light, shining and glittering, over his noble face. A feeling of lightness entered him and he felt a delightful sense of satisfaction as his imagination wandered at will between the recent past and the extraordinary present. He thought of the moment of departure in Napata and of his grandmother Tetisheri giving him the good news that the spirit of Amun had inspired her to send him to Egypt, while his father Kamose stood nearby and counseled him in his deep, impressive voice. He remembered his mother, the queen Setkimus, as she kissed his brow and his wife Nefertari as she cast upon him a farewell glance from between moist eyelashes. A look of tenderness as pure and modest as the light of the moon appeared in his eyes and droplets of the beauty that charged the space between the sky and the water of the Nile seeped into his heart. He felt refreshed and intoxicated with a divine ambrosia. But an image of light and splendor stealthily invaded his imaginings, causing his body to shudder, and, closing his eyes as to fly from it, he whispered to himself in exasperation, "God, I think of her more than I should. And I shouldn't think of her at all."

13

The day of the feast came. Isfinis spent the daylight hours on board the ship, then, in the evening, put on his best clothes, combed his flowing locks, applied perfume, and left the ship, followed by slaves carrying an ivory casket and a litter with lowered drapes. They took the road to the palace. Thebes was making merry, the air resounding to the beating of tambourines and the sound of song. The moon lit up streets

crammed with drunken soldiers roaring songs and the car-
riages of the nobles and the notables making their way toward
the royal palace, preceded by servants carrying torches. The
youth was plunged into deep dejection and said to himself sorrowfully, "It is my fate to share with these people in the feast
with which they commemorate the fall of Thebes and the
killing of Seqenenra," and directed an angry look toward the
clamorous soldiery, remembering the words of the physician
Kagemni, "When soldiers get used to drinking, their arms
grow feeble and they loathe to fight."

He followed the stream of people till he reached the edge of
the square in front of the palace, whose walls and windows appeared to his eyes like light piled upon light. The sight made
him feel wretched, his heart beat violently, and a perfumed
breeze, fragrant with memories of his youth, found him, as it
passed over his fevered head, sad at heart and distracted. He
went on, his sadness growing ever greater the closer his steps
brought him to the cradle of his childhood and the playground
of his youth.

Isfinis approached one of the chamberlains and showed him
Governor Khanzar's letter. The man looked at it closely, then
called a guard and ordered him to lead the trader and his train
to the waiting area in the garden. The youth followed him,
turning behind him into one of the side paths of the courtyard
because the central path was so crowded with guests, chamberlains, and guards. Isfinis remembered the place very well and
felt as though he had quit it for the last time only yesterday.
When they reached the great colonnade that led to the garden,
his heart beat faster and he became so agitated that he bit his
lower lip, remembering how he had used to play in this colonnade with Nefertari, blindfolding himself until she had hidden
herself behind one of the huge pillars, then removing the blind-
fold and searching everywhere until he found her. At that moment it seemed to his imagination that he heard her small feet
and the echo of her sweet laugh. They used to carve their

names on one of the pillars . . . would it still bear the traces? He would have liked to forget about his guard and search for the vestiges of that beautiful past, but the man hurried on, unaware of the melting heart an arm's length from him. When they reached the garden, the guard pointed to a bench and said to the youth, "Wait right here until the herald comes."

The garden was alight with brilliant lamps and the breeze wafted the scent of sweet herbs and the fragrance of flowers from all sides. His eyes sought the place where the statue of Seqenenra used to stand at the end of the grassy pathway that divided the garden in two. In its place he found a new statue, lacking in artistry, representing a stocky individual with a huge frame, large head, curved nose, long beard, and wide, protuberant eyes. He had no doubt that he was before Apophis, King of the Herdsmen. He gazed at it long and balefully, then threw a bitter glance, burning with anger and hatred, at the guards. Everything in the palace and the garden was as he remembered it. He caught sight of the summer gazebo on its high mound, surrounded by bowing palms with their tall graceful trunks, and he recalled the happy days when the whole family would hurry there in spring and summer, his grandfather and father to become absorbed in a game of chess while Nefertari sat between Queen Setkimus and her grandmother Queen Ahotep and he sat in Tetisheri's lap. The hours would pass thus unnoticed as they whiled away the time in soft talk, reading verse, and eating ripe fruit. Isfinis sat for some time reading his memories in the pages of the garden, the pathways, and the arcades, absorbed and at ease, until the herald came and asked him, "Are you ready?"

He stood up and said, "Quite ready, sir."

The other said, as he set off back, "Follow me."

He followed the herald, his men coming behind. They mounted the stairs and crossed the royal arcade until they arrived at the threshold of the royal hall. There they waited for permission to enter. The sound of loud laughter, of dancing feet

and of violent music, reached him. He observed bands of cup-
bearers carrying jugs and cups and flowers and realized that
these people knew neither shame when indulging themselves
nor any restraint in their conduct of their feast days, and that
the king excused them from maintaining their dignity and discipline, allowing them to revert to their original beastly nature.
Then one of the slaves called his name and he advanced with
unhurried steps till he found himself in the empty center of the
hall, the company seated around him in their finest official cos-
tumes, peering at him with interest. A certain embarrassment
overtook him. He realized that the governor knew well how to
excite the people's interest in what he had told them about him
and his gifts so as to magnify his exploits in the eyes of the
king, and he took a good omen from this. When he reached the
middle of the hall, he ordered his retinue to halt and approached the throne alone, bowing his head in respect and saying in tones of slavish submission, "Divine Lord, Master of the
Nile, Pharaoh of Upper and Lower Egypt, Commander of the
East and the West!"

The king replied in a deep, resonant voice, "I grant you
safety, slave."

Isfinis straightened up and was able to steal a quick glance at
the man seated on the throne of his fathers and grandfathers,
recognizing in him without a doubt the original of the statue in
the garden. At the same time he deduced, from the redness of
his face, the look in his eyes, and the glass of wine before him,
that he was drunk. The queen was sitting on his right and
Princess Amenridis on his left. To the youth as he gazed at her
she seemed in her royal clothes like a scintillating star, looking
at him calmly and proudly.

The king threw a penetrating look at him and what he saw
pleased him. He smiled slightly and said in his thick voice, "By
the Lord, this face is worthy to be that of one of our nobles!"

Isfinis bowed his head and said, "It pleased the Lord to give
it to one of Pharaoh's bondsmen."

The king guffawed and said, "I see you speak well. It is with sweet words that your people seek to gain our sympathy and our cash. Seth, in his wisdom, gives the sword to the strong master and glibness of tongue to the weak slave. But what has this to do with you? Our friend Khanzar has told me that you bear us a gift from the lands of Nubia. Show us your gift."

The youth bowed his head and moved aside. He made a signal to his men and two of them approached with the ivory casket and placed it before the throne. The youth went up to it, opened it, and drew forth a pharaoh's double crown of pure gold, studded with rubies, emeralds, pearls, and coral. As he lifted it, it attracted all eyes and the people, dazzled, broke out in a clamor of astonishment and admiration. Apophis, for his part, stared, his eyes bulging and avaricious, and unthinkingly he removed his own crown and took the new crown between his large hands and placed it on his bald head, so that he appeared clothed in new majesty. The king was jubilant and his face glowed with satisfaction. He said, "Trader, your gift is accepted."

Isfinis bowed respectfully. Then he turned to his men and gave them a special sign and they drew aside the closed curtain of the litter, revealing the three pygmies seated and clinging to one another. Their sudden appearance caused great astonishment among all the people. Most of them got to their feet and craned their necks. The young trader called to them, "Bow to your lord Pharaoh!" and the three pygmies jumped down as one and formed a line, then approached the throne with firm, deliberate steps, made a triple obeisance before Pharaoh, and then stood silently, their faces expressionless. The king exclaimed, "Trader, what might these creatures be?"

"They are people, my lord, whose tribes live in the furthest reaches of southern Nubia. They believe that the world contains no other peoples than themselves. If they see one of us, amazement ties their tongues and they call to one another in wonder. These three I raised and I have trained them well. My lord will find them a model of obedience and a form of entertainment and recreation."

The king shook his large head and laughed his mighty laugh, saying, "Anyone who claims to know everything is a fool. You, young man, have brought joy to our hearts and I grant you my favor."

Isfinis bowed his head and then retraced his steps, walking backward. When he reached the center of the hall, he found someone barring his way and grasping his arm. Isfinis turned to look at the owner of the thick hand and saw a man in fine military clothes with a beautiful beard and thick moustaches, his veins throbbing with rage. His flushed face, and the flash of madness in his eyes, indicated how drunk he was. He greeted his lord and said, "I have no doubt that it pleases our lord to witness the arts of valiant combat at our national feasts, as our sacred traditions require. I have saved up for my lord's sacred person a bloody duel that will delight the onlookers."

Lifting the glass to his thick lips, the king said, "How delightful that the blood of warriors be spilled on the floor of this hall to dispel our boredom! But who is the happy man whom you have honored with your enmity, Commander Rukh?"

The drunken commander pointed to Isfinis and said, "This, my lord, shall be my opponent."

The king was amazed, as were many of the nobles, and he asked, "How has this Nubian trader attracted your anger?"

"He rescued a peasant woman—she had had the impudence to direct an insult at my person—from punishment, by paying fifty pieces of gold to ransom her."

The king laughed his mighty, ringing laugh and asked the commander, "Are you willing to have a peasant as your opponent?"

"My Lord, I see that he is well-built and his muscles are strong. If his heart is not that of a bird, I will close my eyes to his lowly origin, to please my lord and make my contribution to the joy of the feast."

Governor Khanzar, however, would not contemplate a duel and had fixed his brother Judge Samnut with a reproachful glance, realizing that it was he who had alerted the commander to Isfinis's presence, without heed for the situation, while he, for his part, thought what a waste it would be should Rukh's sword deny him the precious treasures of Nubia. Going up to Commander Rukh, he told him firmly, "It is inconceivable that the decorations you wear should be scratched in a fight with a peasant trader, Commander."

But Rukh replied, forestalling him, "If it is shameful for me to fight a peasant, then it is disgraceful for me to allow a slave to challenge me without exacting upon him the punishment that he deserves. But when I saw Pharaoh grant this trader his favor, I preferred to treat him fairly and give him a chance to defend himself."

Those who heard the commander thought that what he said was right and just; they hoped earnestly that the trader would agree to fight, so that they could watch the duel and bring their feast-day pleasure to its climax. Isfinis was at a complete loss and could think of no way out. At one moment he would feel the eagerness of the people to hear his response and the look of challenge and contempt directed at him by the stubborn, drunken commander, which made his blood boil in his veins. Then he would think of the advice of Tetisheri and Latu, and how, if that gross commander were to kill him, the fruits that he was so close to plucking would be lost and this favorable opportunity would pass his family by; at this his blood would cool and his resolution grow numb. Dear God! He could not refuse and he could not flee, for if he did so the commander would despise him, all eyes would look at him with contempt, and he would leave the place with his tail between his legs and his heart broken, even if he did thus obtain his noble goal. At this point he heard the commander say to him, "You have challenged me, peasant. Are you ready to face me?"

Isfinis was silent, feeling crushed and numb. Then he heard a voice say, "Leave the boy! He knows nothing of fighting." And another voice said, "Leave the boy! A warrior fights with his soul, not with his body." At this, rage took possession of him, and he became aware of a hand on his shoulder and a voice saying to him, "You are not a warrior, and it is no disgrace if you excuse yourself." He looked and saw Khanzar, and felt a shudder pass through his body at the touch of the hand that slew his grandfather. At that dreadful moment, he glanced toward the throne, and saw Princess Amenridis regarding him with interest. Anger overcame him and, unaware of what he was doing, he said in a clear voice, "I thank the commander for condescending to fight with me and I accept the hand that he has extended to me."

The people were overjoyed and the king laughed and drank another cup, as heads on all sides turned to look at the two opponents. The commander's face relaxed and he smiled a vengeful smile. He asked Isfinis, "Do you fight with the sword?"

He bowed his head in assent and the other gave him a sword. Isfinis removed his cloak to reveal his upper garment and trousers. His tall, strong body attracted looks, as did the slenderness and rectitude of its form and the beauty of his face. He was given a shield and he grasped the sword in his right hand and put the shield on his left, standing at one arm's length from the commander like one of those statues on which the doors of the temples had closed.

The king gave the word for the fight to start and each unsheathed his sword. The angry commander was the first to attack, directing at his enemy a murderous blow that he imagined would be fatal, but the youth avoided it with amazing alacrity and it struck the air harmlessly. The commander allowed him no respite but, quick as lightning, aimed a still harder blow at his head. With a quick movement, however, the youth received it on his shield. Cries of admiration arose from every part of the hall and the commander realized that he was fighting with a man who knew well how to parry and thrust. He took heed and the fight started once more, following a new plan: they attacked, clinched, and separated, and feinted and turned back to the fight, the commander furious and violent, the youth amazingly calm, warding off his enemy's attacks with easy deftness and confidence. Every time that he parried a blow with his amazing skill, his enemy grew more agitated and crazed in his anger. Everyone realized that Isfinis was well able to defend himself and scarcely moved onto the offensive unless to thwart a strategy or make a blow miscarry; his skill was plain for all to see and he excelled his opponent in this and in agility to a degree that caught the enthusiasm of the audience, whose delight in the fight had caused them to forget the difference of race. Rukh became frantic and attacked him again and again, violently and strongly, never tiring or flagging, aiming blow after blow at him, some of which Isfinis warded off with his shield and some of which he skillfully avoided, remaining unhurt, serene, and full of boundless confidence, neither losing his temper nor discarding his insouciance, like some impregnable fortress. Despair started to overcome the exasperated commander and, as he became aware of how delicate and embarrassing was his position, he was driven to take risks. He raised the arm with which he held his sword and gathered all the strength and resolution he could muster to deliver a mortal blow, confident that his opponent's strategy was limited to defending himself. To his surprise, however, Isfinis directed a brilliant blow at the hilt of his sword, the point of his sword wounding the commander's palm. His hand lost its grip and the youth struck the sword a second blow that sent it flying, to fall close to Pharaoh's throne. Rukh was left defenseless, the blood dripping from his hand, and unable to contain his fury, while the audience hooted with pleasure, delighted at the trader's valor and the exquisite manner with which he refrained from pressing his advantage. The commander yelled at him, "Why don't you get on with it and finish me off, peasant?"

Isfinis replied calmly, "I have no reason to do so."

The commander ground his teeth and bowed to the king in salute, then turned on his heel and left the hall. The king laughed till his body was convulsed, then gestured to Isfinis, who gave his sword and shield to a chamberlain and, approaching the throne, bowed to the king, who said to him, "Your fighting is as strange as your pygmies. Where did you learn to fight?"

"Divine King, in the land of Nubia the trader cannot guarantee the safety of his caravan if he does not know how to defend himself and his companions."

The king said, "What a country! We too, men and women, were mighty fighters when we used to wander the cold northern marches of the desert, but when we took to living in palaces and became comfortable with affluence and ease and took to drinking wine instead of water, peace seemed good to us and now I have to watch a commander of my army defeated in combat with a peasant trader."

The king's face was beaming and his mouth smiling as he spoke, so Governor Khanzar approached the throne and, after bowing in salute, said, "My lord, the youth is brave and deserves to be granted safe-conduct."

Pharaoh nodded drunkenly and said, "You are right, Khanzar. The fight was fair and honorable and I grant him safe-conduct."

The governor thought this an excellent opportunity, so he said, "My lord, the youth is prepared to perform exceptional services to the throne, including bringing to it amazing valuables taken from the treasures of Nubia, in return for Egyptian grain."

The king looked at the governor for a while, thinking of the crown that was on his head. Then he said with no hesitation, "He has our permission to do so."

Khanzar bowed in thanks and Isfinis prostrated himself in front of Pharaoh and stretched out his hand to kiss the hem of the royal robe. Then he stood submissively, resisting the temptation to look to the left of the throne, and retreated until the door of the Great Hall hid him from sight. He was overjoyed but asked himself, "I wonder what Latu would say, if he found out about the duel?"

Isfinis and the slaves got back to the ship after midnight and found Latu unsleeping, looking out for them. He approached the youth anxiously, eager to hear his news, and Isfinis related to him the successes and the tribulations that he had faced in the palace. Latu said to him, "Let us praise the Lord Amun for the success that He has granted us! Yet I would be betraying my duty if I did not tell you frankly that you committed a grave error in giving in to your anger and pride. You should never have exposed our great hopes to the risk of collapse for the sake of a sudden surge of anger. Might not the commander have beaten you? Might not the king have struck you down? You must never forget that here we are slaves and they are masters, and that we are seeking a boon that they hold in their possession. Never lose sight of the fact that you must appear to be grateful and loyal to them, and above all to that governor who directed at your mighty grandfather, and at the whole of Egypt, the fatal stroke. Do this for Egypt, and for those we left behind us, fearful and prayerful, in Napata!"

The man could not contain himself and burst into tears, then went into his chamber and prayed earnestly.

Next morning, the two men proceeded to Lady Ebana's hut, as they had previously promised their companions. Lady Ebana, her son Ahmose, and some friends, among them Seneb, Ham, Deeb, and Kom, received them. All were anxious and burning to hear the news. Ham told them, "Our hearts are impatient, tortured by fear yet blazing with hope. And we leave behind in the nearby huts hundreds of friends whose eyelids never closed throughout the past night."

Isfinis smiled sweetly and said, "Good tidings, friends! The king has given us permission to trade between Egypt and Nubia."

Joy filled their faces and their eyes shone with the light of hope. Latu said decisively, "The time has come for work, so do not waste any on trivialities! Know that the way is long, so we must mobilize as many men as we can. Be unflagging in urging the common folk to join our voyage. Attract them with promises of the great profits to be made and do not confide the truth of the matter to them, so that rather we may tell them of our goal once we have crossed the border. I have no doubt that we shall find them to be loyal, as we have always found the people of Thebes and of all of Egypt to be. Off with you all and bundle up your belongings!"

A wide-scale movement covertly spread, pervaded by a sense of enthusiasm and faith. The men, dressed in the garb of fishermen, hurried to the ships, occupying every possible space above and below their decks. Isfinis next faced a difficult problem. How could he disguise the women and children as men and employ them in places better suited to men and youths? Or should he leave them behind alone, with all the pain to them and theirs that this implied? The youth decided to bring the matter up and he consulted his closest friends. They argued back and forth, until Ahmose son of Ebana finally burst out, "Lord Isfinis, we must have an invincible army composed of men. The women cannot be allowed to delay the formation of this mighty army nor will it harm them to remain in Thebes until we return as victors. I call on our enthusiasm for the cause to make us fight while our women are at home, rather than leaving them behind us in Nubia. While this may mean pain for us, let each bear his share of the burden of pain and sacrifice for the sake of our sublime cause!"

Ebana, much affected by these words, said, "What a wise opinion! Our place is here. We shall share their fate with the people of Thebes. If death, then death; if life, life."

None hesitated to agree and the women accepted the separation from their husbands and sons. Southern Thebes almost melted from the ardor of their farewells, the flowing of their tears, and the fervidness of their prayers and hopes.

Isfinis tasted no rest in those few days charged with magnificent deeds and silent sacrifices. He met with men, visited families, and organized the voyagers, keeping himself going by dreaming of his hopes, thinking of the present and the future, and doctoring his upsurges of anger and desire for revenge with doses of patience. Along with all this, he had also to suppress longings that burned in his heart and overcome blazing passions that ate away at him from the inside, weakening the forces of hatred that within him battled those of love. How hard he struggled and how much he bore in those few days! How much he patiently endured and suffered!

14

The governor of the South finally granted Isfinis permission to set off after giving him a permit allowing him to cross the border whenever he wished. The convoy raised anchor and set sail in the cool of dawn, Isfinis, Latu, and Ahmose son of Ebana taking their seats in the deck cabin of the first ship, their hearts filled with longing and yearning, while the tears with which he had made his last farewell to his mother still stood in Ahmose's eyes. Isfinis was lost in his dreams: he thought of Thebes and its people—Thebes, the greatest of the cities of the earth, the city of a hundred gates, of obelisks that reached up to the Heavenly Twins, of stupendous temples and towering palaces, of long avenues and huge squares, of markets that knew no peace or rest either by day or by night; Thebes the glorious, the Thebes of Amun, who had decreed that His gates should be closed before

His worshippers for ten years of captivity, Thebes which, in the end, had been taken by barbarians who now sat in power as ministers, judges, commanders, and nobles and whose people they had enslaved, so that Fate rubbed their faces in the dirt of those who yesterday had been slaves to them. The youth sighed from the depths of his wounded heart, then thought of the men crouched in the bellies of his ships, all driven by a single hope, all propelled by an unshakable love of Egypt passed down from generation to generation. How they suffered from the pain of separation from the wives, daughters, and sons that they had left behind them at the mercy of their enemies! All of them might have been that brave youth Ahmose who had suppressed his longings and curbed his yearning and on whose face resolution and strength were engraved. Among these crowding thoughts an entrancing image rose to the surface of his mind and he looked downward, hiding his eyes from Latu of the piercing glance, who, if he were to discern what he was thinking of, would grow angry once more. He wondered at how his thoughts hovered around her image, unable to drag themselves away from her. In confusion he asked himself, "Is it possible for love and hate to have the same object?" A sad look appeared in his eyes and he said to himself, "However it be with me, I shall not set eyes on her again, so there is no call for disquiet. Can anything in the world defeat forgetfulness?" Latu interrupted his dreams, saying in tones that betrayed concern, "Look to the north! I see a convoy coming on fast."

The two youths looked behind them and saw a convoy of five ships cutting through the crests of the waves at speed. The eye could not make out who was on board but the convoy was approaching fast and its component parts soon became distinct. Isfinis caught sight of a man standing at the front of the convoy and recognized him. Anxiously he said, "It's Commander Rukh."

Latu's face paled and he said with increasing agitation, "Do you think he is trying to overtake us?"

The other had no idea how to answer and they watched the convoy anxiously and warily. A number of fears swept over Latu and he asked in exasperation, "Is that imbecile going to try and delay our departure?"

It dawned on Isfinis that he had not yet escaped the consequences of his mistake and that peril was about to descend on the convoy, just as it neared safety's shores. Training his eyes on Rukh's convoy, he saw that it was approaching so fast that it had already overtaken some of the ships of his own. There were five warships, with detachments of guards standing on their decks, whose presence, without a doubt, did not bode well. The lead ship turned toward his own and came alongside and he saw the commander looking at him with a cruel expression and heard him yell at him in his thick voice, "Stand to and drop anchor!"

The other ships changed their course to pen the convoy in, and Isfinis ordered his sailors to stop rowing and drop anchor. They obeyed, fearfully noting that the Herdsmen's ships were loaded with soldiers bristling with weapons as though ready for a battle. Isfinis grew more anxious still, fearing that the hate-consumed commander would take his rancor out on the convoy, thus dashing the hopes of his whole people. He said to his companion, "If the man wants my head, it is no bad thing that I should be the first to fall in the new struggle. Should I die, you, Latu, must carry on on the same path and not let anger take control of you and so put an end to all our hopes."

The older man gripped his hand, overcome by a sudden despair, but Isfinis resumed, saying firmly, "Latu, I give you the very advice you gave me yesterday: avoid unwise anger. Let me pay the price for my mistake. If, tomorrow, you return to my father and pay him your condolences for my death while congratulating him on the Egyptian troops you have brought him, it will be better than your returning to him with me while our hopes have been lost forever."

He heard Commander Rukh shouting at him, "Come out to the middle of the ship, peasant!"

The youth gripped Latu's hand and left with firm steps. The commander, who was standing on the deck of his own ship, said to him, "You made me drop my sword, crazed peasant, when I was drunk and staggering. Now here I am waiting for you, with strong heart and steady arm."

Realizing that the commander had a vengeful nature and wanted to challenge him so that he could wipe away the stain on his honor, Isfinis said to him quietly, somewhat reassured as to the fate of his convoy, "Would you like to return to the attack, Commander?"

The other replied insolently, "Indeed, slave. And this time I shall kill you with my own hands in the most horrible fashion."

Isfinis asked him quietly, "I do not fear your challenge. But do you promise to do no harm to my convoy whatever the outcome of the duel?"

The commander said contemptuously, "I shall leave the convoy out of respect for my master's wishes. It will proceed without your carcass."

"And where do you want to fight?"

"On the deck of my ship."

Without uttering a word, the youth jumped into a boat and rowed with his strong arms till he reached the commander's ship. There he climbed the ladder onto its deck and stood face to face with his enemy. The commander threw a cruel look at him, angered by the calmness, self-possession, and disdain that appeared on the other's beautiful face. He gestured to one of the soldiers, who gave the youth a sword and shield. As he prepared himself for the fight, the commander said to him, "Today there will be no mercy, so defend yourself." Then he attacked him like a ravening beast and the two joined in violent combat surrounded by a circle of heavily armed soldiers, while, at the prow of the other ship, Latu and Ahmose stood watching the battle with often-averted eyes. The commander delivered a succession of blows, which Isfinis warded off with his amazing skill. Then the latter directed a hard blow at his opponent that fell on his shield, striking it with a force that left its mark. The youth seized the opportunity and began his assault with strength and skill, forcing the commander to retreat, pushing away from himself the blows leveled at him by his powerful opponent, who gave him no opportunity to rest or counter-attack. Exasperation appeared on the man's face and, grinding his teeth in insane fury, he threw himself upon his opponent in desperation. The youth, however, stepped aside and directed at him an elegant stroke that gashed his neck, causing the man's hands to go limp, and he ceased fighting and staggered as though drunk, only to fall finally on his face, flailing in his own blood. The troops, letting out an angry cry, drew their long swords in readiness for an assault on the youth at the first signal from the officer commanding them. Certain that he would perish, Isfinis realized the futility of resistance, especially as so many had their arrows trained on him, and he awaited the taste of death submissively, his eyes never leaving the commander sprawled at his feet. At that delicate juncture, he heard a voice nearby calling out angrily, "Officer, tell your men to sheathe their swords!"

It seemed to him that he knew the voice and, his heart leaping in his breast, he turned to its source and saw a royal ship almost touching the death ship. Princess Amenridis was leaning on its railing, the lineaments of anger sketched on her lovely face.

———————

The soldiers sheathed their swords and saluted. Isfinis bowed his head respectfully before he had time to recover from his astonishment and credit that he truly had been saved from death. The princess asked the officer, "Has he killed Commander Rukh?"

The officer approached the commander, felt his heart, and

examined his neck. Then he stood up and said, "I see a very dangerous wound, Your Highness, but he is still breathing."

Coldly she asked him, "Was it a fair fight?"

"It was, Your Highness."

The princess said angrily, "How then did it enter your minds to kill a man to whom the king has granted safe-conduct?"

Embarrassment showed on the officer's face and he said nothing. The princess said in an imperious tone, "Release this trader and take the wounded commander to the palace physicians!"

The officer obeyed the order and let Isfinis go free and the youth climbed down into his boat and turned it toward the royal ship, saying to himself with relief, "How did the princess manage to arrive at the right moment?" Then he climbed onto the deck of the ship, unimpeded by any of the guards, to find that the princess had returned to her cabin, to which he directed his firm steps, asking a slave girl for permission to enter. The girl disappeared inside for a moment and then returned with permission, and he entered, his heart beating. He found the princess seated on a luxurious divan, her back resting on a silken cushion, her face radiating a brilliant light. He bowed before her with genuine respect and, as he straightened his back, saw his necklace with the green emerald around her neck. He blushed. Nothing of the emotions passing over his face and eyes escaped her, and she said in a sweet and melodious voice, pointing to the necklace with her finger, "Have you come to ask me for the price of the necklace?"

The youth was reassured by her sweet tone and pleased by her jesting. He said honestly, "Indeed no. I have come, Your Highness, to thank you in all sincerity for the blessing of life that you have bestowed upon me, for which I shall remain in your debt as long as I live."

She smiled a dazzling smile that passed over her lips like a lightning flash. She said, "Indeed, you owe me your life. Do not wonder if I say so, for I am not one of those whom hypocrisy compels to put on a show of false modesty. I discovered this morning that the commander had set sail with a small fleet to cut off your convoy, so I caught up with him in this ship and I saw a part of your fight. Then I intervened at the right moment to save your life."

Her graciousness was to his heart as water to one dying of thirst. The look in her drowsy eyes and her announcement of her desire to save his life intoxicated him with happiness and he asked her, "May I hope that my lady will tell me frankly, in view of what I know to be her hatred of hypocrisy and affectation, what made her take upon herself the inconvenience of saving my life?"

She replied gaily, as though making light of his attempts to embarrass her, "To make you my debtor for it."

"It is a debt that makes me richer, not poorer."

She raised to him her blue eyes, making him feel as though he was about to stagger and fall at her feet, and said, "What a liar you are! Is that what a debtor says to his creditor as he turns his back on him to set off on a journey from which he will never return?"

"On the contrary, my lady, it is a journey from which he will return soon."

As though addressing herself, she said, "I am wondering to myself what benefit I might derive from this debt."

Heart throbbing, he looked into the blueness of her eyes and saw in them a look of surrender and of tenderness sweeter than the life that she had given him. The air between them seemed to him to pulsate with a profound heat and a magic that drew their two souls into itself, to meet and mingle. All inhibition thrown aside, he fell at her feet.

With strands of golden hair straying over her shining forehead and her ears, she asked him, "Will you be gone for long?"

He replied, sighing, "A month, my lady."

A look of sorrow passed over her eyes and she said, "But you do intend to come back, don't you?"

"I do, my lady, by this life of mine which belongs to you and by this sacred cabin!"

She held her hand out to him and said, "Till we meet again."

He kissed her hand and said, "Till we meet again."

———————

Latu met him with open arms and tears in his eyes, hugging him to his chest, and Ahmose threw his arm around his neck and kissed his brow. The convoy then raised anchor and set off at full tilt, the men standing gazing after the princess's ship, which pushed on to the north as they did to the south, until their eyes turned away in weariness. Returning to the cabin, they took their seats as though nothing had happened.

Isfinis distracted himself by watching the villages and their hardy menfolk with their coppery bodies, but his heart kept pulling him back to the cabin. Did Latu suspect anything? Latu was a noble man, whose heart had grown old and renounced everything but love of Egypt. And he could not shake himself free either of a thought that haunted him: had he acted wrongly or rightly? But what mortal could reach the goal that he had first set himself without taking into account what he might find along the way? How many a man had set out to climb a mountain and found himself descending into a deep chasm! And how many a man, having fledged his arrows for the hunt, had found the quarry had turned and was chasing him!

15

———————

The convoy safely crossed the borders of Egypt, and the men prayed an ardent collective prayer to the Lord Amun. They thanked their Lord for the paths of success that he had paved for them and they called on Him to bring their hopes within reach and preserve their women from all harm. The convoy proceeded upstream for some days and nights till it anchored at a small island for rest and recuperation. Latu invited the men to leave the ships for the island and, standing among them with Isfinis on his right, he said to them, "Brothers, let me reveal to you a secret that I have concealed from you for reasons that you will understand. Know that we are envoys to you from the family of our martyred sovereign Seqenenra and that your sovereign Kamose awaits your arrival now in Napata."

Astonishment appeared on the men's faces and some, unable to contain themselves for joy, asked, "Is it true, Lord Latu, that our royal family is in Napata?"

Smiling, he bowed his head in reply. Others asked, "Is our Sacred Mother Tetisheri there?"

"She is, and soon she will congratulate you herself."

"And our sovereign Kamose, son of Seqenenra?"

"He is, and you will see him with your own eyes, and hear him with your own ears."

"And the Crown Prince, Ahmose?"

Latu smiled and pointed to Isfinis, then bowed his head, saying, "I present to you, gentlemen, the Crown Prince of the Kingdom of Egypt, His Royal Highness Prince Ahmose."

Many exclaimed, "The trader Isfinis is the Crown Prince Ahmose?"

Ahmose Ebana, however, prostrated himself at the prince's feet, weeping, and the rest then did the same behind him, some weeping, some cheering, their cries rising from the depths of their hearts.

The convoy resumed its journey with joy unconfined, the men almost wishing the ships could fly with them to Napata, where their divine sovereign Kamose and sacred mother Tetisheri awaited them. Days and nights passed, then Napata appeared on the horizon with its simple huts and modest buildings, its features continuing to grow closer and more distinct until the convoy cast anchor in its harbor. Some soldiers noticed the convoy and went to the palace of the governor and a crowd of Nubians gathered on the shore to watch the ships and those that they brought. The Egyptians disembarked with Prince Ahmose and Chamberlain Hur at their head. Then a fast chariot arrived, from which descended Ra'um, governor of the south. He greeted the prince and those with him, conveying to them the greetings of the king and his family, and informed them that His Majesty was waiting for them in the palace. The men cheered the king at length, then proceeded in large companies behind their prince, a throng of Nubians in their wake.

The royal family was sitting beneath a large sunshade in the courtyard of the governor's palace. The ten years that had passed had wrought their changes. Seriousness of purpose, sternness of outlook, and sorrow had all left traces that time would never erase. Those most affected by the passing of time were the two queens, Tetisheri and Ahotep. The sacred mother's physique was less supple, her body tending to stoop a little, and her travails had engraved their lines on her radiant brow. All that was left of the old Tetisheri was the gleam in her eyes, and her looks evincing wisdom and patience. As for Ahotep, white hair had brought venerability to her head and sorrow and anxiety had left their mark on her comely face.

Beholding their sovereign, the people prostrated themselves to him. Then Ahmose went up to his father, kissed the hands of his mother Queen Setkimus, of his grandmother Ahotep, and of Tetisheri, and kissed the brow of his wife, Princess Nefertari. Next he addressed himself to the king, saying, "My lord, Amun has granted success to our work. I present to Your Majesty the first battalions of the Army of Deliverance."

Pleasure lit up the king's face and he arose and raised his scepter in salute to his people, who cheered him long. Then they approached him and kissed his hand one by one. Kamose said, "The Lord grant you life, you good, courageous men whom injustice first separated from us, then fated to suffer humiliation, just as we were fated to taste the bitterness of exile for ten long years! But I see that you are men who reject in-equity and prefer the hardships of separation from their loved ones and the difficulties of the struggle to the acceptance of se-curity in the shadow of ignominy. Such have I always known you to be, as did my father before me. You have come to rally to my cause, when it is in tatters, or nearly so, and to strengthen my heart, when it has been shaken by Fate's indif-ference. It was one of the Lord Amun's mercies to us that He came to the purest of us in heart and the greatest of us in hope, Mother Tetisheri, in a dream, and ordered her to send my son Ahmose to the land of our fathers and grandfathers to bring back soldiers who would deliver Egypt from her enemy and her humiliation. Welcome, soldiers of Egypt, soldiers of Kamose! Tomorrow others will come, so let us adopt an attitude of pa-tience, and set to work. Let our slogan be 'the Struggle,' our hope, Egypt, and our faith, Amun!"

As one man, all cried out, "The Struggle, Egypt, and Amun!" Then Tetisheri arose and advanced a few steps, leaning on her royal staff, and said to the men in a strong, clear voice, "Sons of sad, glorious Thebes, accept the greetings of your old mother and allow me to present you with a gift that I made with my own hands for you, that you may all labor in its shadow."

She made a sign with her staff to one of the soldiers, who ap-proached the men and presented to them a large flag that bore the image of the temple of Amun, surrounded by the wall of Thebes with its hundred gates. Eager hands seized it and the men uttered ardent prayers for their Mother and cheered for her and for glorious Thebes. Tetisheri smiled and a joyful light illumined her face. She said, "Dear sons, let me tell you that I have never given in to that despair against which Seqenenra, on the day of his farewell, warned us and have never ceased to pray to the Lord that He extend my fated term so that I might see Thebes again, with our flags fluttering above its palace and Kamose sitting on its throne as Pharaoh of Upper and Lower

Egypt. Today I am closer to my hope, now that your youthful hands are joined to mine."

The people's plaudits rose again and the king started asking about the great men of Egypt, the priest of Amun, and the Lord's temple, while the chamberlain answered him as best he could. Then Prince Ahmose led Ahmose Ebana, son of Commander Pepi, to his father. The king welcomed him and told him, "I hope that you will be to me as your father was to mine—a valiant commander, who lived for his duty and died in doing it."

Then the king invited the new arrivals to a midday banquet and they ate and drank in health and good cheer. Afterward, all started to think of the morrow and what lay after that, and Napata slept for the first time in ten years in joy and optimism, its heart filled with hope.

AHMOSE AT WAR

1

The life of the royal family in exile had been one not of listlessness and inactivity but of work and preparation for the distant future, with the heart of Tetisheri, which knew neither despair nor rest, as the point around which all of them revolved. As soon as she arrived, she had asked of Ra'um, governor of the south, to summon to Napata the most skilled Nubian craftsmen and Egyptian technicians residing in Nubia and the man had sent his messengers to Argo and Atlal and other Nubian towns, and these had returned to him with craftsmen and workers. The old queen demanded that her son contract them to make weapons, helmets, and the accoutrements of war and to build ships and war chariots. To encourage him she told him, "You will decide one day to attack the enemy who has usurped your throne and taken possession of your country. When that day comes, you must attack with a large fleet and a force of chariots that cannot be overcome, as the enemy did with your father."

Over the past ten years, Napata had been turned into a great factory for the building of ships, chariots, and instruments of war in all their forms. As the days passed, the fruits of these labors grew, becoming the pillars of new hope. When the men came with the first convoy, they found the weapons and materiel that they needed present in full supply and they presented themselves for training with hearts full of enthusiasm and honest optimism. The day after their arrival in Napata they were all inducted into the army and trained under the supervision of officers of the Egyptian garrison in the arts of combat and the use of a variety of weapons. They drove themselves hard during the training, working from dawn to dusk.

Everyone worked, the mighty and the lowly alike. King Kamose personally supervised the training of the troops and the formation of the nuclei of the different battalions and picked out those most suited to serve with the fleet, Crown Prince Ahmose assisting him in this. The three queens and the young princess insisted on going to work with everybody else. They straightened and fledged arrows or worked at sewing military clothing and they mixed constantly with the soldiers and craftsmen, eating and drinking with them to encourage them and strengthen their hearts. How wonderful it was to see Mother Tetisheri bent over her work with a dedication that knew no fatigue or moving among the troops to observe their training and offer words of enthusiasm and hope! Seeing her, the men would forget themselves and tremble with excitement and dedication and the woman would smile in delight at these auspicious signs and say to those around her, "The ships and the chariots will become the graves of those who ride in them if they are not propelled by hearts yet harder than the iron of which they are made. See how the men of Thebes work! Any one of them would fall on ten of the Herdsmen, with their filthy beards and white skin, and put their hearts to rout."

And indeed, the men had been turned, by the force of their excitement, their love, and their hate, into ravening beasts.

Chamberlain Hur now departed to prepare the second convoy, doubling the number of ships and filling them with gold and silver, pygmies and exotic animals. Mother Tetisheri was of the opinion that he should take with him companies of loyal Nubians to present to the gentry of Thebes, to work for them overtly as slaves, while covertly they would be their helpers, ready to attack the enemy from behind if the enemy one day were to become involved in a clash with them. The king was delighted with the idea, as was Chamberlain Hur, who worked unhesitatingly to bring it about.

Once Hur had completed the preparations for his convoy, he sought permission to set off. Prince Ahmose had been waiting for this moment with a heart wrung by longing and preoccupied with passion. He asked that he be allowed to make the voyage as leader of the convoy but the king, who had found out about what had befallen him and the dangers to which he had been exposed, refused to take the needless risk of letting him travel again. He told him, "Prince, your duty now calls you to stay in Napata."

His father's words took the prince by surprise, dashing the burning hope in his breast like water dashed on fiery coals. Candidly he pleaded with him, "Seeing Egypt and mixing with its people would bring relief to my heart from certain maladies that afflict it."

The king said, "You will find complete relief the day you enter it as a warrior at the head of the Army of Deliverance."

Once more the youth pleaded his case, "Father, how often I have dreamed of seeing Thebes again soon!"

But the king said resolutely, "You will not have to wait long. Be patient until the day of struggle dawns!"

The youth realized from the king's tone that he had spoken his final word and feared his anger were he to plead with him again, so he bowed his head in a sign of submission and acceptance even though the pain pierced his heart and choked his breathing. His days passed in hard work and he had only a short time to himself before sleeping in which to summon up, in his private chamber, the sweetest of memories, and to hover in imagination about the beautiful cabin on the deck of the royal ship that had witnessed, at the moment of farewell, the most blinding loveliness and tenderest passion. During such moments it would seem to him that he heard that melodious voice telling him, "Till we meet again!"—at which he would sigh from the depths of his soul and say sorrowfully, "When will that meeting be? That was a farewell that no reunion can follow."

Napata in those days, however, was a fit place to make a man forget himself and his cares and focus his attention on whatever was most important and urgent. The men gave their all to their work, struggling unceasingly, and if the wind of Thebes sprang up and longing for those whom they had left behind its walls shook them, they sighed awhile then bent again to what they were at with increased determination and greater resolve. Days passed in which they could not believe that there was anything in the world but work, or anything in the future but hope.

The convoy returned with new men, who cheered as the first had cheered the day of their arrival and who shouted with the same excitement, "Where is our sovereign, Kamose? Where is our mother, Tetisheri? Where is our prince, Ahmose?" then joined the camp, to work and be trained.

Chamberlain Hur came to Prince Ahmose and greeted him. He handed him a letter, saying, "I have been charged with bearing this letter to Your Highness."

Ahmose asked in astonishment as he turned the letter over in his hands, "Who is the sender?"

Hur, however, maintained a gloomy silence and an idea struck the prince that made his heart flutter, and he tore open the letter and read the signature. His limbs gave way and the fire in his heart flared up as his eyes ran over the lines, where he read:

It saddens me to inform you that I chose one of your pygmies to live with me in my private quarters and that I took care of him, feeding him the most delicious foods, dressing him in the most beautiful clothes, and giving him the best treatment, so that he became fond of me and I of him. Then I noticed his absence one day and I could not find him, so I ordered my slave girls to look for him and they found that he

*had fled to his brothers in the garden. His inconstancy
pained me and I turned my face from him. Is it possible for
you to send me a new pygmy, one who knows how to be true?*

Amenridis

As he finished reading the letter, Ahmose felt a blow like the
thrust of a heavy spear into his heart and the ground seemed to
shake beneath his feet. He shot a glance at Hur, who was regarding him closely as though trying to discover what was in
the letter by reading his face.

Turning away from him, Ahmose continued on his way sorrowing and brokenhearted, telling himself how impossible it was
that she would ever know what it was that had prevented him
from coming back to her and how impossible it was that he
would ever be able to communicate to her his grief and emotion.
She would, indeed, always see him as the inconstant pygmy.

He kept his sorrows to himself, however, and none were
aware of the struggle raging in his heart but the person closest
to him: Nefertari. She was at a loss as to what to do with him
and perplexed as to what might lie behind his distractedness
and absent-mindedness and at the look of sorrow that would
appear in his lovely eyes whenever he stared ahead, looking at
nothing.

One evening she said to him, "You are not yourself, Ahmose."

Her remark disturbed him and, playing with her plaits with
his fingertips, he said smiling, "It's just fatigue, my dear. Don't
you see how we are engaged in a struggle fit to move solid
mountains?"

She shook her head and said nothing and the youth put himself more on his guard.

Napata, however, allowed no man to drown in his sorrows,
for work is the destroyer of care and the city witnessed miracles
of work such as it had never seen before. Men were trained,
ships, chariots, and weapons made, and convoys dispatched

loaded with gold, to return loaded with men, only to be sent back and return once more. Long days and months passed until the happy, long-awaited day arrived and King Kamose, unable to contain his joy, went to his grandmother Tetisheri, kissed her brow, and said in joyful tones: "Good news, Grandmother! The Army of Deliverance is ready!"

2

The send-off drums sounded, the army formed itself into battalions, and the fleet raised anchor. Tetisheri summoned to her the king, the crown prince, and the leading commanders and officers and told them, "This is one of those happy days for which I have waited long. Tell your valiant soldiers that Tetisheri entreats them to set her free from her captivity and smash the shackles that bind the necks of all Egypt. Let the motto of every one of you be to 'Live like Amenhotep or die like Seqenenra.' The Lord Amun bless you and make your hearts steadfast!"

The men kissed her thin hand and King Kamose said to her as he bade her farewell, "The motto of all of us shall be 'Live like Amenhotep or die like Seqenenra!' and those of us who die will die the noblest of deaths, while those of us who remain will live the most honorable of lives."

Napata, the royal family, and Governor Ra'um at its head, turned out to bid farewell to the tumultuous army. Drums beat, bands played, and the army moved, following its traditional order of march and preceded by a force of scouts bearing flags. King Kamose was in the vanguard of the army in the center of a ring of servants, chamberlains, and commanders, followed by the royal guard in elegant chariots. Next came a battalion of chariots, which proceeded rank after rank, further than the eye could see, their wheels sending a deafening squeal into the air, the neighing of their horses like the shrilling of the wind. After these came a battalion of heavy archers with their bows, coats of mail, and quivers of arrows, followed in their footsteps by a battalion of highly trained lancers with their lances and shields. Next was a battalion of light infantry, while the wagons of weapons, supplies, and tents, guarded by horsemen, brought up the rear. At the same time, the fleet, with its huge vessels, set sail, the soldiers that it bore equipped with all the weaponry they might need by way of bows, lances, and swords.

These forces advanced to the music of the band, excitement burning in their youthful, angry hearts, the terrifying sight throwing dread into hearts and minds. They marched all day, eating up the miles, and came to a halt when darkness fell, neither tired nor wearied, seeking help against the hardships of the road and the length of the journey from a resolve that could move mountains. On their way they passed by Semna, Buhen, Ibsakhlis, Fatatzis, and Nafis and they continued to march until they reached Dabod, the last Nubian town. Here the scented breeze of Egypt caressed their faces and they camped and set up their tents to take rest from the privations of the journey and prepare themselves for battle.

The king and his men plotted the first plan of invasion and they plotted it well. Ahmose Ebana, the most skilled man in the whole fleet, was given command of a part of it to take up to the borders of Egypt as though it were a convoy of the sort which the border guards had become accustomed to see pass in recent times. At dawn on the fourth day after the army's arrival at Dabod, the small fleet set sail, reaching Egypt's borders as day was breaking. Ahmose Ebana stood on the deck of the ship in the flowing robes of a trader. He produced the entry permit for the guards and took his fleet safely in. Ahmose knew that the border guard consisted of a few ships and a small garrison, so his plan consisted of taking the ships unawares and overpowering them, then laying siege to the island of Biga until the army and the rest of the fleet could enter Egypt. Thereafter it would be easy for him to strike Sayin before it could prepare itself to resist. The convoy proceeded in open formation and when it drew close to the southern shore of Biga, where the Herdsmen's ships were moored, the soldiers appeared on deck with bows in their hands, while Ahmose, throwing off his trader's cloak, appeared in the dress of an officer and ordered his men to fire their arrows at the men guarding the ships. The fleet approached the moored ships rapidly, swooped down upon them before help could reach them from the shore, and cast nets over them, while the soldiers jumped onto their decks to take possession of them. They clashed with the few guards who were to be found on board in a small battle and crushed them swiftly. During this maneuver, Ahmose's ship fired its arrows at the guards on the bank and prevented the soldiers from coming to the aid of their companions on the ships. Thus, the vessels were quickly subdued without high cost to the attackers and the fleet laid siege to the island to prevent contact with the cities of the north. The Biga garrison took note of the sudden maneuver and rushed to the shore, only to find itself surrounded and imprisoned, its small fleet captive.

The battle was barely over before units of the Egyptian fleet appeared, plowing through the billows on the horizon, its course set straight for the border. This it passed safely without meeting any resistance. Then it joined itself to Ahmose Ebana's fleet, placing the island in the middle of a circle of huge ships and causing the Biga garrison to retreat into its center, out of reach of the arrows of the fleet, which poured down on them from all quarters.

As soon as the forward units of the army had entered Egyptian territory and descended on the eastern shore, followed by the clamoring battalions, those besieged on Biga realized that the newcomers were invaders, not pirates, as they had first imagined. The commander of the fleet, Qumkaf, now gave his order to attack the island and the ships descended on it from all directions, the soldiers disembarking, bristling with weapons, under the protection of the bowmen. The soldiers then marched from all sides on the garrison besieged in the middle. The soldiers of the latter, in addition to finding themselves in a critical position militarily, had observed the impetuous charge of the Egyptian forces on land and on the Nile, and their hands betrayed them, their courage abandoned them, and they threw down their weapons and were taken prisoner. Ahmose Ebana was at the head of the attackers and entered the governor's palace in triumph. He raised the Egyptian flags above it and ordered that the Herdsmen officials and notables there be seized just like the soldiers.

When the peasants, workers, and servants of the island saw the Egyptian soldiers, they could not believe their eyes and they hurried, men and women, to the palace of the new governor and gathered in front of it to find out what was going on, hopes and fears struggling in their breasts. Ahmose Ebana went out to them and they stared at him in silence. He said to them, "May the Lord Amun, protector of Egyptians and destroyer of Herdsmen, bless you!"

The word "Amun," of whose sound they had been deprived for ten years, fell on their ears like beautiful magic and joy lit up their faces. Some asked, "Have you really come to save us?"

In a trembling voice, Ahmose Ebana said, "We have come to save you and to save enslaved Egypt, so rejoice! Do you not see these mighty forces? They are the Army of Deliverance, the army of our lord King Kamose, son of our martyred sovereign Seqenenra, come to liberate his people and reclaim his throne."

The assembled people repeated the name of Kamose in astonishment. Then joy and excitement swept through them and they cheered him at length, many kneeling in prayer to the Divine Lord Amun. Some of the men asked Ahmose Ebana, "Is our slavery really over? Are we free men again, as we were ten years ago? Are the days of the lash and the stick, of our being abused for being peasants, gone?"

Ahmose Ebana grew angry and said furiously, "Be sure that the era of oppression, slavery, and the lash is gone, never to return. From this moment, you shall live as free men under the benevolent protection of our sovereign Kamose, Egypt's rightful pharaoh. Your land and your houses will be returned to you and those who usurped them throughout this time will be thrown into the depths of the dungeons."

Joy engulfed those suffering souls, who fell spontaneously into a collective prayer, whose words ascended to Amun in Heaven, and to Kamose on earth.

3

In the freshness of the morning, King Kamose, Crown Prince Ahmose, Chamberlain Hur, and all the members of pharaoh's entourage descended to the island, where the people received him enthusiastically, falling prostrate in front of him and kissing the ground before his feet. Their cheers for the memory of Seqenenra, and for Tetisheri, the king, and Prince Ahmose, rose high and Kamose greeted them with his own hands, speaking to a great throng of men, women, and children, eating the doum palm and other fruit that they brought them and drinking, along with his entourage and commanders, cups full of the wine of Maryut. All went to the governor's palace and the king issued an order appointing one of his loyal men, named Samar, governor over the island, charging him to provide justice for all and to apply the laws of Egypt. At the same meeting, the commanders agreed that they must surprise Sayin at first light, so as to strike the decisive blow before it awoke from its torpor.

The army slept early and awoke just before dawn, then marched north, the fleet accompanying it to block the Nile inlets. The soldiers marched through the darkness watched with shining eyes by the wakeful stars, anger boiling in their breasts as they yearned for revenge and battle. They drew close to Sayin as the last of night's darkness mixed with the bashful blue light of morning and the eastern horizon shimmered with the first rays of the sun. Kamose issued an order to the charioteers to advance on the city from south and east, supported by troops from the archers' and lancers' battalions. Likewise, he ordered the fleet to lay siege to the western shore of the city. These forces attacked the city from three sides at the same time. The chariots were led by experienced officers, who knew the city and its strategic points, and these directed their chariots against the barracks and police headquarters. After them came the infantry, bristling with weapons, who fell on the enemy in a massacre in which rivers of blood flowed. The Herdsmen were able to fight in certain positions and they defended themselves desperately, falling like dry leaves in autumn caught by a tempestuous wind. The fleet, for its part, met with no resistance and came across no warships in its path. Having once secured the beach, it disembarked parties of its troops, who assaulted the palaces that overlooked the Nile and seized their owners, among them the governor of the city, its judges, and its major notables. Then the same forces set out across the fields, heading straight for the city.

Surprise was the decisive element in the battle, which was short, but saw the fall of many Herdsmen. As soon as the sun rose on the horizon and sent its light out over the city, parties of the invaders might be seen occupying the barracks and the palaces and driving captives before them. Corpses were to be beheld flung down in the streets and the barracks' courtyards, drained of their blood. It was bruited about in the outskirts of the city and the nearby fields that Kamose son of Seqenenra had entered Sayin with a huge army and taken possession of it, and a bloody uprising broke out in the wake of this news, the local people attacking the Herdsmen and killing them in their beds. They mutilated them and beat them mercilessly with whips, so that many Herdsmen fled in terror, as the Egyptians had done when Apophis marched on the South with his chariots and his men. Then tempers cooled and the army established order and King Kamose entered at the head of his army, the flags of Egypt fluttering at the front and the guards preceding him with their band. The people rushed to welcome him and it was a glorious day.

The officers conveyed to the king that a large number of young men, including some who had been soldiers in his former army, had come forward with striking enthusiasm to volunteer for the army. Kamose was delighted and set over the city a man of his called Shaw, whom he commanded to organize and train the volunteers so that they could be inducted into the army as battle-ready troops. The commanders also gave the king an accounting of the chariots and horses they had taken as spoils of war and it was a great number.

Chamberlain Hur proposed to the king that they should advance without delay, so as not to give the enemy any respite in which to ready itself and gather its armies. He said, "Our first real battle will be at Ombos."

Kamose replied, "Indeed, Hur. Dozens of refugees may have knocked on the gates of Ombos already, so from now on there is no room for surprise. We will find our enemy prepared. Apophis may even be able to confront us with his barbaric forces at Hierakonpolis. So on with us to our destiny!"

The Egyptian forces proceeded, by land and by river, northward on the road to Ombos, entering many villages but meeting no resistance whatsoever. They did not come across a single Herdsman, indicating to the king that the enemy had loaded up their belongings and driven off their animals, fleeing toward Ombos. The peasants came out to welcome the Army of Deliverance and greet their victorious sovereign, calling out to him with hearts revived by joy and hope. The army hurried on until it arrived at the outskirts of Ombos, where the forward parties of scouts arrived to report that the enemy was camped to the south of the city, ready for battle, and that a fleet of middling size was moored to the west of Ombos. The king divined that the first major battle would be at the gates. He wanted to know the number of the enemy's troops but it was difficult for the scouts to find this out, as the enemy was camped on a broad plain that was not easy to approach. A young commander called Mheb said, "My lord, I do not believe that the forces of Ombos can exceed a few thousand."

King Kamose replied, "Bring me all our officers or soldiers who are from Ombos."

Chamberlain Hur grasped what the king wanted and said, "Pardon, my lord, but the face of Ombos has changed in the past ten years. Barracks have been constructed that did not exist before, as I saw with my own eyes on one of my trading voyages. The Herdsmen have probably taken these as a center to defend the towns that fall close to the borders."

Commander Mheb said, "In any case, my lord, I believe that we should attack with light forces, so that we do not sustain a heavy loss."

Prince Ahmose, however, did not favor this opinion and he said to his father, "My lord, I hold the opposite view. I think that we should attack with forces too heavy to be resisted and throw the main body of our forces into the battle, so as to deal the enemy the final blow as quickly as possible. In so doing, we will dismay the forces that are gathering now at Thebes to fight us and in the future we will be doing battle with men who believe that to fight us is to die. There is no fear of risking our troops, for our army will double in size with the volunteers who join it at every town we take, while the enemy will never find replacements for its own losses."

The idea pleased the king, who said, "My men will sacrifice themselves willingly for the sake of Thebes."

The king was aware of the decisive effect that the fleet's victory had had in winning the battle, because of the significant role that fleets can play in laying siege to the beaches of rich cities or landing troops behind enemy lines. He therefore issued an order to Commander Qumkaf to attack the Herdsmen's ships that lay at anchor to the west of Ombos.

All that now lay between the two armies was a broad plain. The Herdsmen were warlike and tough, intrepid and strong, and they harbored an ingrained contempt for the Egyptians. Ignorant of the Egyptians' strength, they attacked first, sending against them a battalion of a hundred war chariots. Then Kamose gave the order to attack and more than three hundred chariots sprang forward and surrounded the enemy. Dust rose, horses neighed, bows twanged. A violent fight occurred, with Prince Ahmose determined to put paid to the enemy once and for all. He launched a further two hundred chariots against the enemy's infantry, which was awaiting the outcome of the chariot battle in front of the gates of Ombos. These were followed by units from the archers' battalion and others from that of the spearmen. The chariots swept down on the infantry and broke through their lines, throwing them into confusion and terror and raining arrows upon them. Their ranks gave way, with some wounded, some dead, and some in flight, but they were met by Ahmose's attacking infantry in irresistible numbers and wiped out in their entirety. The enemy was taken by surprise, not having expected that it would meet with forces of this size, and its forces rapidly collapsed, its horsemen falling and its chariots disintegrating. The Egyptians had mastery of the field in a time so short as to be barely believable, having fought with anger and fury, striking with arms whose sinews were hardened by age-old hatred and blazing resentment.

Armed forces broached the gates of Ombos and forced an entry in order to occupy the barracks and cleanse them of the remnants of enemy troops, and officers went over the field, organizing their battalions and carrying off the wounded and the dead. King Kamose stood in the midst of the field on his chariot surrounded by his commanders, with Prince Ahmose on his right and Chamberlain Hur on his left. News had arrived that his fleet had borne down on the enemy ships and attacked them fiercely and that the enemy had retreated before them in disarray. The king was pleased and said to those around him, smiling, "A successful beginning."

Prince Ahmose, his clothes covered with dust, his face smeared with grime, and his forehead dripping with sweat, said, "I am looking forward to plunging into battles more terrible than that."

Kamose, throwing at his lovely face a look of admiration, said, "You will not have to wait long."

The king then descended from his chariot, his men following, and took a few steps that brought him into the midst of the corpses of the Herdsmen. He looked at them and, seeing that the blood that had gushed from them had stained their white skin and that arrows and lances had lacerated it, he said, "Do not imagine that this blood is the blood of our enemies: it is the blood of our people whom they sucked dry and left to die of hunger."

Kamose's face was drawn, hidden behind a dark mask of sorrow. Raising his head to the heavens, he murmured, "May your soul, my dear father, live in peace and felicity!"

Then he looked at those about him, and said in a voice bespeaking strength and courage, "Our strength will be tested in two fierce battles, at Thebes and at Avaris. If victory there be ours, we shall have cleansed the motherland of the Herdsmen forever and restored Egypt to the days of glorious Amenhotep. When, then, shall we stand as we do now, on the corpses of the defenders of Avaris?"

The king turned to go back to his chariot and, at that very moment, one of the bodies sprang upright with the speed of lightning, aimed its bow at the king, and let fly. Nothing could prevent what was fated and none could strike the warrior before he released his arrow, which struck the king's chest. The men let out a yell of alarm and fired their arrows at the Hyksos warrior, then hurried to the king with hearts full of horror and pity as a deep sigh issued from Kamose's chest. Then he staggered like one intoxicated and fell in front of the crown prince, who cried, "Bring a litter and call the physician!"

He bent his head over his father and said in a trembling voice, "Father, Father, can you not speak to us?"

The physician came quickly and the litter with him, and they picked the king up and laid him on it with exquisite care. The physician knelt at his side and set to removing the king's armor and his upper garment, so as to reveal his chest. The entourage surrounded the litter in silence, their eyes darting from the wan face of the king to that of the physician. News spread through the field, and the noise died down. Then a heavy silence reigned, as though all that mighty army had been obliterated.

The physician tugged on the arrow and the blood immediately started gushing copiously from the wound. The king's face contracted with the pain and the eyes of the prince darkened in sorrow as he murmured to Hur, "Dear God, the king is in pain."

The man washed the wound and placed herbs on it but the king showed no improvement and his limbs shook visibly. Then he sighed deeply and opened his eyes, with a dark, lifeless look. Ahmose's breast tightened still more and he said to himself in a plaintive voice, "How you have changed, Father!" The king's eyes moved until they fell on Ahmose, a smile appeared in them, and he said in a voice so weak as barely to be audible, "A moment ago I thought I was going on to Avaris but the Lord wishes my journey to end here, at the gates of Ombos."

In a sorrowing voice, Ahmose cried out, "Let Him take my soul for yours, Father!"

The king returned in his weak voice, "Never! Take care of yourself, for you are much needed! Be more cautious than I and remember always that you must not give up the struggle until Avaris, the Herdsmen's last fortress, has fallen and the enemy has withdrawn from our lands to the last man!"

The physician feared for the king because of the effort that he was making in speaking and gestured at him to say no more, but the king was lost in a higher realm of experience, that which divides extinction from immortality, and he said in a voice whose accents had changed and which fell strangely on their ears, "Say to Tetisheri that I went to my father a brave man like him!"

He stretched out his hand to his son and the prince went down on his knees and held him to his breast, the king clinging to his shoulder for a while in farewell. Then his fingers relaxed and he surrendered his spirit.

4

The physician covered the body and the men prostrated themselves about it in a prayer of farewell, then rose as though drunk with sorrow. Chamberlain Hur sent out a call for the battalion commanders and upper officers and when they appeared addressed them as follows: "Comrades, it grieves me to announce to you the death of our brave sovereign, Kamose. He was martyred on the field of battle, fighting for Egypt, as was his father before him, and, snatched from our bosoms, has been transported to dwell next to Osiris. But first he left it as his testament to us that we cease not the struggle until Avaris has fallen and the enemy withdrawn from our lands. As chamberlain of this noble family, I offer you my condolences for this mighty loss and announce to you the succession of our new sovereign and glorious commander, Ahmose son of Kamose, son of Seqenenra, may the Lord preserve him and grant him clear victory!"

The commanders saluted the king's body and bowed to Ahmose, the new king, and the chamberlain gave them permission to go back to their troops and announce the death and succession.

Hur, consumed by grief, ordered the soldiers to raise the litter on their shoulders. Drying his eyes, he said, "May your sublime soul live in happiness and peace next to Osiris! You were on the verge of entering Ombos at the head of your victorious army but the Lord has decreed that you should enter it on your bier. However it be, you are the noblest among us."

The army entered Ombos in its traditional order, the king's bier at its head. The grievous news had spread throughout the city and the rapture of victory and the anguish of death were drunk in a single draught. Multitudinous throngs came from every place to welcome the Army of Deliverance and bid farewell to their departed sovereign with hearts confused between joy and sorrow. When the people saw the new king, Ahmose, they prostrated themselves in silent submission but not a cheer went up that day. The priests of Ombos received the mighty body and Ahmose withdrew from public view and wrote a letter to Tetisheri as his father had bidden him and sent it with a messenger.

Dispatch riders brought news of the fleet that was both pleasing and sad. They said that the Egyptian fleet had defeated the Herdsmen's and taken some of its units captive; however, the commander, Qumkaf, had fallen and officer Ahmose, having taken the helm after the commander's death, had achieved total victory and killed the Herdsmen's commander with his own hand in a fierce battle. To reward Ahmose Ebana, the king issued an order giving him command of the fleet.

Following his father's wise policy, he made his friend Ham governor of Ombos and charged him to organize it and induct the able-bodied there into the army. The king said to Hur, "We shall advance quickly with our troops, for, if the Herdsmen tormented our people in time of peace, they will double their sufferings in time of war. We must make the period of suffering as short as we can."

The king summoned Governor Ham and told him before his entourage and commanders, "Know that I promised myself from the day that I went to Egypt dressed as a trader that I would take Egypt for the Egyptians. Let that then be our motto in ruling this country; and let your guiding principle be to cleanse it of the whites, so that from this day on none but an Egyptian may rule here and none but an Egyptian may hold property, and that the land be Pharaoh's land and the peasants his deputies in its exploitation, the ones taking by right what they need to guarantee them a life of plenty, the other taking what is in excess of their needs to spend on the public good. All Egyptians are equal before the law and none of them shall be raised above his brother except by merit; and the only slaves in this country shall be the Herdsmen. Finally, I commend to you the body of my father, to perform for it its sacred rites."

5

The army left Ombos at dawn, the fleet set sail, and the forward units passed through village after village to the warmest and loveliest reception until they reached the outskirts of Apollonopolis Magna, where they readied themselves to plunge into a new battle. However, the vanguard met with no resistance and entered the city in peace. The fleet sailed downstream with the Nile current and a favorable wind, finding no trace of the enemy's ships. Hur, ever cautious, advised the king to send some of his scouts into the fields to the east, lest they fall into a trap. The army and the fleet spent the night at Apollonopolis Magna and left it at dawn, the king and his guards traveling at the front of the army, behind the scouts, with the chariot of Chamberlain Hur to the king's right, and, surrounding them both, members of the king's entourage who were familiar with the territory. The king asked Hur, "Are we not moving toward Hierakonpolis now?"

The chamberlain replied, "Indeed, my lord. It is the forward defense center for Thebes itself, and the first tough battle between two equal forces will take place in its valley."

In the forenoon, intelligence came that the Egyptian fleet had engaged with a fleet belonging to the Herdsmen, which, from its size and the number of its units, was thought to be the entire enemy navy. It was also said that the battle was being fought strongly and fiercely. The king turned his head to the west, hope and entreaty on his handsome face. Hur said, "The Herdsmen, my lord, are newcomers to naval warfare."

The king was silent and did not reply, and the sun made its way toward the middle of the sky as the army with its battalions and equipment continued its progress. Ahmose surrendered himself to meditation and thought. A vision of his family came to him as they received the news of the killing of Kamose: how shocked his mother Setkimus would be, how his grandmother Ahotep would grieve, how the long-suffering Sacred Mother Tetisheri would moan, and how his wife Nefertari, now Queen of Egypt, would weep. Dear God! Kamose had fallen to treachery, the army thus losing his bravery and experience, while he had been bequeathed an inheritance weighed down with the most onerous responsibilities. Then his imagination traveled ahead, to Thebes, where Apophis ruled and the people suffered every kind of torment and humiliation. He thought of Khanzar, the brave, terrible governor, against whom his soul would never rest until he had taken revenge for his father who had been made a martyr at his hands and had felled him with a fatal blow. Then the thought of Princess Amenridis came to him and he remembered the cabin where passion had consumed them both with sacred fire, and he asked himself, "Does she still cling to the memory of the handsome trader Isfinis and hope that he will be faithful to his promise?"

At this point Hur coughed, which reminded him that he should not yearn for Amenridis while at the head of the army that was marching to cleanse Egypt of her people. He tried to expel the thought and his sight fell on his huge army whose rearguard stretched away beyond the horizon behind him; then he turned away and his thoughts returned to the battle that was taking place on the Nile. At midday, dispatch riders arrived and said that the two fleets were engaged in a violent battle, that the dead were falling in great numbers on either side, and that the two forces were still so evenly matched that it was impossible to predict the outcome. A frown appeared on the king's face and he could not hide his anxiety. Hur said, "There is no call for anxiety, my lord. The Herdsmen's fleet is no mean force that it should be easily overcome and our fleet is now plunged into the decisive battle on the Nile."

Ahmose said, "If we lose it, we shall have lost half the war."

Hur replied with certitude, "And if we win it, my lord, as I expect us to do, we shall have won the whole war."

Evening found the army several hours away from Hierakonpolis and it became necessary to halt to rest and make ready. However, it had not been halted for more than a short time before news came that the vanguard was battling scattered forces of the enemy's army. Ahmose said, "The Herdsmen are rested. No doubt they welcome an engagement with us now."

The king ordered a force of chariots to be sent to the aid of the scouts, should they be attacked by forces that outnumbered them. He also summoned his commanders and ordered them to be ready to enter the battle at any time.

Ahmose felt the grave burden that he bore in leading the army for the first time in his life, conscious that he was both the protector of this mighty army and the one responsible for the eternal destiny of Egypt. He said to Hur, "We must send our forces to destroy the Herdsmen's chariots."

The chamberlain replied, "That is what both armies will try to do; and if we succeed in destroying the enemy's chariots and gain the upper hand in the field, then its army will be at the mercy of our bowmen."

At this moment, as Ahmose was preparing himself to hazard his troops in the battle, messengers came from the direction of the Nile and informed the king that the Egyptian fleet had suffered serious blows, that Ahmose Ebana had thought that it was better to retreat with his main vessels in order to regroup, and that the battle continued unabated. Anxiety overwhelmed the youth and he had premonitions of the loss of his great fleet. Before he had time to think, however, news came that the enemy's troops had commenced their assault and he bade farewell to Hur and his courtiers and, advancing with his guard, ordered the chariot battalion to attack. The army attacked using a three-pronged formation that leapt forward in serried ranks with a speed and clamor that made the earth shake like an earthquake. No sooner did they see the Herdsmen's army advancing, swooping down like a hurricane in dense companies of chariots, than it bore home on them that their enemy was throwing at them those savage forces at whose hands they had so long been forced to suffer ignominy, and the Egyptians' anger rose up in their breasts and they cried out with a voice like a clap of thunder "Live like Amenhotep or die like Seqenenra!" and threw themselves into the battle, their hearts thirsting for combat and revenge. The two sides fought hard, with relentless savagery, and the earth turned red with blood. The cries of the soldiers mixed with the neighing of the horses and the twanging of the bows. The fight continued in its cruelty and violence until the sun inclined toward the horizon and melted in a lake of blood. As the miasma of darkness filled the sky, the two armies drew back, each returning to its camp. Ahmose proceeded in the midst of a circle of his guards, who had defended him during his sallies. When he met his men, Hur at their head, he told them, "It was a tough fight that has cost us some brave heroes."

Then the king enquired, "Is there no news of the battle of the Nile?"

The chamberlain answered, "The two fleets are still fighting."

"Is there nothing new concerning our fleet?"

Hur said, "It fought all day long as it retreated. Then the majority of the ships grappled units of the enemy with ladders and they were unable to separate when darkness fell. The fighting continues and we are waiting for further news."

Fatigue showed on the king's face and he said to those around him, "Let us all pray to the Lord that He come to the aid of our brothers who are fighting on the Nile."

6

The army woke with the dawn and started to equip and ready itself. Spies brought important intelligence: there had been movement all night long in the enemy camp. Some who had risked pushing their way into the fields surrounding the battle ground reported that new forces, both men and chariots, had poured toward Hierakonpolis throughout the night, the stream continuing until just before dawn. Hur thought a moment, then said, "The enemy, my lord, is gathering the greater part of his forces here in order to face us with his whole army. This is no surprise, since, if we penetrate the gates of Hierakonpolis, there will be nothing to delay our advance, but the walls of Glorious Thebes."

Good news came from the Nile, the king learning that his fleet had fought desperately and that the enemy had not been able to do with it as it wished. On the contrary, its soldiers had been driven off many of those of his ships that they had been able to board and the Herdsmen's fleet had been compelled to detach itself after losing a third of its forces. The fleets had then ceased fighting for some hours. They had re-engaged in a new battle just after daybreak, with Ahmose Ebana's fleet launching the attack. The king rejoiced at this news and prepared himself for battle with high spirits.

As morning grew bright, the two armies advanced to do battle. The ranks of chariots hove into view and the Egyptians gave their famous cry of "Live like Amenhotep or die like Seqe-nenra!" then rushed onto the killing grounds like men possessed. They encircled the enemy in mortal clashes, giving them as good as the enemy gave them, fighting with bows, lances, and swords. King Ahmose, despite the fierceness of the battle, noticed that the center of the enemy's army was directing the battle with extreme skill, sending forces here and there with discipline and precision. He caught sight of the capable commander and it turned out to be not the governor of Hierakon-polis but Apophis himself, with his obese build, long beard, and sharp look, to whom he had given the gem-studded crown in the palace at Thebes. Ahmose undertook a number of fierce forays, fighting like a brave hero, his guard repelling the enemy's attacks. Not a horseman of the enemy's did he meet whom he did not bring down in the twinkling of an eye, till they dreaded his approach and despaired of overcoming him. As the battle wore on, fresh forces from both sides threw themselves into the field and the fighting continued at the same pitch of violence and intensity until the day was almost over. At that moment, when the troops on both sides were exhausted, a force of Herdsmen chariots, led by an intrepid man, descended on the Egyptians' left wing and drove their attack home so hard that the exhausted resistance could do nothing to stop it and it made itself a breach through which it poured either to encircle the opposing force or to attack the infantry. Ahmose realized that this dauntless commander had waited for their fatigue to offer an appropriate opportunity and had held his men back to strike the final blow. Fearing that the man would in-

deed obtain his objective and strike confusion among the serried ranks of his army or massacre his infantry, he decided to
lead a spearhead attack on the enemy's heart to beleaguer it, so
that that formidable commander would find himself partially
besieged. He did not hesitate, for the situation was dangerous
and critical, but ordered his troops to attack and assaulted the
center with a strong surprise maneuver that brought the fighting to a terrible peak, compelling the enemy to retreat under
the fierce pressure. At the same time, Ahmose sent a force of
chariots to encircle the force that was pressing on the left wing.
Their commander, however, was formidably capable and adjusted his plan after he had almost managed to create the
breach that he had been seeking, throwing a small force of his
chariots into an attack on the enemy while he retired rapidly to
his army with the rest. During this delicate operation, Ahmose
was able to set eyes on the daring commander and recognized
Khanzar, the great governor of the South, with his solid build
and steely muscles. His mighty assault had cost the Egyptians
many fallen among the flower of its charioteers. Shortly after
this, the fighting came to an end and the king and his army retired to their camp, Ahmose saying in angry threat, "Khanzar,
we shall meet for sure, face to face." At camp, his men received
him with prayers. Among them he found a new arrival, Ahmose Ebana. Drawing hope from his presence in the camp, he
asked him, "What news, Commander?"

Ahmose Ebana said, "Victory, my lord. We brought defeat
down upon the Herdsmen's fleet and captured four of its large
ships and sank half of it, while other ships fled in a state in
which they could neither be helped nor help."

The king's face lit up and he placed a hand on the commander's shoulder, saying, "With this victory you have won half the
war for Egypt. I am very proud of you."

Ahmose Ebana blushed and he said with pleasure, "There is
no doubt, my lord, that we paid a high price for this victory but
we are now the undisputed masters of the Nile."

The king said solemnly, "The enemy has inflicted heavy losses on us which I am afraid we shall not be able to replace. The one who wins this war will be the one who destroys his enemy's charioteers."

The king fell silent for a moment, then resumed, "Our governors in the south are training soldiers and building ships and chariots. However, training charioteers takes time and the only thing that will help us in the battle that lies ahead will be our own bravery in making sure that our infantry do not face the enemy's chariots again."

7

The army woke at daybreak once more and started to ready and equip itself. The king donned his battle dress and received his men in his tent, telling them, "I have decided to fight Khanzar in single combat."

Hur, alarmed at the king's words, said in earnest entreaty, "My lord, one reckless blow must not be allowed to bring down our whole enterprise."

Each one of the commanders begged the king to allow him to fight the governor of the South but Ahmose declined their offers with thanks, saying to Hur, "No mishap can bring down our enterprise, however great, and my fall will not hold it up should I fall. My army does not want for commanders nor my country for men. I cannot forego an opportunity to face the killer of Seqenenra, so let me fight him and pay a debt that I bear to a noble soul that watches over me from the Western World; and the Lord curse vacillators and weaklings!"

The king sent an officer to present his wish to his opponent, the man going out into the middle of the field and crying out,

"Enemy, Egypt's Pharaoh wishes to fight Commander Khanzar in single combat to settle an old score."

A man came out to him from Khanzar's corps and said, "Say to the one who calls himself Pharaoh, 'The commander never denies an enemy the honor of dying by his sword.'"

Ahmose mounted a fine-bred steed, put his sword in its scabbard, his lance in its holder, and urged the horse out onto the field, where he saw his enemy dashing toward him on a gray steed, haughty and proud, his body like a mighty block of granite. Little by little, they drew closer, until the heads of their two steeds were almost touching. As each looked his opponent up and down, Khanzar could not prevent his face from registering astonishment and he shouted in amazement, "Dear God! Who is this before me? Is it not Isfinis, the trader in pygmies and pearls? What a jest! Where is your trade now, trader Isfinis?"

Ahmose looked at him, quietly and serenely, then said, "Isfinis is no more, Commander Khanzar, and I have no trade now but this" and he pointed to his sword. Khanzar regained control of his emotions and asked him, "Who, then, are you?"

Ahmose said simply and quietly, "Ahmose, Pharaoh of Egypt."

Khanzar gave a loud laugh that echoed around the field and said sarcastically, "And who appointed you ruler of Egypt, when its king is the one who wears the double crown that you presented to him on bended knee?"

Ahmose said, "He appointed me who appointed my father and my forefathers before him. Know, Commander Khanzar, that he who is about to kill you is the grandson of Seqenenra."

A look of gravity appeared on the governor's face and he said quietly, "Seqenenra. I remember that man whose ill fortune dictated that he should one day seek to bring me down. I am starting to grasp it all—excuse me for my slowness of understanding. We Hyksos are heroes of the battlefield and we do not excel at cunning or know any language but that of the sword. As for you Egyptians who lay claim to the throne, you disguise yourselves for long in the clothes of traders before you can pluck up the courage to wear the dress of kings. Let it be as you wish; but do you really desire to fight me single-handed, Isfinis?"

Ahmose said vehemently, "Let us wear whatever clothes we desire, for they are our clothes. You, however, never learned to wear clothes at all until Egypt took you in. And do not call me Isfinis, since you know that I am Ahmose, son of Kamose, son of Seqenenra, a lineage venerable in nobility and age, descended from the loins of Glorious Thebes, one that never roamed shelterless in the deserts or shepherded flocks. Indeed, I wish to fight you single-handed. This is an honor you will gain that I may quit myself of a debt that I bear toward the greatest man Thebes has ever known."

Khanzar shouted, "I see that conceit has blinded you from a true knowledge of your own worth. You think that your victory over Commander Rukh is good cause for you to stand before me. God have mercy on you, conceited youth! What do you choose for your weapon?"

Ahmose said, a mocking smile on his lips, "The sword, if you will."

Khanzar said, shrugging his broad shoulders, "It is my dearest friend."

Khanzar got off his horse and handed its reins to his squire. Then he unsheathed his sword and grasped his shield. Ahmose did likewise and they stood in silence, two arms-lengths apart. Ahmose asked, "Shall we begin?"

Laughing, Khanzar replied, "How lovely these moments are, in which Life and Death exchange whispers! Have at you, young man!"

At this the king leapt forward and assailed his huge opponent courageously, aiming at him a mighty blow that the governor met with his shield. Then the governor attacked in his turn, saying, "A clean blow, Isfinis! Methinks the ringing of your sword on my shield sings the melody of Death. Well met, well met! My breast welcomes the envoys of Death. How often has Death wanted me as I played between its claws, then, baffled, let me go, realizing at the end that it had really come for someone else!"

The man never ceased speaking as he fought, as though he were a skillful dancer who sang while he danced. Ahmose, realizing that his opponent was stubborn and intrepid, with muscles of steel, a foe full of tricks, light on his feet, a master of attack and feint, exerted all his strength and skill in avoiding the blows aimed at him, knowing that these were mortal blows for which there would be no cure should they reach their mark. Despite this, he took a blow on his shield whose heft he felt and he saw his opponent smile confidently, at which anger and fury arose within him and he aimed at the man a terrible blow that he in turn took on his shield. Struggling to master nerves and will alike, he asked Ahmose, "Where was this stout sword made?"

Controlling himself likewise, Ahmose replied, "At Napata, in the far south."

As he dodged a hard blow aimed at him with exquisite skill, the man said, "My sword was made in Memphis, by the hands of Egyptian craftsmen. The man who made it had no idea that he was providing me with the tool that I will use to slay his sovereign, who trades and fights for him."

Ahmose said, "How happy he will be tomorrow when he finds out that it brought the enemy of his country bad luck!"

Ahmose, seeking an opportunity for a violent attack, had scarcely finished speaking before he aimed at his mighty opponent three strokes one after the other with lightning speed. Khanzar warded them off with armor and sword but was forced to retreat a few steps and the king sprang after him and fell upon him brutally, directing blow after blow at his foe. Realizing the danger of this development, Khanzar stopped jesting with his opponent and closed his mouth, from which the smile had disappeared. He furrowed his brow and defended himself against his enemy's attacks with great strength and terrible courage, displaying unimaginable feats of skill and valor. The point of his sword gashed Ahmose's helmet and the Herdsmen, thinking that he had finished off his stubborn opponent, cheered loudly, to the point that Ahmose thought to himself, "I wonder if I am hurt?" However, he felt no fatigue or weakness, and, gathering his strength, struck his enemy a mighty blow that the latter met with his shield. The blow struck it hard and he let it fall uselessly from his hand, his arm trembling. Shouts of joy and anger arose from the two sides and Ahmose ceased fighting, looking at this opponent with a smile of triumph. The other brandished his sword and prepared to fight without a shield. Ahmose immediately took off his own shield and threw it to one side. Astonishment appeared on Khanzar's face and, giving him a strange look, he said, "What nobility, worthy of a king!"

The fight resumed in silence and they exchanged two mighty blows, of which Ahmose's was the faster to the huge neck of his opponent. The latter, seized by a terrible convulsion and his hand losing its grip on the hilt of his sword, fell to the ground like a building demolished. Approaching with slow steps, the king looked into his face with eyes filled with respect and said to him, "What a valiant and doughty fighter you are, Governor Khanzar!"

The man said, as he breathed his last, "You spoke truly, king. After me, no other warrior will bar your way."

Ahmose took Khanzar's sword and placed it next to his body, then mounted his steed and returned to his camp, knowing that the Herdsmen would fight with fury and a lust for revenge. As he approached his charioteers, he called out to them, "Soldiers, repeat our immortal cry 'Live like Amenhotep or die like Seqenenra!' and remember that our destiny is forever tied to the outcome of this ongoing battle. Never accept that the patience of years and the struggle of generations be lost in the weakness of an hour!"

Then he attacked, and they attacked, and the fighting continued fiercely till sunset.

For ten whole days, the fighting went on in this way.

8

On the evening of the tenth day of fighting, King Ahmose returned from the field exhausted, his strength all spent, and he called together his entourage and commanders. Though the fall of Khanzar had inflicted on the Herdsmen's army an irreplaceable loss, their chariot battalion continued to resist and repel the attacks of the Egyptians, causing them terrible losses. The king was absorbed by anxiety and feared that day by day the huge chariot battalion would be destroyed. On that particular evening, he was angry and sad at the fall of so many of his brave charioteers who had stood firm in the face of death, indifferent to their fate. As though talking to himself, he said, "Hierakonpolis, Hierakonpolis, will your name, I wonder, be coupled with our victory or with our defeat?"

The others present were no less sad and angry than the king, but the tiredness and agitation that they saw on his handsome face alarmed them. Chamberlain Hur said, "My lord, our charioteers are fighting the Herdsmen's chariot battalion in its full strength and with all the equipment it possesses; thus our losses do not scare us. If soon we triumph over the enemy and destroy his chariots, his infantry will have no power over us. They will take refuge behind the walls of their fortresses, in flight from the assaults of our chariots."

The king said, "My main goal was to destroy the enemy's chariots while preserving a large force of our own chariots that could maintain permanent domination on the field, as the Herdsmen did in their attack on Thebes. But now I fear that both our forces will be destroyed and we shall be exposed to a long-term war that will leave no city unspared."

The king asked to review the latest count of the losses, which an officer brought. The Egyptian chariot battalion had lost two thirds of its force of men and vehicles.

Ahmose paled and looked into the faces of his men, where gloom prevailed without exception. He said, "We have only two thousand charioteers left. How do you estimate the enemy's losses?"

Commander Deeb said, "I don't imagine, my lord, that they are any less than ours. Indeed, they are likely to be greater."

The king bowed his head and remained for a moment in thought. Then he looked at his men and said, "Everything will be clear tomorrow. Tomorrow will be the decisive day, there is no doubt. Our enemy may be suffering anxiety and doubt as much as we, or even more. In any case, none can blame us and we will blame none, and the Lord knows that we fight with hearts that care nothing for life."

Deeb enquired, "Our fleet is not fighting now, so why not use it to disembark troops behind the enemy, between Hierakonpolis and Nekheb?"

Ahmose Ebana said, "Our fleet now has complete control of the Nile, but we cannot risk disembarking troops behind enemy lines unless its whole army is engaged in the fighting. And the fact is, that the fighting so far has been confined to the two battalions of charioteers, while the rest of the enemy's army is lurking behind the battlefield, rested and wakeful."

One of the priests of Ombos asked, "My lord, do we not have a reserve force of charioteers?"

Ahmose said, "We brought six thousand charioteers, the fruit of an exhausting campaign and much patience, and we have lost four thousand of them in twelve days of hell."

Hur said, "My lord, Sayin, Ombos, and Apollonopolis Magna are ceaselessly building chariots and training charioteers."

Ahmose Ebana, for his part, said with his usual unflagging enthusiasm, "Enough for us the slogan that Sacred Mother Tetisheri taught us, 'Live like Amenhotep or die like Seqenenra!' Our charioteers cannot be subdued and our infantry burn with longing for the fight. Let us always remember that the Lord who sent you to the land of Egypt did not do so wantonly."

The men were reassured by the young commander's words and the king smiled radiantly. The army passed the night and awoke at dawn, as was their custom, and made themselves ready for the fight. As the day's first rays appeared, the chariot battalion advanced, the king and his guard at its center. To his amazement, when he looked at the field he found it empty. Looking again more closely, he saw in the distance the walls of Hierakonpolis, with not a single Herdsman standing between them and him. His surprise did not last long, however, as some of his spies came to him and reported that Apophis's army with all its huge divisions had withdrawn from the field and left Hierakonpolis by night to march fast toward the north. Commander Mheb could not help saying, "Now the truth is clear. There can be no doubt that the Herdsmen's chariot forces have been smashed and that Apophis preferred to flee to his fortresses rather than face our charioteers with his infantry."

Commander Deeb said joyfully, "My lord, we have won the great battle of Hierakonpolis."

King Ahmose enquired, "Do you think the cloud has really passed? Do you think that the dangers are really gone?" Then he turned to Deeb and said, "Just say that we have smashed the chariots of the Herdsmen, no more."

The news spread to the army and joy overcame all. The men of the royal entourage hurried to the king and congratulated him on the incontestable victory that the Lord had granted to him. Ahmose entered Hierakonpolis at the head of his army, the local people hurrying there with him from the fields to which they had fled in fear of the Herdsmen's revenge, and welcomed their king ardently, cheering the Army of Deliverance with cries that pierced the highest heavens.

The first thing that the king did was to pray to the Lord Amun, who had extended to him a helping hand when he had been on the very brink of despair.

9

After this fierce twelve-day battle, the army rested at Hierakonpolis a few days and Ahmose himself took charge of organizing the city and restoring an Egyptian character to its government, farms, markets, and temples. He consoled its people for the various kinds of oppression, in the form of plunder, pillage, and destruction, to which they and their city had been subjected during the Herdsmen's retreat.

Then the army marched north, the fleet setting sail at the same time, and entered the city of Nekheb on the afternoon of the same day, without resistance. It stayed there until dawn the following morning, when it resumed its progress, occupying villages and raising over them the flags of Egypt, without coming across any of the enemy's forces. After three days, they came to the edge of the valley of Latopolis. The king and his men thought that the enemy would defend it, so Ahmose sent forward units of his army to the city, while Ahmose Ebana laid siege to its western shores. However, the vanguard entered the city without resistance and the army entered in peace. The people told them how the army of Apophis had passed them by, carrying its wounded with it, and how Herdsmen who owned houses and farms had loaded their furniture and wealth and joined up with their king's army in an awful state of terror and chaos.

The army with its terrible forces continued to advance, entering villages and cities without the slightest resistance, until it

reached Tirt, then Hermonthis. All yearned to make contact
with the enemy so that they might vent the spleen that was in
their breasts; yet their faces shone with pleasure whenever they
raised the flag over a town or village and felt they had liberated
a piece of their noble homeland. News of the defeat of the
Herdsmen's chariots had revived the troops and kindled hope
and enthusiasm in their hearts and they marched to rousing
songs, pounding the earth of the valley with their copper-
colored legs, until the walls of the city of Habu, an outlier of
Thebes, towered above them. Here the valley descended
toward the south in a sudden, steep incline. The vanguard went
to the city but it was unguarded, like the cities before it, and
the army entered peacefully. The entry into Habu shook the
hearts of all the soldiers, because Habu and Thebes were like
limbs of a single body, and because many of the army's soldiers
were numbered among its valiant sons. Hearts and souls embraced in its squares and the men's spirits shouted out loud with
longing and affection. Then the army moved north, their hearts
full of anticipation and souls straining toward their goal, knowing that they were approaching the action that would determine
their history and the critical battle that would decide the destiny
of Egypt. They descended the great valley that the Thebans
called "Amun's Way," which grew wider the further they went
into it, until they saw the great wall with its many gates block-
ing their path and running to the east and the west; the obelisks,
temple walls, and towering buildings rising above it, all speaking of glory and immortality, and all enveloped in memories of
greatness. A tempest of excitement and nostalgia flowed into
them from these things that shook their hearts and minds, and
the sides of the valley echoed to the cry of "Thebes! Thebes!"
The name was on every tongue and the burning hearts pro-
claimed it and went on shouting it until tears swept aside their
pride and they wept; and Hur, the old man, wept with them.

The mighty army struck camp and Ahmose stood in its
midst, the flag of Thebes that Tetisheri had sewn with her own

hands fluttering above him, as he directed his eyes, shining with dreams, to the city and said, "Thebes, Thebes, land of glory, refuge of our fathers and our grandfathers, be of good cheer, for tomorrow a new day rises upon you!"

10

The king summoned Commander Ahmose Ebana and said to him, "I entrust to you Thebes' western shore. Attack it or lay siege to it as you think fit, taking the inspiration for your plans from the conditions around you."

The men set to thinking about the plan of attack for Thebes. Commander Mheb said, "The walls of Thebes are well-built, and intimidating, and will cost the attackers many lives. However, they must be assailed, for the southern gates are the city's only point of access."

Commander Deeb said, "It is more effective for attackers to lay siege to a city and starve it into submission, but we cannot think even for a moment of starving Thebes. Thus, the only way open to us is to attack its walls. We are not without means of attack for the walls such as ladders and siege towers, but what we have is still not sufficient and we hope that adequate quantities of these will reach us. In any case, if the price of Thebes is high, we will pay it cheerfully."

Ahmose said, "That is right. We must not waste time, for our people are penned up inside the city's walls and they are likely to be exposed to our barbaric enemy's revenge."

The same day, the fleet advanced toward the western shore of Thebes and found before it a fleet belonging to the Herdsmen, which they had collected from the ships that had fled from Hierakonpolis. The Egyptian navy fell upon it and the two fleets engaged in a violent battle, but the Egyptians' superiority in numbers of men and ships was large and they tightened the noose around the enemy and subjected it to a withering fire.

Ahmose sent battalions of bowmen and lancers to test the defending forces. They shot their arrows at widely separated points along the great wall and discovered that the Herdsmen had filled it with the toughest guards and an inexhaustible supply of weapons. The Egyptian commanders had been organizing their forces and when the order to attack was issued, they sent successive platoons of their men to different parts of the valley to attack the walls at widely separated points, the men protected by their long armor. The enemy's arrows fell on them in a devastating rain and the men aimed their bows at the openings in the impregnable walls. The fighting proceeded without mercy, the camp sending out company after company of soldiers eager for the fight. These fought with death-defying boldness and paid dearly for their daring, and the day ended with a terrible massacre, so that the king, alarmed at the sight of the wounded and fallen, cried out in anger, "My troops care nothing for Death, and Death reaps them like a harvest."

Casting glances of fascination and horror at the field, Hur said, "What a battle, my lord! I see bodies everywhere on the field."

Commander Mheb, his face dark, his clothes dust-stained, said, "Are we not staring Death itself in the face as we attack?"

Ahmose said, "I will not drive my army to certain destruction. It seems better to me to send a limited number of men behind siege towers, so that the openings in the enemy's wall fill with the dead."

The king remained in a state of high excitement, which the news borne by the messengers, that the Egyptian fleet had overcome the remains of the Herdsmen's fleet and become the unchallenged master of the Nile, did nothing to reduce. That evening, the messenger whom he had sent to his family in Napata returned carrying a message from Tetisheri. Ahmose smoothed the letter in his hands and read as follows:

From Tetisheri to my grandson and lord, Pharaoh of Egypt, Ahmose son of Kamose, whose dear life I pray the Generous Lord may preserve, guiding his judgment to the truth, his heart to the faith, and his hand to the slaying of his enemy. Your messenger reached us bringing the announcement of the death of our brave departed Kamose and informing me of his final words addressed to me. It seems to me proper that, while you are fighting our enemy, I should write a few lines devoted to the mention of that which has wrung the hearts of us all, for my heart has tasted death twice in one short life. But condolences are no stranger to one who lives in the furnace of a terrible battle, where lives are sold cheap and the courageous man rushes to meet Death. I will not hide from you that, despite my pain and grief, a messenger bringing me news of the death of Kamose and our army's victory is dearer to me than Kamose himself would be if he came with news of our defeat. So continue on your course, may the Merciful Lord watch over you with His care, and may the prayer of my heart and of the tender hearts of those gathered around me, torn as they are between sorrow, fortitude, and hope, preserve you! Know, my lord, that we shall journey to the town of Dabod, close to the borders of our country, in order to be closer to your messengers. Farewell.

Ahmose read the letter and glimpsed the agonizing pain and burning hope that lay behind its lines. The faces that he had left behind in Napata appeared to him: Tetisheri with her thin face crowned with white hair, his grandmother Ahotep with her majesty and sorrow, his mother Setkimus with her gentleheartedness, and his wife Nefertari with her wide eyes and slender form. He murmured to himself, "Dear God, Tetisheri takes these murderously painful blows with composure and hope and her sorrow never makes her forget the goal to which we aspire. May I always remember her wisdom and take it as an example for my mind and heart!"

11

The fleet set about its task after taking the Herdsmen's fleet captive. It blockaded the city's western shore, striking terror into the hearts of the inhabitants of the palaces overlooking the Nile, and exchanged arrow fire with the forts on the shore. It did not, however, try to attack those forts, as these were too well-defended and too elevated, given the low level of the Nile during the harvest season. Instead, it contented itself with probing actions and a siege. Ahmose Ebana's heart tugged him toward the town's southern shore, where the fishermen lived and where a tender heart beat with love for him, and he thought that that place might provide a point of entry for him into Thebes. However, the Herdsmen had been more cautious than he expected and had taken the shore from the Egyptians and occupied its extensive area with well-armored guards.

King Ahmose had decided against attacking with massed companies and sent into the field an elite force of trained men sheltered by tall shields. They vied with the defenders of the mighty wall in a war based on technique and precision targeting. The men were tireless in displaying their traditional skill and high efficiency and the war went on in this way for several days without providing a glimpse of the likely outcome or giving a hint of what the end might be. Growing restive, the king said, "We must give the enemy no respite in which to reorganize or rebuild a new force of chariots." Ahmose then grasped the hilt of his sword and said, "I shall give orders for the resumption of all-out attack. If lives must be lost, then let us offer ourselves, as befits men who have sworn to liberate Egypt from the heavy yoke of its enemy. I shall dispatch my messengers to the governors of the south to urge them to make siege armory and well-armored siege towers."

The king issued his order to attack and himself supervised the distribution of the archers' and lancers' battalions in the wide field, in the form of a center and two wings, putting Commander Mheb on the right wing and Commander Deeb on the left. The Egyptians started to advance in broad waves, and no sooner had one of these caught up with the one in front than it took its place and immediately engaged in battle the enemy sheltering behind the awe-inspiring wall. As the day of fighting wore on, the field started to overflow with the soldiers pressing on the wall of Thebes and the Egyptians started to deal their enemy terrible losses, though they themselves also lost large numbers of men; however, no matter how bad these losses were, they were smaller than those of the first day. The fighting continued in this way for several more days, the number of dead on both sides increasing. The Egyptians' right wing redoubled its pressure on the enemy until it was able on one occasion to silence one of the numerous defensive positions and destroy all those firing from its openings. Some brave officers seized the opportunity and attacked this position with their troops, setting up an attack ladder and climbing it with a brave force, while the arrows of their companions concealed them like clouds. The Herdsmen noticed the threatened side and rushed to it in large numbers, subjecting the attackers to withering fire until they wiped them out. The king was delighted with this attack, which set an excellent example for his army, and he told those around him, "For the first time since the siege started, one of my soldiers has been killed on the wall of Thebes."

And indeed, this operation had great impact and was repeated on the second day, and then, the following day, took place at two more points on the wall, the Egyptians' pressure on the enemy increasing to the point that victory turned into a readily realizable hope. At this juncture, a messenger came from Shaw, governor of Sayin, at the head of a force of troops, bristling with arms, that had recently completed training and accompanied by a ship loaded with siege armor and ladders and a number of siege towers. The king received the soldiers with pleasure, his faith in victory doubling, and ordered them to be paraded in the field in front of his camp so that the existing troops could greet them and find in them new hope and strength.

The following day, the fighting took on a terrifying aspect. The Egyptians put their all into one attack after another and faced Death with heedless hearts. They wrought huge losses on their enemy, which started to show its fatigue and despair and whose sword arms, one by one, began to falter. Commander Mheb was able to tell his lord as he returned from the field, "My lord, tomorrow we shall take the wall."

As all the commanders were of one mind on this, Ahmose sent a messenger to his family summoning them to Habu, where the Egyptian flag fluttered, so that they might enter Thebes together in the near future; and the king passed the night strong in faith, great in hope.

12

The promised day broke and the Egyptians awoke crazy with excitement, straining at the leash, their hearts yearning for the music of battle and of victory. Their companies advanced to their places behind the armor and the siege towers and gazed angrily at their objectives, only to be met with a sight incredible and unforeseen that caused them to raise a clamor of astonishment and confusion and exchange looks of perplexity and shock. What they beheld on the encircling wall were, shackled to it, naked bodies. They saw Egyptian women and their small children whom the Herdsmen had taken as shields to protect them from their pitiless arrows and projectiles and behind whom they stood, laughing and gloating. The sight of the naked women, their hair loosed and their modesty violated, and of the small children with their hands and feet bound, wrung the hearts of all who beheld them and not just of those who were their husbands and sons. The men's hands fell to their sides, their sword arms paralyzed, and confusion spread through their hearts till the news reached the king, who received it as though it were a lightning bolt from the sky and cried out in anger, "What barbaric savagery! The cowards have taken refuge behind the bodies of women and children!"

Silence and despondency reigned among the king's entourage and commanders and no one uttered a word. As daylight grew and they saw the wall of Thebes in the distance protected by the bodies of the women and children, their skins crawled with dread, their faces turned pale with anger, their limbs shook, and their souls went out to the tormented captives and to their brave families who stood in the field before them helplessly, tormented and oppressed by their powerlessness. Hur cried out, his voice trembling, "Poor wretches! The exposure day and night will kill them, if the arrows do not shred their bodies."

Confusion enveloped the king and he stared with horror-stricken, sorrowful eyes at the captives and their children who protected their enemy with their bodies. What could he do? The struggle of months was threatened with failure, and the hopes of ten years with disappointment and despair. What plan could he devise? Had he come to deliver his people or to torture them? Had he been sent as a mercy or as an affliction? He started to murmur in his sorrow "Amun, Amun, my Divine Lord, this struggle is for your sake and for the sake of those who believe in you. Tell me what I should do, before I am forced to find a way out for myself!" The rattling of a chariot coming from the direction of the Nile roused him from his prayer. He and those with him looked at its rider closely and saw that it was the commander of the fleet, Ahmose Ebana. The commander descended and greeted the king, then enquired, "My lord, why is our army not attacking the tottering Herdsmen? Were our troops not supposed to be on the wall of Thebes by now?"

In a sad voice and with heavy accents, gesturing in the direction of the wall, the king said, "Look and see for yourself, Commander!"

However, Ahmose Ebana did not look as they were expecting but said quietly, "My eyes have informed me of the vile, barbaric act, but how can we permit ourselves to be made accomplices with Apophis, when we know him so well? Are we to give up the struggle for Thebes and for Egypt out of concern for a few of our women and children?"

King Ahmose said bitterly, "Do you think I should give the order to shred the bodies of these wretched women and their children?"

The commander replied enthusiastically and confidently, "Yes, my lord! They are a sacrifice offered up to the struggle. They are just the same as our brave soldiers, who fall all the time. Indeed, they are just the same as our martyred sovereign Seqenenra, and the brave departed Kamose. Why should we care for their going so much that it incapacitates our struggle? My lord, my heart tells me that my mother Ebana is among those unfortunate captives. If my feelings speak truly, then I do not doubt that she is praying to the Lord that He put your love for Thebes above your pity for her and her unfortunate sisters. I am not the only one among our soldiers to bear this wound, so let each one of us place around his heart the armor of faith and resolution and let us attack!"

The king looked long at the commander of his fleet. Then, grim and pale, he turned his face toward his entourage, the commanders, and Chamberlain Hur and said in a quiet voice, "Mighty Ahmose Ebana has spoken the truth."

A deep breath escaped from the men's bodies and they

shouted with one voice, "Yes, yes! The commander of the fleet has spoken the truth. Let us attack!"

The king turned to the commanders and spoke decisively, "Commanders, go to your troops and tell them that their sovereign, who for Egypt lost grandfather and father, and who does not hesitate to give himself for its sake, commands you to attack the walls of Thebes that are shielded by our flesh and blood and to take them, at whatever cost."

The commanders went quickly and sounded the bugles and the ranks of the troops advanced, bristling with weapons, their faces dark. The officers called out in resounding tones, "Live like Amenhotep or die like Seqenenra!" and immediately the most horrible battle into whose perils man had ever thrown himself commenced. The Herdsmen shot their arrows and the Egyptians returned the fire, their shafts immediately cleaving the breasts of their women and piercing the hearts of their children, so that the blood flowed unchecked. The women nodded their heads to the soldiers and called out in high, hoarse voices, "Strike us, may the Lord grant you victory, and take revenge for us!"

The Egyptians went berserk, attacking like ravening beasts whose hearts know no mercy and thirst for blood and their screams resounded against the sides of the valley like the pealing of thunder or the roaring of lions. They hurled themselves forward heedless of the death that poured down upon them, as though they had lost all sensation or comprehension and been turned into instruments of Hell. The fighting was fierce, the exchange of blows intense, and the blood flowed like gushing springs from breasts and necks. Each attacker felt a crazed urge that would not slacken until he had buried his lance in a Herdsman's heart. Before noon, the right wing had managed to silence a number of defensive positions and some men took the lead in erecting siege ladders, upon which they climbed with death-defying hearts, thus transferring the battle from the field to the top of the fortified wall, where some of them leapt onto the inner parapet, engaging the enemy with lance and sword.

The attacks followed one another violently and courageously as the king observed the fight with watchful eyes and sent reinforcements to places where the enemy was attacking hard. After watching his soldiers ascend the wall in the middle and at two points on the right as the sun rose to the zenith of the sky, he said, "My troops are making the effort of giants, but I fear that darkness will overtake us before we take the whole wall and we shall have to start tomorrow from the beginning."

The king issued orders to new contingents to attack and the pressure of his men on the defenders of the near-impregnable wall increased as they made themselves new paths to its summit. Despair seemed to start to overcome the Herdsmen after the Egyptians had inflicted terrible losses on them and they saw that the flow was never ending, the Egyptians climbing the siege ladders like ants marching up the trunks of trees. Defenses collapsed with a rapidity that no one had expected, and Ahmose's troops occupied whole sections of the wall, so that its fall became only a matter of time. Ahmose was continuing to send strong reinforcements, when an officer of a force of scouts that had penetrated into the fields surrounding Thebes came to him in the camp, his face beaming with joy. He bowed to the king and said, "Wonderful news, my lord! Apophis and his army are leaving the northern gates of Thebes like fugitives."

The king, amazed, asked the officer, "Are you sure of what you say?"

The man said confidently, "I saw the cavalcade of the Herdsmen's king and his guards with my own eyes, followed by companies of the army, armed to the teeth."

Ahmose Ebana said, "Apophis must have realized the pointlessness of defending the wall of Thebes after witnessing our troops' attacks, while his army inside the city could not properly defend itself, so he fled."

Hur said, "Now no doubt he knows that taking shelter behind the women and children of the fighters was a calamitous act of wickedness."

Hur had scarcely finished speaking before a new messenger from the fleet came. He saluted the king and said, "My lord, an uprising is spreading like wildfire in Thebes. From the fleet, we saw a fierce battle taking place between the peasants and the Nubians on one side and the owners of the palaces and the guards of the shore on the other."

Ahmose Ebana appeared anxious and asked the officer, "Did the fleet do its duty?"

"Indeed, sir. Our ships drew in close to the shore and fired numerous arrows at the guards, so that they could not free themselves to fight the insurgents."

The commander's face relaxed and he asked permission of the king to return to his fleet to carry out an attack on the shore, which the king granted, saying to Hur in delight, "The estate owners will not escape this time with their wealth."

Hur replied in a voice trembling with joy, "Indeed, my lord, and soon Thebes the Glorious will open its gates to you."

"But Apophis has taken his army with him."

"We will not stop struggling until Avaris has fallen and the last Herdsman has withdrawn from Egypt."

The king resumed his observation of the fighting and found his troops doing battle on the siege ladders and on top of the wall, pressing on the Herdsmen, who retreated before them. Contingents of bow- and lance-carrying troops climbed up in great numbers and scaled the wall on every side, surrounding the Herdsmen and setting about the work of slaughtering them. Before long, he saw his troops rip up the Hyksos flag and raise the fluttering flag of Thebes. Then he witnessed the great gates of Thebes open wide, while his troops poured inside acclaiming his name. In a low voice, he murmured, "Thebes, wellspring of my blood, my body's first home and playground of my soul, open your arms and clasp to your tender breast your brave and vindicated sons!" Then he bowed his head to hide a tear wrung from the depths of his being, while Hur, on his right, prayed and wiped his eyes, his thin cheeks bedewed with tears.

13

More hours passed and the sun started to incline toward the west. Commanders Mheb and Deeb approached the king, Ahmose Ebana following in their footsteps. They bowed to Ahmose respectfully and congratulated him on the victory. Ahmose said, "Before we congratulate one another, we must perform our duty toward the bodies of the heroes and soldiers, and the women and children, who were martyred for the sake of Thebes. Bring them all to me!"

The bodies, begrimed with dust and stained with blood, were strewn at the sides of the field, on top of the wall, and behind the gates. The iron helmets had fallen from their heads and the terrible silence of death hung over them. The soldiers picked them up respectfully, took them to one side of the camp, and laid them side by side, just as they brought the women and children whom their soldiers' arrows had cut to pieces, and put them in a separate place. The king proceeded to the resting place of the martyrs followed by Chamberlain Hur, the three commanders, and his entourage. When he got close to the rows of bodies, he bowed in silent, sorrowing reverence, and his men did likewise. Then he walked on with slow steps, passing before them as though he were reviewing them at some official occasion before spectators. Next, he turned aside to the place where the women and children lay, their bodies now wrapped in linen coverings. A cloud of sadness cast a shadow over the king's face and his eyes darkened. In the midst of his grief, he became aware of the voice of Commander Ahmose Ebana, crying out despite himself in a choking voice, "Mother!"

The king turned back and saw his commander kneeling in pain and agony beside one of the corpses. The king cast an enquiring look at the body and saw that it was Lady Ebana, the terrifying shadow of extinction sketched on her visage. The king stopped beside his kneeling commander, humbled and sad at heart. He had had a great respect for the lady, and knew well her patriotism, her courage, and her merit in raising Ahmose to be, without contest, his best commander. The king raised his head to the heavens and said in a trembling voice, "Divine Lord Amun, creator of the universe, giver of life and arranger of all according to His high plan, these are your charges who now are returned to you at your desire. In our world they lived for others and thus they died. They are dear fragments broken from my heart. Grant them your mercy and compensate them for the ephemeral life that they lost with a happy eternal life in the Hereafter!"

The king turned to Chamberlain Hur and said, "Chamberlain, I wish that these bodies all be preserved and placed in Thebes' western cemetery. By my life, those worthiest of the earth of Thebes are those who died as martyrs for its sake!"

At this point, the messenger whom the king had sent to his family in Dabod returned and presented his lord with a message. Surprised, the king asked, "Have my family come back to Habu?"

The man replied, "Indeed not, my lord."

Ahmose spread open the message, which was sent by Teti-sheri, and read:

My lord, aided in triumph by the spirit of the Lord Amun and His blessings, may the Lord grant that this letter of mine reach you to whom Thebes has opened its gates so that you might enter at the head of the Army of Deliverance to tend to its wounded and make happy the souls of Seqenenra and Kamose. For ourselves, we shall not leave Dabod. I have thought long about the matter and have found that the best way for us to share with our tormented people in their pain is to remain in our exile where we are now, living the agonies

*of separation and homesickness until such time as we smash
the shackles that bind them and they are relieved of their tri-
als, and we may enter Egypt in security and take part with
them in their happiness and peace. Go on your way aided by
the Lord's care, liberate the cities, suppress the fortresses,
and cleanse the land of Egypt of its enemy, leaving it not one
single foothold on its soil. Then summon us and we shall
come in safety.*

Ahmose raised his head and folded the message, saying dis-
contentedly, "Tetisheri says that she will not enter Egypt until
we expel from it the last Herdsman."

Hur said, "Our Sacred Mother does not want us to cease
fighting until we have liberated Egypt."

The king nodded his head in agreement and Hur asked,
"Will my lord not enter Thebes this evening?"

Ahmose said, "I will not, Hur. My army shall enter on its
own. As for me, I shall enter it with my family when we have
thrown out the Herdsmen. We shall enter it together as we left
it, ten years ago."

"Its people will suffer great disappointment!"

"Tell anyone who asks after me that I pursue the Herdsmen,
to throw them beyond our sacred borders; and let those who
love me follow me!"

14

The king returned to the royal tent. It had been his intention to
issue an order to his commanders telling them to enter the city
in their traditional fashion, to the tunes of the military band.
However, an army officer came and said, "My Lord, a group of
the leaders of the uprising have charged me to ask permission

for them to appear before you and offer your High Person gifts chosen from the spoils they took during the uprising."

Ahmose smiled and asked the officer, "Have you come from the city?"

"Indeed, sir."

"Have the doors of Amun's temple been opened?"

"By the insurgents, my lord."

"And why has the Chief Priest not come to greet me?"

"They say, my lord, that he has sworn that he will not leave his retreat so long as there is a single Herdsman in Egypt who is not either a slave or a captive."

The king smiled and said, "Good. Call my people."

The man left the tent and went to the city. He returned followed by large numbers of people walking company by company, each pushing before it its gift. The officer asked permission for the first company to enter and a band of Egyptians, naked but for kilts around their waists, did so, their faces bespeaking hardship and poverty. They were pushing before them some Herdsmen with bared heads, matted beards, and brows stained with grime. The Egyptians prostrated themselves to the king until their foreheads touched the ground. When they raised their faces to him, he saw that their eyes were flooded with tears of happiness and joy. Their leader said, "Lord Ahmose, son of Kamose, son of Seqenenra, Pharaoh of Egypt, its liberator and protector, and the lofty branch of that towering tree whose roots were martyred for the sake of Thebes the Glorious, who came to bring us mercy and make amends for our past ill-treatment . . ."

Ahmose said, smiling, "Welcome, my noble people, whose hopes are my hopes, whose pains spring from the same source as mine, and the color of whose skin is as the color of my skin!"

The faces of the people lit up with a radiant light and their leader now addressed the Herdsmen, saying, "Prostrate yourselves to Pharaoh, you lowest of his slaves!"

The men prostrated themselves without uttering a word. The leader said, "My lord, these Herdsmen are among those who took over estates without right, as though they had inherited them from their forefathers generation after generation. They humiliated the Egyptians, treated them unjustly, and demanded of them the most onerous tasks for the most miserly pittance. They made them prey to poverty, hunger, sickness, and ignorance. When they called to them, they addressed them contemptuously as 'peasants' and they pretended that they were granting them a favor by letting them live. These are yesterday's tyrants and today's captives. We have driven them to your High Person as the most abject of your slaves."

The king smiled and said, "I thank you, my people, for your gift, and I congratulate you on the recovery of your sovereignty and your liberty."

The men prostrated themselves to their sovereign a second time and left the tent, the soldiers driving the Herdsmen to the captives' enclosure. Then a second company entered, a man of huge stature with a brilliantly white complexion and torn clothes walking before them. Whips had left clear marks on his back and arms and he fell in exhaustion before the king, to the indifference of his tormentors, who prostrated themselves long before their sovereign. One of them said, "My lord, Pharaoh of Egypt, son of the Lord Amun! This evil man, dressed in the garments of abjection, was the chief of police of Thebes and used to flay our backs with his cruel whip for the most trivial of reasons. The Lord placed him in our possession and we flayed his back with our whips until his skin was in tatters. We have brought him to the king's camp that he be added to his slaves."

The king dismissed the man, the soldiers took him away, and the king thanked his people for what they had done.

The king gave permission for the third company to enter. They approached him, driving before them a man whom the king recognized as soon as he set eyes upon him. It was Samnut, Judge of Thebes and brother of Khanzar. The king looked at him calmly, while Samnut looked at him in astonishment with anxious, startled, scarce-believing eyes. The men greeted the king and their spokesman said, "To you, Pharaoh, we bring him who yesterday was Judge of Thebes. He swore by justice but meted out only injustice. Now he has been made to drink of injustice, that he may taste that whereof he gave the innocent to drink."

Ahmose said, addressing his words to the judge, "Samnut, all your life you sat in judgment over the Egyptians; now prepare yourself for them to sit in judgment over you."

Then he handed him over to his soldiers and thanked his loyal men.

The last company came. It was very excited and boiling over with anger. In its midst was a person whom they had wrapped in a linen covering from head to foot. They saluted the king with cheers, and their spokesman said, "Pharaoh of Egypt and protector and avenger of the Egyptians, we are some of those whose wives and children the Herdsmen took to use as shields in the battle for Thebes. The Lord wished to avenge us on the tyrant Apophis and we attacked his women's quarters during his retreat, and there we kidnapped one who is dearer to him than his own soul. We have brought her to you that you may revenge yourself on her for what was done to our women."

The man approached the person hidden in the linen wrap and ripped the covering from her, revealing a woman, naked but for a diaphanous skirt around her waist. She was white, pure as light, and hair like threads of gold floated around her head, while exasperation, fury, and pride showed in her bewitching face. Ahmose turned pale. He gazed at her and she at him. Then confusion appeared on his face, and on hers an astonishment that wiped away the exasperation, fury, and pride. He murmured in an inaudible voice, still shocked, "Princess Amenridis!"

Hur took off his cloak, went up to the woman, and threw it over her. Ahmose shouted at his men, "Why have you maltreated this woman?"

The leader of the group said, "She is the daughter of the great murderer Apophis."

Ahmose awoke to the delicacy of his situation among these angry people thirsting for revenge and he said, "Do not allow anger to corrupt your sacred ways. The truly virtuous man is he who holds fast to his virtue when passion erupts and anger flares. You are a people that respect women and do not kill captives."

One of them, who had lost a relative but still not tasted revenge, said, "Protector of Egypt, our rage will be appeased when we send the head of this woman to Apophis."

Ahmose said, "Are you urging your sovereign to be like Apophis, a shedder of innocent blood and a killer of women? Leave the matter to me and leave in peace."

The people prostrated themselves to Pharaoh and left. The king called an officer of his guard and ordered him in a low voice to take the princess to his royal ship and guard her closely.

The king was experiencing a tempest in his heart and soul. Unable to remain idle, he issued an order to his commanders to make a triumphal victory entrance into Thebes at the head of the army. When he turned to Hur, he found that he was staring at him with startled, puzzled, pitying eyes.

15

The field emptied and the king made his way toward the Nile followed by his guards. He urged the drivers of his chariot to hurry and plunged into his private dreams and thoughts. What a shock his heart had been subjected to today! What a surprise he had endured! It had never occurred to him that he might meet Amenridis again. He had despaired of ever seeing her and she had become for him a dream that had illumined his night for a brief moment, then been swallowed by the darkness. Then he had seen her again, unexpectedly and without design. The fates had thrown her on his mercy and put her all of a sudden under his control. In such a state of ferment was his breast, so hard was his heart beating, and so heated were the emotions that had been awoken in him, that sweet memories were brought back to life and he surrendered himself to their tender current, forgetful of all else.

But she, could it be that she had recognized him? And if she had not, did she still remember the happy trader Isfinis, whose life she had rescued from a certain death and to whom she had said, with beating heart and welling tears, "Till we meet again!"? And whom she had yearned for in his exile and to whom she had sent a message in whose lines she had hidden her love as fire is hidden in the flint? Did her heart still beat as it had the first time in the cabin of the royal vessel? Dear God! How was it that he felt that he was approaching a boundless happiness? Should he trust his heart or suspect it? The king thought of her wretched appearance when the insurgents had thrust her toward him. His strong body trembled and a shudder ran through it. He asked himself sadly—as he thought of her with the angry people around her spitting on her, abusing her, and insulting her father, and remembered the anger, fury, and pride that had shown in her face—would her anger abate if she knew that she was the prisoner of Isfinis? He felt an anxiety that had never assailed him in the most trying of circumstances. His cavalcade having reached the shore, he descended and went to the royal vessel, where he summoned the officer to whom he had entrusted her and asked him, "How is the princess?"

"She has been put, my lord, in a private chamber and brought new clothes. Food has been offered her, but she refuses to touch it and she treated the soldiers with contempt and called them slaves. Nevertheless, she has been given the best treatment, as Your Majesty commanded."

The king looked uneasy and went with quiet steps to the chamber. A guard opened the door, closing it after the king had entered. The chamber was small and elegant, lit by a large lamp suspended from the ceiling. To the right of the entrance the princess, in simple clothes of linen, sat on a luxuriously upholstered couch. She had combed her hair, which the insurgents had disarranged, and let it fall in a large plait. He looked at her, smiled, and found that she was looking at him in astonishment and disbelief, seemingly confused and mistrustful, as though she could not believe her eyes. He greeted her, saying, "Good evening, Princess."

She did not answer him but, on hearing his voice, seemed to become yet more confused and mistrustful. The youth held her in a long look of love and infatuation, then asked her, "Do you lack anything?"

She looked closely at his face, raised her eyes to his helmet and lowered them to his armor, and asked him, "Who are you?"

"I am called Ahmose, Pharaoh of Egypt."

Distaste appeared in her eyes. He wanted to confuse her yet more, so he took off his helmet and placed it on a table, telling himself that she would not be able to believe her eyes. He saw her looking at his curly hair in disbelief. As though it was he who was startled, he said to her, "Why do you look at me thus, as though you knew someone who resembled me?"

She did not know what to say and made no reply. He longed to hear her voice and feel her tenderness, so he said to her, "Suppose I told you my name was Isfinis, would you answer me?"

No sooner did she hear the name Isfinis than she stood up and shouted at him, "So you are Isfinis!"

He took a step toward her, looked at her tenderly, and grasped her wrist, saying, "I am Isfinis, Princess Amenridis."

She tore her wrist away and said, "I understand nothing."

Ahmose smiled and said gently, "What do names matter? Yesterday I was called Isfinis and today I am called Ahmose, but I am one person and one heart."

"How strange! How can you say that you are one person? You were a trader who sold trinkets and pygmies and now you fight and wear the clothes of a king."

"And why not? Before, I was prying around Thebes in disguise, and now I lead my people to liberate my country and reclaim my stolen throne."

She gave him a long look, whose meaning he could not fathom, and he tried to approach her once again but she repelled him with a gesture of her hand and her features hardened, harshness and pride appearing in her eyes. He felt disappointment and rejection overwhelm his hopes and murder the nightingales of anticipation that sung in his breast. He heard her saying vehemently, "Keep away from me!"

He entreated her, saying, "Don't you remember . . . ?"

But, the anger for which her people were famous taking control of her, she cut him short before he could finish, saying, "I remember and I shall always remember that you are a common spy."

The terrible shock made him grimace and he said angrily, "Princess, are you not aware that you are speaking to a king?"

"What king, fellow?"

Anger getting the better of him, he said vehemently, "The Pharaoh of Egypt."

Contemptuously she replied, "And my father would be one of your agents, then?"

The king's anger grew and his pride overwhelmed all other feelings. He said, "Your father is not worthy to be one of my agents. He is the usurper of my country's throne and I have defeated him utterly and made him flee from the northern gates of Thebes, leaving his daughter to fall captive to the people whom he mistreated. I shall follow him with my armies until he takes refuge in the deserts that spat him out into our valley. Are you not aware of this? As for me, I am the lawful king of this valley because I am of the line of the pharaohs of glorious Thebes and because I am a victorious general who is reclaiming his country by strength and by skill."

Coldly and sarcastically she replied, "Are you proud to be a king whose people excel at fighting women?"

"Amazing! Do you not know that you are indebted to those people of mine for your life? You were at their mercy and if they had killed you, they would not have violated the code that your father established when he exposed women and children to the arrows of the foe."

"And do you place me on an equal footing with those women?"

"Why not?"

"Pardon, King. I cannot bring myself to imagine that I am like one of your women or that any of my people are like any of yours, unless masters are like slaves. Do you not know that our army felt nothing of the humiliation of defeat when they quit Thebes, but said, in derision, 'Our slaves have revolted and we shall come back and deal with them'?"

The king lost his temper completely and shouted at her, "Who are the slaves and who the masters? You understand nothing, conceited girl! You were born in the bosom of this valley that inspires men to glory and honor, but had you been born a century earlier you would have been born in the most savage deserts of the cold north and never heard anyone call you 'princess' or your father 'king.' From those deserts came your people, usurping the sovereignty of our valley and turning its great men into serfs. Then, in their ignorance and conceit, they said that they were princes and we were peasants and slaves, that they were white and we were brown. Today, justice has returned, and will restore the master to his proper place while the slave will be turned back into a slave. Whiteness will become the badge of those who roam the cold deserts and brownness the emblem of the masters of Egypt, who have been cleansed by the light of the sun. This is the indisputable truth."

Rage now blazed in the princess's heart and the blood rushed to her face. Contemptuously she said, "I know that my forefathers descended onto Egypt from the northern deserts, but how has it escaped you that they were lords of those deserts before they became, by their strength, masters of this valley? They were already masters, people of pride and dignity, who knew no path to their goal but the sword and did not disguise themselves in the clothes of traders so that today they might attack those to whom only yesterday they had prostrated themselves."

He stared at her with a harsh, scrutinizing look and saw that she was possessed of a pride, imagination, and cruelty that never softened or gave way to fear and that the overbearing, haughty characteristics of her people were all present in her. Overwhelmed by fury, he felt a burning desire to subdue and humble her, especially after she had belittled his emotions with her pride and boasting. In a haughty, quiet voice he said to her, "I can see no reason to continue this debate with you and I should not forget that I am a king and you a captive."

"Captive if you wish, but I shall never be humbled."

"On the contrary, you are protected by my mercy, so this courage becomes you well."

"My courage never abandons me. Ask your men who snatched me by treachery and they will tell you of my courage and my contempt for them at the most critical and dangerous of all times for me."

He shrugged his broad shoulders disdainfully and, turning to the table, took his helmet and placed it on his head. But before he could take another step, he heard her say, "You spoke the truth when you said that I am a captive, and your ship is not the place for captives. Take me and put me with the captives of my people!"

He looked at her in anger and exasperation and said, to provoke and scare her, "The matter is not as you imagine. The custom is that the male captives are taken as slaves, while the females are added to the victorious king's harem."

Eyes widening, she said, "But I am a princess."

"You were a princess. Now you are just a captive."

"Whenever I think that one day I saved your life, I go mad."

Quietly he said, "Long may the memory stay with you! It was for its sake that I saved your life from the insurgents who wished to send your head to Apophis."

He turned his back on her and left the chamber in anger and fury. The guards saluted him and he ordered them to set sail to the north of Thebes. Then he went to the front of the ship with heavy, dragging steps, filling his chest with the moist night air, while the ship continued on its way, descending with the ever-flowing Nile current and cleaving the darkness toward the north of Thebes.

The king set his eyes on the city, fleeing to it from the troubles of his soul. The light radiated from the fleet moored at the city's shore, while the lofty palaces, now that their owners had left them and fled, were plunged in darkness. In the distance, among the palaces and gardens, the light of the torches carried by joyful revelers appeared and the breeze brought the echo of their voices as they rose in cheers and hymns. A smile passed over his broad mouth and he realized that Thebes was giving the Army of Deliverance the reception it reserved for its triumphant armies and immortal feasts.

The ship drew close to the royal palace, passing alongside it on its course, and the king saw that its lamps had been lit, the light radiating from its windows and garden. From this he gathered that Hur was attending to its preparation and cleansing and that he had returned indeed to the performance of his original role in the palace of Seqenenra. Ahmose observed the palace garden anchorage and the painful memory came back to him of the night when the royal ship had carried his family away to the furthest south, while the blood spurted behind them.

The king paced back and forth on the deck of the ship, his look turning often to the princess's locked chamber, at which he would ask himself in displeasure and annoyance, "Why did they bring her to me? Why did they bring her to me?"

16

On the morning of the following day, Hur, the commanders, and the counselors went early to visit the king on his ship moored north of Thebes. The king received them in his cabin and they prostrated themselves before him. Hur said in his quiet voice, "May the Lord make your morning joyful, triumphant king! We have left behind us the gates of Thebes, whose heart flutters with joy and shakes with longing to see the light of its savior and liberator's brow."

Ahmose said, "Let Thebes rejoice. Our meeting, however, will come only when the Lord decrees us victory."

Hur said, "Word has spread among the people that their sovereign is on his way to the north and that he welcomes any who has the ability to join him. Do not ask, my lord, about the enthusiasm that overflowed in the hearts of the young men or how they swarm around the officers asking to be inducted into the army of the Divine Ahmose!"

The king smiled and asked his men, "Have you visited the temple of Amun?"

Hur replied, "Indeed, my lord; we visited it all together and the soldiers hurried to it, stroking its corners, rubbing their faces in its dust, and embracing its priests. The altar overflowed with offerings, the priests sang the hymn of the Lord Amun, and their prayers echoed from the sides of the temple. Affection melted all hearts and the Thebans organized themselves altogether in collective prayer. Nofer-Amun, however, has yet to leave his seclusion."

The king smiled and, happening to turn, saw Commander Ahmose Ebana standing silent and oppressed. He signaled to him to draw close and the commander approached his master. The king placed his hand on his shoulder and said to him, "Bear your portion of injury, Ahmose, and remember that the motto of your family is 'Courage and Sacrifice.'"

The commander bowed his head in thanks, the king's sympathy bringing him some solace. Ahmose looked at his men and said, "Counsel me on whom I should choose as governor of Thebes and charge with the onerous task of organizing it."

Commander Mheb said, "The best man for this critical post is the wise, loyal Hur."

However, Hur quickly intervened to say, "My duty lies in watching vigilantly over my lord's servants, not in absenting myself from his presence."

Ahmose said, "You are right and I cannot do without you."

Then Hur said, "There is a man of great virtue and experience, known for his wisdom and originality of thought, and that is Tuti-Amun, agent of the temple of Amun. If my lord wishes, let him charge this man with the affairs of Thebes."

Ahmose said, "We declare him our governor of Thebes."

Then the king invited his men to take breakfast at his table.

17

The army passed the daylight hours dressing its wounds and taking its share of rest and recreation, song and drink. Those soldiers who were from Thebes raced one another to get to their homes, where hearts embraced and souls mingled. So great were the joy and emotion, that Thebes seemed as though it were the beating heart of the very world. Ahmose, however, did not leave his ship, and, summoning the officer charged with guarding the princess, asked him about her. The man told him that she had gone the night without tasting food. It occurred to him to put her on another ship, under the charge of trustworthy officers, but he could not arrive at a definite decision. He had no doubt that Hur was displeased at her presence on his ship and sure that the chamberlain found it difficult to understand why the daughter of Apophis should be given this honored status in his eyes. Ahmose knew the man inside out and that his heart had no place for anything but Thebes' struggle. He, on the other hand, found his emotions athirst and overflowing. He was making himself sick with the effort of holding himself back from hovering about the chamber and its occupant or of distracting himself from his obsessive desire for her, despite his displeasure and anger. Anger does not destroy love, but conceals it briefly, just as mist may cloud briefly the face of a polished mirror, after which it is gone and the mirror's original purity returns. He did not, therefore, give in to despair and would say to himself consolingly that maybe it was remnants of defeated pride and fallen conceit from which she suffered, that maybe her anger would go away and then she would discover the love that lay behind the outward show of hatred and relent, submit, and give love its due, just as she had anger. Was she not the one in the cabin, who had saved his life and granted him sympathy and love? Was she not the one who had become so upset by his absence that she had written him a message of reproof to hide the moans of suppressed love? How could these emotions of hers wither just because of an upsurge of pride and anger?

He waited until the late afternoon, then shrugged his broad shoulders, as though making light of the matter, and went to the chamber. The guard saluted him and made way, and he entered with great hopes. He found her seated unmoving and silent, dejection and ennui showing in her blue eyes. Her dejection pained him and he said to himself, "Thebes for all its vastness was too narrow for her, so how must she feel now that she is a prisoner in this small chamber?" He stood unmoving before her and she straightened her back and raised her insolent eyes to him. He asked her gently, "How was your night?"

She did not answer and lowered her head to look at the ground. He cast a longing look at her head, shoulders, and bosom and repeated the question, feeling at the same time that his hope was not far off, "How was your night?"

She appeared not to want to abandon her silence, but raised her head sharply, and said, "It was the worst night of my life."

He ignored her tone and asked her, "Why? Is there anything you lack?"

She replied without changing her tone, "I lack everything."

"How so? I gave orders to the officer charged with guarding you to . . ."

She interrupted him with annoyance, "Don't even bother to speak of such things! I lack everything I love. I lack my father, my people, and my liberty. But I have everything that I hate: these clothes, this food, this chamber, and these guards."

Once again he was stricken by disappointment and felt the collapse of his hopes and the disappearance of all he longed for. His features hardened and he said to her, "Do you want me to release you from your captivity and send you to your father?"

She shook her head violently and said vehemently, "Never!"

He looked at her in amazement and confusion but she resumed in the same tones, "So that it not be said that the daughter of Apophis abased herself before the enemy of her great father or that once she needed someone to comfort her."

Aroused by anger and exasperation at her conceit and pride, he said, "You are not embarrassed to display your conceit because you feel sure of my compassion."

"You lie!"

His face turned pale and he stared at her with a harsh look and said, "How callow you are, you who know nothing of sorrow or pain! Do you know the punishment for insulting a king? Have you ever seen a woman flogged? If I wished, I could have you kneeling at the feet of the least of my soldiers begging for pardon and forgiveness."

He looked at her a long time to ascertain the effect of his threat on her and found her challenging him with her harsh, unflinching eyes. Anger swept over her with the same speed that it overtook all those of her race and she said sharply, "We are a people to whose hearts fear knows no path and our pride will not be brought low though the hands of men should grasp the heavens."

He asked himself in his anger, should he attempt to humiliate her? Why should he not humiliate her and trample her pride into the ground? Was she not his captive, whom he could make into one of his slave girls? However, he did not feel at ease with this idea. He had had ambitions for something sweeter and lovelier, so that when his disappointment caught up with him, his pride rose up and his anger grew sharper. He renounced his desire to humiliate her, though he made his outward demeanor conceal his true thoughts, saying in tones as imperious as hers, "What I want does not require that you be tortured and for that reason you will not be tortured. And indeed, it would be bizarre for anyone to think of torturing a lovely slave girl like you."

"No! A proud princess!"

"That was before you fell into my hands as a prisoner. Personally, I would rather add you to my harem than torture you. My will is what will decide."

"You should know that your will may decide for you and your people, but not for me, and you will never put a hand on me alive."

He shrugged his shoulders as though to make light of this, but she went on, "Among the customs passed down among us is that if one of us should fall into the snares of abjection and has no hope of rescue, he abstain from food until he die with honor."

Contemptuously he said, "Really? But I saw the judges of Thebes driven to me, and prostrate themselves before me, groveling, their eyes pleading for pardon and mercy."

Her face turned pale and she took refuge in silence.

The king, unable to listen to more of her words and suffering the bitterness of disappointment, could stay no longer. As he got ready to leave the chamber, he said, "You will not need to abstain from food."

He left the chamber angry and depressed, having decided to transfer her to another ship. No sooner, however, had his anger died down and he was alone in his cabin than he changed his mind, and he did not give the order.

18

Chamberlain Hur appeared before the king in his cabin and said, "My lord, envoys from Apophis are come seeking permission to appear before you."

Ahmose asked in surprise, "What do they want?"

The chamberlain said, "They say they carry a letter for your High Person."

Ahmose said, "Summon them immediately!"

The chamberlain left the cabin and sent an officer to the envoys, returning to his master to wait. The envoys soon appeared with a small party of guards' officers. They were three, the leader in front, and two others carrying an ivory chest. They were, as their flowing garments evidenced, chamberlains, white-faced and long-bearded. They raised their hands in greeting, without bowing, and then stood, with obvious insolence. Ahmose returned their greeting proudly and asked, "What do you want?"

Their leader said in an arrogant, foreign accent, "Commander . . ."

Hur, however, did not let him complete what he intended to say, and said to him with his customary calm, "Envoy of Apophis, you are speaking to the pharaoh of Egypt."

The leader said, "The war is still ongoing and its outcome is still to be decided. As long as we are still men and there are weapons in our hands, Apophis is pharaoh of Egypt, without partner."

Ahmose gestured to his chamberlain to be quiet and said to the envoys, "Speak of the matter about which you came."

The leader said, "Commander, on the day of the withdrawal from Thebes, the peasants abducted Her Royal Highness, the Princess Amenridis, daughter of our lord king, Apophis, Pharaoh of Egypt, son of the Lord Seth. Our lord desires to know whether his daughter is alive or did the peasants kill her."

"Does your master remember what he did to our women and children at the siege of Thebes? Does he not remember how he exposed them to the arrows of their sons and husbands, which tore their bodies to pieces, while your cowardly soldiers sought shelter behind them?"

The man said sharply, "My lord does not shirk responsibility for what he does. War is a struggle to the death and mercy cannot be called on to prevent defeat."

Ahmose shook his head in disgust and said, "On the contrary, war is an encounter between men, whose outcome is decided by the strong, while the weak suffer. For us it is a struggle that must not be allowed to suppress our gallantry and religious values . . . though I wonder at how the king can ask about his daughter, when such are his understanding of and opinions on war."

The envoy said with disdain, "My master enquires for a reason that he alone knows and he neither asks for mercy, nor will show it himself."

Ahmose thought for a moment, not unaware of the motive that drove his enemy to ask after his daughter. He therefore asked clearly and in accents born of contempt, "Go back to your master and tell him that the peasants are a noble people who do not murder women and that the Egyptian soldiers think it below them to kill captives, and that his daughter is a captive who enjoys the magnanimity of her captors."

Relief appeared on the man's face and he said, "These words of yours have saved the lives of many thousands of your people, women and children, whom the king has taken captive and whose lives are hostage for the life of Princess Amenridis."

Ahmose said, "And hers for theirs."

The man was silent for a moment and then he said, "I have been commanded not to return before I see her for myself."

Displeasure appeared on Hur's face but Ahmose hastened to tell the envoy, "You shall see her yourself."

The leader then indicated the ivory chest that his two followers were carrying and said, "This chest contains some of her clothes. Will you permit us to leave it in her room?"

The king was briefly silent, then said, "You may do so."

However, Hur inclined his head toward his master and whispered, "We must search the clothes first."

The king agreed with his chamberlain's opinion and the chamberlain ordered the chest placed before the king, who opened it with his own hands and took out the contents, garment by garment. In the course of so doing, he came across a small casket. This he took and opened, only to find therein the necklace with the emerald heart. The king's heart trembled when he saw it as he remembered how the princess had picked it out from among his other jewelry at the time when he was called Isfinis and sold gems, and his face reddened. Hur, however, said, "Is prison a proper place for baubles?"

The envoy said, "This necklace is the princess's favorite piece of jewelry. If the commander wishes, we shall leave it. If he does not, we shall take it with us."

Ahmose said, "There is nothing wrong with leaving it."

Then the king turned to the officers and ordered them to accompany the envoys to the princess's chamber, and the envoys left, the officers behind them.

19

The same evening, forces coming from the south, recently trained at Apollonopolis Magna and Hierakonpolis, caught up with the army and small ships loaded with weapons and siege towers sent from Ombos moored at the harbor of Thebes. The captain gave the king the good tidings that a force of chariots and trained horsemen would arrive soon. Men from Thebes and Habu were inducted into the army, with the result that Ahmose's army both replaced the men it had lost and increased its number beyond that it had possessed the day it first crossed the borders in its invasion. The king saw no reason to remain in Thebes any longer, so he ordered his commanders to get ready to march north at dawn. The soldiers said their farewells to Thebes and its people and turned from recreation and calm to face struggle and fighting. At daybreak, the soldiers blew the bugles and the huge army moved forward in ranks like the waves of the sea, preceded by the vanguards with the king and his guard at the head and the chariot battalion and others following. The fleet, under the command of Ahmose Ebana, set sail, its sturdy vessels cleaving the waters of the Nile. All were eager for battle; their will had been honed by victory till it was like iron, or harder still. In the villages, the army was met with boundless enthusiasm and the peasants hurried to its route, cheering and waving flags and fronds of palm. It continued on its way without mishap until it found itself at the forenoon at Shanhur, which it entered without resistance, and in the evening at Gesyi, which opened its gates to it. Everyone spent the night at Gesyi and they resumed their march at dawn. They made fast progress, so that they reached the edge of the Field of Koptos and could see the valley that ends up at that city. Here a sad silence enveloped the army at the memories that arose in people's minds, and Ahmose recalled the defeat that had overtaken the army of Thebes in that valley ten or more years ago. He remembered the fall of his brave grandfather Seqenenra, who had watered this ground with his blood, and his eyes scanned the sides of the valley as he asked himself, "Where, I wonder, did he fall?" He happened to look at Hur and saw that his face was pale and his eyes brimming with tears, which affected him yet more. "What a painful memory!" he said to him.

Hur replied, with trembling voice and labored breath, "It is as though I hear the souls of the martyred with whom the air of this sacred place is populated."

Commander Mheb said, "How much blood of our fathers has watered this place!"

Hur dried his tears and said to the king, "Let us all pray, my lord, for the soul of our martyred sovereign Seqenenra and his brave soldiers!"

Ahmose, his commanders, and his entourage all descended from their chariots, and prayed together ardently.

20

The army entered the city of Koptos and the flag of Egypt fluttered above its walls, the soldiers cheering long to the memory of Seqenenra. Then the army marched to Dendara, without finding the least resistance. Diospolis Parva was reclaimed the same way. Then it proceeded along the road to Abydos, expecting to find the Herdsmen in the valley there. It failed, however, to come across a single one of the enemy. Ahmose was amazed and asked himself, "Where is Apophis and where are his mighty armies?"

Hur said, "Perhaps he does not want to meet our chariots with his infantry."

"So how long will this chase go on?"

"Who knows, my lord? It may go on until we face the walls of Avaris, the Herdsmen's impregnable fortress, whose walls took them a century to build, and which likely will cost Egypt dear in blood before our soldiers can break in."

Abydos opened its gates to the Army of Deliverance and it entered them in triumph and rested there that day.

Ahmose craved war, partly because he looked forward to meeting his enemy in a decisive encounter and partly because he yearned to plunge himself into the fighting, forget the upheavals in his soul, and erase the sorrows in his heart. Apophis, however, denied him that comfort, so he found his thoughts hovering about the obstinate captive and his heart tugging him toward her, in spite of the ill will she felt for him. He remembered his dreams when he had thought that the happiest of fates was the one that had turned her over to his keeping and when he had been greedy to make the vessel of captivity a paradise of love. Then he thought of what her disdain and anger had done to him and how they had made him a sick man, deprived of the most delicious fruit, ripe and ready for the picking though it was. His desire for love was irresistible, its rushing torrent sweeping away the barriers of hesitation and pride. He went to the ship, made for the magic chamber, and entered. She was sitting in her usual position on the divan, enveloped in one of Memphis's most delicate robes. She seemed to have recognized his footfall, for she did not raise her head to him and remained looking at the floor between her feet. His infatuated vision ran over the parting of her hair, her brow, her lowered eyelashes, and he felt a thundering in his chest, desire tugging at him to throw himself upon her and press her between his arms with all the strength and resolution that he possessed. However, she raised her head unexpectedly in an insolent stare and he remained where he was, frozen. He asked her, "Did the envoys visit you?"

She replied, in a tone that betrayed no emotion, "Yes."

His gaze passed over the room, until it came to rest on the ivory chest and he said, "I gave them permission to deliver this chest to you."

She said offhandedly and in a voice that was not without asperity, "Thank you."

He felt better and he said, "In the chest was the necklace with the emerald heart."

Her lips trembled and she wanted to speak but suddenly decided against it and shut her mouth in a way that indicated confusion. Ahmose said gently, "The envoys said that this necklace was dear to you."

She shook her head violently, as though rejecting an accusation made against her and said, "Indeed, I used to wear it frequently, because the palace witch had made it into a talisman to drive away harm and evil."

He discerned her evasiveness but, not despairing, said, "I thought it might be for other causes, to which the cabin of the royal vessel might bear witness."

Her face turned deep red and she said angrily, "I do not remember today the whims of yesterday; and it would be proper for you to talk to me as the enemy must talk to a captive."

He saw her face was cruel and hard, so he swallowed his disappointment yet again. However, in an attempt to suppress his emotions, he said, "Are you not aware that we add the women of our enemies to our palace harems?"

She said sharply, "Not such as me."

"Are you going to go back to your threats of fasting?"

"I do not need to anymore now."

He examined her suspiciously and asked her sarcastically, "Then how will you defend yourself?"

She showed him that in her hand she had a small weapon, no longer than a fingernail, and said with assurance, "Look! This is a poisoned dagger. If I scratch my skin with it, the poison will pass into my bloodstream and kill me in moments. The envoy gave it to me secretly, unnoticed by your watchers. Thus, I knew that my father had placed in my hand something with which to do away with myself should any dishonor touch me or any person provoke me."

Ahmose grew angry and, frowning, he said, "Was that the secret of the chest? To hell with anyone who believes the word of a Herdsman pig with his filthy beard! Treachery runs in your veins like blood. However, I see that you misunderstood your father's message, for he secretly sent you this dagger so that you could kill me."

She shook her head as though mocking him and said, "You do not understand Apophis. He will accept nothing but that I live honorably or die honorably. As for his enemy, he will kill him himself, as he is accustomed to kill his enemies."

Ahmose struck the ground with his foot and said in extreme exasperation, "Why all this trouble? How little do I need a slave girl like you, blinded by conceit, pride, and a corrupt nature! In the past, I imagined you to be something that in reality you have nothing in common with, so to hell with all illusions!"

The king turned away from her and left the chamber. Outside, he summoned the chief of the guards and said to him, "The princess is to be transferred to another ship, under tight guard."

Ahmose left the ship downcast, his face dark, and returned in his chariot to the camp.

21

─────────

Finding inactivity oppressive, the king ordered his commanders to prepare themselves. At dawn on the second day, the army marched off with its myriad companies and the fleet set sail. In two days it reached Ptolemais. There was no sign of the enemy to be seen nearby, so the vanguard entered the city peacefully, the army in its footsteps. The vanguard probed as far as Panopolis, the northernmost city under the aegis of Thebes and entered it without resistance. The good tidings were brought to King Ahmose that Panopolis was in Egyptian hands and he cried out, "The Herdsmen have been cleared from the Kingdom of Thebes!"

Said Hur, "And soon they will be cleared from Egypt."

The army continued toward Panopolis and entered it proudly and triumphantly to the patriotic music of the band and blew on the bugles to announce victory. The flags of Egypt were raised over the wall of the city and the soldiers spread out through the markets and mixed with the people, cheering and singing. A crazy joy, beating in every breast and resonating in every soul, filled the city. The king invited the army and navy commanders and his entourage to a luxurious banquet, at the end of which cups brimming with vintage wines of Maryut were offered, along with lotus flowers and sprigs of basil. The king told his men, "Tomorrow we cross the borders of the Northern Kingdom and the flags of Egypt will be raised above its walls for the first time in a hundred years or more."

The men called blessings on him and cheered his name at length.

However, in the late afternoon of the same day, the guards saw a squadron of chariots flying a white pennant moving fast toward the city from the north. The soldiers surrounded them and asked them where they were headed and one of the squadron told them that they were envoys of King Apophis to Ahmose, so the soldiers took them to the city. On learning of their arrival, Ahmose went to the palace of the governor of the city, summoned Hur, the commander of the fleet, and Commanders Mheb and Deeb to him, and took his seat on the governor's throne, his commanders around him, and, around them, the guard in their dress uniforms. Then he gave permission to the envoys to enter. The Egyptians, not knowing what the envoys carried with them this time, waited impatiently. The envoys of the Herdsman king came. They were a mixture of commanders and chamberlains, in military and civilian dress, their flowing beards preceding them. There was no sign in their faces of the defiant demeanor or obstreperousness that Ahmose had expected. On the contrary, they approached the king's seat and bowed together with the greatest reverence and respect, so that the king almost gave voice to his astonishment. Then their leader said, "The Lord grant you life, King of Thebes! We are envoys to you from the Pharaoh of Upper, Middle, and Lower Egypt."

Ahmose cast a look at them that revealed nothing of the turmoil that was taking place in his breast and said to them calmly, "The Lord grant you life, envoys of Apophis! What do you want?"

The envoys appeared displeased at the king's ignoring of their sovereign's titles. However, their leader said, "King, we are men of war. We were raised on its fields and we live according to its code, bravely and courageously, as you know from long experience. We admire the hero, though he be our enemy, and we cede to the judgment of the sword, though it be against us. You are victorious, King, and have regained the throne of your kingdom. Thus it is your right to possess it, just as it is our obligation to surrender it; it is your kingdom and you are its sovereign. Pharaoh now extends to you his greetings and proposes to you an end to the bloodshed and an honorable settlement that respects the rights of all, restoring the friendly relations between the Kingdom of the South and the Kingdom of the North that have been severed.

The king listened intently to the envoys with outward calm and inner astonishment. Then he looked at the spokesman and asked him wonderingly, "Are you really come to sue for peace?"

The man said, "We are, King."

Ahmose said in a voice indicating decisiveness and resolution, "I refuse such a peace."

"Why do you insist on war, King?"

Ahmose said, "People of Apophis, this is the first time you address an Egyptian with respect, and the first time you do not insist, because you cannot, on describing him in terms reserved for slaves. Do you know why? Because you have been beaten. For you, my good people, are wild beasts when you win but sheep when you are beaten. You ask me why I insist on war. This is my answer: I did not declare war on you in order to regain Thebes, but because I gave an undertaking to my Lord and to my people that I would liberate the whole of Egypt from the yokes of injustice and oppression, and that I would restore to it its freedom and glory. If he who sent you truly wants peace, let him leave Egypt to its people and return with his to the deserts of the north."

The envoy asked him in a peremptory voice, "That is your final answer?"

Ahmose replied confidently and strongly, "It is what we opened our struggle with and what we shall end it with."

The envoys stood and their chief said, "Since you desire war, it will be unrelenting war between us and you until the Lord imposes the end He sees fit."

The men bowed to the king again and left the place with heavy steps.

22

Ahmose remained at Panopolis two whole days. Then he sent the vanguard to cross the borders of Apophis's state. Strong companies advanced north of the city and made contact with small forces of the enemy, which they scattered, preparing the way for the army encamped at Panopolis. Ahmose marched at the head of an army the like of which Egypt had not seen before, either in numbers or equipment and materiel, while Ahmose Ebana's huge fleet with its triumphant vessels set sail. While on the road, spies informed Ahmose that the Herdsmen's army was encamped to the south of Aphroditopolis in innumerable companies. The Herdsmen's numbers did not worry the king. However, he asked Chamberlain Hur, "Do you think that Apophis still has a force of chariots that he can send against us?"

Hur said, "There is no doubt, my lord, that Apophis has lost the greater number of his charioteers. If he still had a force of them sufficient to make a difference in the coming battle, he would not have asked for a settlement or pressed for peace. In any case, the Herdsmen have lost something more valuable than charioteers and chariots: they have lost confidence and hope."

The army's advance continued until it was close to the enemy camp, and the harbingers of the battle appeared on the horizon. Commanded by the king, the chariot battalion prepared to plunge into the heart of the battle. Ahmose cried to his commanders, "We shall fight on ground on which we have been forbidden to tread for a hundred years and more. Let us strike a terrible blow such as will put an end to the sufferings of millions of our enslaved brothers and let us advance with hearts ready for heroic deeds, for the Lord has given us the numbers and the hope and has abandoned our enemy to extinction and despair; and I am at your head, as were Seqenenra and Kamose."

The king ordered his vanguard to attack and they descended like predatory eagles, throwing themselves into the attack while he watched to see how the enemy met them. He observed a force of around two hundred chariots returning the attack in an attempt to encircle them. Eager to destroy the enemy's chariots, the king attacked the head of the chariot column and descended on the enemy from all sides. The Hyksos realized that their charioteers could not stand firm against forces that vastly outnumbered them, so Apophis threw in squadrons of archers and lance-bearers to support his limited number of chariots. A fierce battle ensued, but the Herdsmen's courage was of no help to them and their mounted force was destroyed.

The army passed the night with Ahmose not knowing whether Apophis would throw his infantry against him in desperation or flee with his army, as he had done at Hierakonpolis, preferring peace. Things became clear in the morning, when the king saw companies of Herdsmen advancing to occupy their positions, bows and lances in their hands. Hur saw them too and said, "Now the tables are turned against them, my lord, and Apophis will be exposed with his infantry to the onslaught of our chariots, as was our sovereign Seqenenra south of Koptos ten years ago."

The king rejoiced and made ready to attack with the chariot battalion, supported by selected forces of lancers and others. The chariots descended on the Herdsmen's position, filling the air ahead of them with flying arrows, and burst through their lines at many points, the lancers behind them protecting their backs and pursuing those of the enemy who scattered, killing or capturing them. The Herdsmen fought with their usual courage but they fell like dry leaves before the furious winds of autumn. The Egyptians took possession of the field. Ahmose was afraid that he would allow Apophis to escape from his grip, so he attacked Aphroditopolis at the same time as the fleet attacked its beaches. Inside its walls, however, he found no sign of the Herdsmen and did not come across his archenemy. Then spies provided him with the information that Apophis had left the city with some of his forces after the nightmare of the previous night, leaving some men behind to delay the Egyptians' advance. Hur said to the king, "From today on, resistance will be futile. Apophis may already be making haste toward Avaris, to take shelter behind its impregnable walls."

Ahmose did not sorrow for long. His joy at conquering a city of Egypt that had been forbidden to his people for two hundred years knew no bounds and he distracted himself with the inspection of the city and its people from all else.

23

The army continued its great march, meeting with no resistance and finding no sign of the enemy. The people of the villages and cities welcomed it, stupefied with joy, unable to believe that after two full centuries, the gods had lifted from them their anger and that he who was conquering their cities and had driven off their enemy was a king drawn from among them to revive the glories of the pharaohs. Ahmose found that the Herdsmen had fled from the cities, leaving their palaces and estates and carrying whatever they could of their possessions and wealth. Every place he came to, he heard that Apophis was fleeing fast with his army and his people to the north. Thus, the king regained in one month Habsil, Lykopolis, and Kusai, ending up finally at Hermopolis. Their entry into the latter had great significance for Ahmose and his soldiers, for Hermopolis was the birthplace of Sacred Mother Tetisheri, her birth having taken place in her ancient house before the occupation. Ahmose celebrated its liberation, and the men of his entourage, the commanders of the army and the fleet, and all the troops took part in the great festivity, the king then writing his grandmother a letter congratulating her on the independence of her first home, and assuring her of his feelings and of those of his army and people. The king, the commanders, and the leading officers all signed this.

The army continued its triumphant march. It entered Titnawi, Sinopolis, Hebennu, and finally Arsinoe, descending between the pyramids on the great Memphis road, indifferent to the hardships of the journey and the length of the way. Along the way, Ahmose smashed the shackles with which his wretched people were bound, breathing into them, from his great soul, a new life, so that one day Hur said to him, "Your military greatness, my lord, has nothing to compare to it except your political skill and your administrative proficiency. You have changed the features of the cities, eliminating systems and constructing systems. You have drawn up the practices that should be followed and the customs that must be observed and you have appointed patriotic governors. Life flows again in the valley's veins and the people have witnessed, for the first time since the distant past, Egyptian governors and Egyptian judges. Bowed heads have risen and a man no longer suffers or is looked down on because of his dark complexion. On the contrary, it has become a source of strength and pride for him. May the Lord Amun indeed protect you, grandson of Seqenenra!"

The king worked wholeheartedly and untiringly, knowing neither despair nor fatigue, his unswerving goal being the restoration to his people, whom abjection, hunger, poverty, and ignorance had brought close to the breaking point, of honor, self-esteem, a well-provided-for life without deprivation, and knowledge.

His heart, however, despite his labors and preoccupations, had not been rescued from its private concerns. Love made him suffer and pride wore him out. Often he would strike the ground with his foot and say to himself, "I was tricked. She is just a heartless woman." He had hoped that work would force him to forget and bring him solace, but he found that his spirit slipped away despite him to a ship tossing in the waves at the rear of his fleet.

24

The army made good progress in its march and began to draw close to Immortal Memphis of the glorious memories, whose lofty white walls now started to appear. Ahmose thought that the Herdsmen would defend the capital of their kingdom to the death. However, he was wrong, and the vanguard entered the city in peace. He found out that Apophis had withdrawn with his army toward the northeast. Ahmose thus entered the Thebes of the north in a festival the likes of which none had seen before, the people welcoming him with enthusiasm and reverence, prostrating themselves to him and calling him "Son of Merenptah." The king stayed in Memphis a number of days, during which he visited its quarters and inspected its markets and manufacturing areas. He made a circuit of the three pyramids and prayed in the temple of the Sphinx, making offerings. Their joy at the conquest of Memphis was unrivaled by anything but the retaking of Thebes. Ahmose marveled at how the Herdsmen could fail to defend Memphis but Commander Mheb said to him, "They will never expose themselves to the onslaught of our chariots after what they experienced in Hierakonpolis and Aphroditopolis."

Chamberlain Hur said confidently, "Ships come to us constantly, laden with chariots and horses from the districts of the south, while all Apophis has to worry about are the walls of Avaris."

They consulted together on the direction to take, spreading out the map of the invasion in front of them. Commander Mheb said, "There is no doubt that the enemy has withdrawn from the north altogether and congregated in the east, behind the walls of Avaris. We must go there with all our forces."

But Ahmose was extremely cautious. He sent a small army to the west via Lenopolis, dispatched another to the north in the direction of Athribis, and went himself with his main forces and his great fleet eastward on the road to On. The days passed as they covered the miles, driven by enthusiasm and the hope that they would deliver the final blow and crown their long struggle with a decisive victory. They entered On, the immortal city of Ra. Then they came to Phakussa, followed by Pharbaithos, where they turned onto the road leading to Avaris. News of Apophis kept coming to them and thus they discovered that the Herdsmen had withdrawn from all other districts to go to Avaris, driving before them thousands of poor wretches. This news caused the king great sadness and his heart went out to those despised captives who had fallen into the Herdsmen's cruel clutches.

Finally, the terrible walls of Avaris appeared on the horizon like a rocky mountain range and Ahmose cried out, "The last fortress of the Herdsmen in Egypt!"

Hur said to him, as he looked at the fortress with his weak eyes, "Smash its gates, my lord, and the lovely face of Egypt will be yours alone."

25

Avaris was located to the east of the branch of the Nile and its wall extended eastward farther than the eye could see. Many of the local inhabitants knew the fortified city and some of them had worked inside it or on its walls. They told their sovereign, "Four circular, massively thick walls surround the city, beyond which is an encircling ditch through which the water of the Nile runs. Within the city are broad fields that provide for the needs of its entire people, most of whom are soldiers, the Egyptian farmers being the exception. The city is watered by channels that draw from branches of the Nile, under the western wall, and are protected by it. From there, they go east toward the city."

Ahmose and his men stood on the south side of the terrible fortress, turning their faces this way and that in amazement at the enormous towering walls, in whose lee the soldiers appeared no larger than dwarfs. The army pitched its tents, the rows of troops extending parallel to the southern wall. The fleet went forward on the river on the western side of the western wall, out of range of its arrows, in order to watch and lay siege. Ahmose listened to the words of the inhabitants concerning the fortress and examined the land around it and the river running to its west, his mind never resting. While thus occupied, he dispatched mounted and infantry forces to the villages around the city, taking possession of them without trouble and quickly completing his blockade of the fortress. However, he and his men knew that the siege would produce nothing, for the city could provide for itself from its own resources, and that the blockade could last for years without having any effect on it, while he and his army would suffer the frustration of waiting without hope amidst the horrors of the weather and its changes. On one of his circuits around the fortress, an idea came to him and he summoned his men to his tent to consult them. He said to them, "Advise me. It seems to me that the siege is a waste of our time and a dissipation of our strength. Likewise, it seems to me that an attack is futile and obvious suicide and it may be that the enemy wants us to assault him so that he can pick off our brave men or drive them into his ditches. So what is your advice?"

Commander Deeb said, "My advice, my lord, is to besiege the fortress with a part of our forces and consider the war over. Then you can announce the independence of the valley and take up your duties as pharaoh of a united Egypt."

Hur, however, objected to the idea, and said, "How can we leave Apophis safe to train his men and build new chariots so that he can assault us later on?"

Commander Mheb said enthusiastically, "We paid a high price for Thebes and struggle is by its nature effort and sacrifice. Why then do we not pay the price for Avaris and attack as we attacked the forts of Thebes?"

Commander Deeb said, "We do not begrudge ourselves, but an attack on four massive walls separated by ditches full of water is a sure destruction for our troops for no gain."

The king was silent, plunged in thought. Then he said, pointing to the river running beneath the western wall of the city, "Avaris is well-defended. It cannot be taken and it cannot be starved. However, it can be made to feel thirst."

The men looked at the river and astonishment appeared on their faces. Hur said in alarm, "How made to feel thirst, my lord?"

Ahmose said quietly, "By diverting from it the waters of the Nile."

The men looked again at the Nile, unable to believe that it would be possible to divert that mighty river from its course. Hur asked, "Can such an enormous task be undertaken?"

Ahmose said, "We have no lack of engineers and laborers."

"How long will it take, my lord?"

"A year, or two, or three. The time is not important, since that is the only way. The Nile will have to be diverted north of Pharbaithos into a new channel that goes west toward Mendes, so that Apophis is forced to choose between death by hunger and thirst and coming out to fight us. My people will forgive me for exposing the Egyptians in Avaris to danger and death just as they forgave me for doing the same to some of the women of Thebes."

26

Ahmose prepared for the great work. He summoned the famous engineers of Thebes and proposed his idea to them. They studied it with diligence and passion, then told the king that his idea was feasible, provided that he gave them enough time and a thousand laborers. Ahmose learned that his project could not be realized in less than two years but did not give up in despair. Instead he sent messengers to the cities to call for volunteers for the great work on which the liberation of the country and the expulsion of its enemy depended. The workers came in bands from all parts and soon there were enough of them to start with. The king inaugurated the great work, taking a mattock and striking the ground with it to announce the beginning. Behind him followed the brawny arms that labor to the rhythm of hymns and songs.

There was nothing for the king and army to do but settle in for a long wait. The troops did their daily training under the supervision of their officers and commanders. The king, for his part, passed his spare time in expeditions to the eastern desert to hunt or hold races, and to escape from the impulses of his heart and the agonies of his passion. During this period of waiting, messengers brought him a letter from Sacred Mother Tetisheri, in which she wrote:

My lord, Son of Amun, Pharaoh of Upper and Lower Egypt, may the Lord preserve him and help him with victory and triumph: little Dabod is today a paradise of happiness and joy by virtue of the news of the incontestable victory granted you by the Lord that the messengers have brought. We do not wait today in Dabod as we waited yesterday, for now

*our waiting is bounded by equanimity and closer to hope.
How happy we all are to learn that Egypt has been freed
from ignominy and slavery and that its enemy and humiliator has imprisoned himself within the walls of his fortress,
waiting cringingly for the blow with which you will destroy
him! The Almighty Lord has willed, in His solicitude and
mercy, that He should present you with a gift—you who
brought low His enemy and raised high His word—and has
provided you with a son as a light for your eyes and a successor to your throne. I have named him Amenhotep in
honor of the Divine Lord, and I have taken him in my arms,
as I took his father, and his grandfather, and his father's
grandfather before him. My heart tells me that he will be
crown prince of a great kingdom, of many races, languages,
and religions, watched over by his dear father.*

Ahmose's heart beat as any father's must, tenderness flowed
in his breast, and he rejoiced with a great joy that made him
forget some of what he suffered from the pains of repressed
passion. He announced the birth of the crown prince Amenhotep to his men, and it was a day to be remembered.

27

The days passed slowly and heavily, though they were filled
with extraordinary works in which the greatest minds,
strongest arms, and most dedicated wills took part. None of
them paid heed to the difficulty of the work or the time that
was taken, so long as it brought them closer to their sublime
hope and highest goal. One day, however, several months after
the start of the siege, the guards saw a chariot coming from the
direction of the fortress, a white flag flying at its front. Some

guards intercepted it and found that it held three chamberlains. On being asked where they were heading, their leader said that they were envoys from King Apophis to King Ahmose. The guards sent the news flying to the king, who called a council of his entourage and commanders in his pavilion, and ordered the envoys to enter. The men were brought. They walked humbly and with downcast mien, so little left of their haughtiness and pride that they seemed not to be of the people of Apophis. They bowed before the king and their leader greeted him by saying, "The Lord grant you life, O King!"

Ahmose replied, "And you, envoys of Apophis. What does your king want?"

The envoy said, "King, the man of the sword is an adventurer. He seeks victory, but may find death. We are men of war. War put your country in our hands and we ruled it for two centuries or more, during which we were divine overlords. Then it was fated that we should be defeated and we were beaten and forced to take refuge in our citadel. We, King, are no weaklings. We are as capable of bearing defeat as we were of plucking the fruits of victory. . . ."

Ahmose said angrily, "I see that you have worked out the meaning of this new channel that my people are digging and have come to propitiate us."

The man shook his huge head, "Not so, King. We do not seek to propitiate anyone but we do admit defeat. My master has sent me to propose to you two plans, of which you may choose what you wish. War to the finish, in which case we shall not wait behind the walls to die of hunger and thirst, but kill the captives of your people, of whom there are more than thirty thousand; then we shall kill our women and children by our own hand and launch against your army three hundred thousand warriors, of whom there will not be one who does not hate life and thirst for revenge."

The man fell silent, as though to gather his breath. Then he resumed and said, "Or you return to us Princess Amenridis and the captives of our people you hold and grant us safe conduct for ourselves, our possessions, and our wealth, in which case we will return to you your people and evacuate Avaris, turning our faces to the desert from which we came, leaving you your country to do with as you wish. This will bring to an end the conflict that has lasted two centuries."

The man fell silent and the king realized that he was awaiting his reply. However, the reply was not ready, nor was it of the kind that could be left to spontaneous inspiration, so he said to the envoy, "Will you not wait until we reach a decision?"

The envoy replied, "As you wish, King. My master has given me till the end of the day."

28

The king met with his men in the cabin of the royal ship and told them, "Give me your opinions."

All were agreed without need for further consultation. Hur said, "My lord, you have achieved victory over the Herdsmen in many engagements and they have acknowledged your victory and their defeat. By so doing, you have wiped out the vestiges of the defeats that we suffered in our grievous past. You have killed large numbers of them and by doing so taken revenge for the wretched dead among our own people. We cannot therefore be blamed now if we purchase the life of thirty thousand of our men and save ourselves an effort that no duty requires of us so long as our enemy is going to evacuate our country in defeat and our motherland is going to be liberated forever."

The king turned his eyes on the faces of his people and found in them a shared enthusiasm for acceptance of the idea.

Commander Deeb said, "Every one of our soldiers has performed his duty to the full. For Apophis, a return to the deserts would be a more punishing disaster than death itself."

Commander Mheb said, "Our higher goal is to liberate the motherland from the Herdsmen's rule and clear them from its territory. The Lord has granted us this, so there is no need for us to prolong the period of abasement of our own volition."

Ahmose Ebana said, "We shall purchase the life of thirty thousand captives at the price of Princess Amenridis and a handful of Herdsmen."

The king listened closely to his men and said, "Your opinion is sound. However, I think that the envoy of Apophis should wait a little longer so that he does not think that our haste to agree to a peaceful solution comes from weakness or weariness with the struggle."

The men left the ship and the king was alone. Despite all the reasons he had to rejoice, he was despondent and ill at ease. His struggle had been crowned with outright victory, his mighty enemy had knelt to him, and tomorrow Apophis would load his belongings and flee to the deserts from which his people came, in submission to irreversible Fate. So why was it that he could not rejoice? Or why was it that his joy was not pure and complete? The critical moment had come, the moment of farewell forever. Even before this moment, he had been truly despairing, though she was there, on the small ship. What would he do tomorrow should he return to the palace of Thebes, while she was taken to the heart of the unknown desert? Could he let her go without fortifying himself with a look of farewell from her? "No!" responded his heart, and smashing the shackles of resignation and pride he rose and left the cabin, whence he took a boat to the captive princess's ship, saying to himself, "Whatever reception she gives me, I will find something to say." He climbed up to the ship and went to the chamber, where the guards saluted him and opened the door.

Heart beating, he crossed the threshold and cast a look around the small, simple chamber. He found the captive sitting in the center of the room on a divan. She seemed not to have been expecting his return, for astonishment and reproach showed on her lovely visage. Ahmose examined her with a deep look and found her as beautiful as ever, her features just as they had been on the day when they were engraved on his heart on the deck of the royal vessel. He bit his lip and said to her, "Good morning, Princess."

She looked up at him with eyes that still held their astonishment and seemed not to know what to reply. The king did not wait long but said in a quiet voice and an inexpressive tone, "Today you are released, Princess."

Her face indicated that she had understood nothing, so he said again, "Do you not hear what I say? Today you are released, free. Your captivity is at an end, Princess, and you have a right to go free."

Her astonishment increased and hope appeared in her eyes. She said impatiently, "Is it true what you say? Is it true what you say?"

"What I say is an accomplished fact."

Her face lit up and her cheeks reddened. Then she hesitated for a second and enquired, "But how can that be?"

"Aha! I read your eager hopes in your eyes. Are you not hoping that your father's victory is the reason for your regaining your liberty? That is what I read. But it is his defeat, alas, that has put an end to your enslavement."

She was tongue-tied and said not a word. He informed her briefly of her father's envoys' proposals and what had been agreed. Then he said, "And soon you will be taken to your father and journey with him wherever he journeys. So this is a blessed day for us."

Shades of sorrow enshrouded her face, her features froze, and she looked away. Ahmose asked her, "Do you find your sorrow at the defeat greater than your joy at your release?"

She replied, "It behooves you not to gloat over me, for we shall leave your country as honorable people, just as we lived in it."

Ahmose said with visible disquiet, "I am not gloating over you, Princess. We ourselves have tasted the bitterness of defeat and these long wars have taught us to acknowledge your courage and bravery."

Comforted, she said, "I thank you, King."

For the first time, he heard her speak in tones empty of anger and pride. Affected, he said to her, smiling sadly, "I see that you call me 'King,' Princess."

Turning her eyes away, she replied, "Because you are the king of this valley, without any to share it with you. I, however, shall never be called 'Princess' after today."

The king was even more affected, for he had not expected her unyieldingness to soften in this way. He had thought that she would become yet more arrogant in defeat. He said sadly, "Princess, the experiences of this world are a register of pleasure and pain. You have experienced life in its sweetness and bitterness and you still have a future."

With amazing serenity she said, "Indeed, we have a future, behind the mirages of the unknown desert and we shall meet our fate with courage."

Silence reigned. Their eyes met and he read in hers purity and gentleness. He remembered the lady of the cabin, who saved his life and fed him the nectar of love and tenderness. It was as though he were seeing her for the first time since then and, his heart shaking violently, he said earnestly and sadly, "Soon we will be parted and you will not care. But I shall always remember that you were uncivil and harsh with me."

Sadness showed in her eyes and her mouth parted in a slight smile as she said, "King, you know little about us. We are a people who find death easier to bear than abasement."

"I never wanted to abase you. But I was deluded by hope,

misled by my misplaced confidence in a standing that I believed I had in your heart."

She said in a low voice, "Would it not be abasement for me to open my arms to my captor and my father's enemy?"

He replied bitterly, "Love knows nothing of such logic."

She took refuge in silence. Then, as though persuaded by his words, she murmured in a low voice that he did not hear, "I blame only myself." Her eyes took on a faraway look and with a sudden motion she stretched out her hand to her bed pillow and took out from beneath it the necklace with the emerald heart and put it around her neck calmly and submissively. His eyes followed her, unbelieving. Then he threw himself at her side, unable to contain himself longer, encircled her neck with his arm and drew her madly and violently to his chest. She offered him no resistance but said sadly, "Beware. It is too late."

The pressure of his arms around her increased and he said in a trembling voice, "Amenridis, how can you bring yourself to say that? How can I discover my happiness only when it is about to disappear? No, I will not let you go."

She gazed at him with sympathy and pity and asked him, "What will you do?"

"I shall keep you at my side."

"Don't you know what my staying with you means? Will you sacrifice thirty thousand captives of your people and many more of your soldiers?"

He frowned, his eyes darkened, and he murmured as though speaking to himself, "My father and grandfather were martyred for my people and I have given them my life. Will they begrudge my heart its happiness?"

She shook her head sadly and said gently, "Listen to me, Isfinis—let me call you by that dear name, because it is the first name I have loved in my life. There is no escape from parting. We shall part. We shall part. You will never agree to sacrifice thirty thousand of your people, whom you love, and I shall never agree to the massacre of my father and my people. So let each one of us bear his lot of pain."

He looked at her distractedly, as though he could not bear that his only lot in love should be the acceptance of parting and pain, and said to her hopefully, "Amenridis, don't rush to despair, and shun thoughts of parting. Hearing the word pass so easily over your tongue brings back the madness to my blood. Amenridis, let me knock on all doors, even that of your father. Why should I not ask him for your hand?"

She smiled sadly and said, gently touching his hand, "Alas, Isfinis, you do not know what you are saying. Do you think my father would accept the marriage of his daughter to the victorious king who subdued him and exiled him from the country in which he was born and on whose throne he sat? I know my father better than you and there is no hope. The only path is patience."

He listened to her distractedly, asking himself, "Is the person who is speaking in this low, broken, sad voice really the Princess Amenridis for whom, in her folly, scorn, and conceit, the whole world was not large enough?" Everything seemed strange and abominable to his eyes and he said angrily, "The least of my soldiers would not so neglect his heart that he would allow anyone to separate it from what it loved."

"You are a king, my lord, and kings have greater pleasures than the rest and heavier duties—like the towering tree, which gets a larger portion of the sun's rays and the breezes than the plants beneath it and greater exposure to the unruliness of the wind and the blustering of the storms."

Ahmose groaned, and said, "Ah, how wretched I am! I have loved you from the first meeting on my ship."

She lowered her eyes and said simply and honestly, "Love knocked at my heart that same day but I did not know it until later. My feelings awoke the night Commander Rukh forced you to fight him and my concern for you showed me my sickness. I spent the night in confusion and turmoil, not knowing

what to do with this newborn . . . until infatuation overwhelmed me a few days later and I lost my senses."

"In the cabin, isn't that so?"

"Yes."

"Oh, God! What will my life be without you?"

"It will be like my life without you, Isfinis."

He clasped her to his bosom and laid his cheek against hers,
as though their touching could drive away the specter of parting that loomed before them. He could not bear it that he
should have discovered his love and bade it farewell within the
same hour. His thoughts ran in all directions seeking a solution
but found their way barred at every turn by despair and grief,
and the best that he could do in the end was to tighten his arms
around her. Both of them felt that the time had come for them
to part but neither moved, and they remained like one.

29

Ahmose left the princess's ship, his feet barely able to carry
him. He was looking at something in his hand, murmuring, "Is
this all that is left to me of my beloved?" It was the chain of the
necklace, the princess having given it to him as a memento
while she kept the heart for herself. The king mounted his chariot and proceeded to the army's camp, where his men met him
with Chamberlain Hur at their head, the latter stealing anxious, pitying glances at his master. The king went to the pavilion and, summoning the envoy of Apophis, told him, "Envoy,
we have studied your proposal carefully. Since my goal has
been to liberate my country from your rule and that is what
you have accepted, I have chosen the solution of peace, to
avoid further bloodshed. We shall exchange prisoners immediately but I shall not give the order to halt work until the last of

your men leaves Avaris. Thus this black page in the history of our country will be turned."

The envoy bent his head and said, "Your decision is wise, O King. War, if not for a valid purpose, is nothing but slaughter and massacre."

Ahmose said, "Now I shall leave you to discuss together the details of the exchange and the evacuation."

The king arose. Everyone stood and bowed to him respectfully and he saluted them with his hand and left the place.

30

The exchange of prisoners took place on the evening of that day. One of the gates of Avaris was opened and the bands of prisoners came out, women and men, cheering joyfully for their sovereign and waving their hands. The Herdsmen prisoners, with Princess Amenridis at their head, left for the city in silence and dejection.

On the morning of the following day, Ahmose and his entourage went early to a nearby hill that looked out over the eastern gates of Avaris to witness the departure of the Herdsmen from the last Egyptian city. The others could not conceal their gaiety and their faces twinkled with joy and happiness. Commander Mheb said, "Soon the chamberlains of Apophis will bring the keys of Avaris to surrender to His Majesty, just as the keys of Thebes were surrendered to Apophis eleven years ago."

The chamberlains came, as Commander Mheb had said, and presented to Ahmose an ebony box in which were laid the keys of Avaris. The king received these and gave them to his grand chamberlain, then returned the salute of the men, who returned whence they came in silence.

The eastern gates were then opened wide, their squealing resounding off the valley's sides as the observers on the hill watched in silence. The first groups of those leaving emerged—charioteers bristling with arms, whom Apophis had sent ahead to scout out the unknown road. Groups of women and children followed them, riding on the backs of mules and donkeys, some of them carried in litters. Their exit took many long hours. Then a great cavalcade appeared, surrounded by horsemen from the guard and followed by ox-drawn carts. The watchers realized that this was Apophis and the people of his house. Ahmose's heart beat hard when he saw it and he resisted a burning tear that he felt tugging at him inside. He asked himself where she might be. Was she looking as hard for him as he for her? Was she thinking of him in the same way that he thought of her? Was she suppressing a tear as he was? He followed the cavalcade with his eyes, not turning to the soldiers pouring out in its wake from all the gates, and continued to follow it with his eyes and his heart, and to hover around it in spirit, until the horizon hid it and the unknown swallowed it up.

The king awoke to the voice of Hur saying, "At this immortal hour, the hearts of our sovereign Seqenenra and of our glorious hero Kamose are happy, and Thebes' struggle, which has known no despair, is crowned with outright triumph."

The Army of Deliverance entered mighty Avaris, occupying its impregnable walls, and there it stayed until dawn of the following day. Ahmose marched eastward with a battalion of chariots headed by his vanguard, and entered Tanis and Difna, where spies came to him and congratulated him on the withdrawal of the last of the Herdsmen from the land of Egypt. Returning to Avaris, the king ordered the army to perform a collective prayer to the Lord Amun. The various battalions formed, their officers and commander at the head of each and the king and his entourage at the head of all. Then all knelt in reverent submission and prayed ardently to the Lord. Ahmose ended his prayer with the following words: "I praise you and thank you, Divine Lord, for you have protected me and made steadfast my heart and honored me by allowing me to achieve the goal for which my grandfather and my father were martyred. O God, inspire me to do what is right, and help me to find the resolution and faith to heal my people's wounds and make them worthy slaves of the best of lords!"

Ahmose then summoned his men to meet with him and they obeyed the summons quickly. He said to them, "Today the war is over and we must sheathe our swords. But the struggle never ends. Believe me when I say that peace is yet more demanding of vigilance and readiness to do great things than war. Lend me then your hearts, that we may make Egypt live anew."

The king looked into the faces of his men for a while and then he continued, "I have decided to start the struggle for the peace by choosing my loyal helpers. Thus, I appoint Hur my minister."

Hur stood and went to his master and knelt before him and kissed his hand. The king said, "I believe that Seneb is the best successor for Hur in my palace. Deeb will be head of the royal guard."

The king looked at Mheb and said, "You, Mheb, are to be commander-in-chief of my army."

Then he turned to Ahmose Ebana and said, "You will be commander of the fleet and the estates of your brave father Pepi will be restored to you."

Then the king addressed his words to all, saying, "Now return to Thebes, capital of our realm, that each may carry out his duty."

Hur asked anxiously, "Will Pharaoh not return at the head of his army to Thebes?"

"No," Ahmose replied, as he prepared to rise. "My ship will set sail with me to Dabod, so that I may take the glad tidings of victory to my family. Then I will return with them to Thebes, that we may enter it together just as we left it together."

31

The royal ship set sail, guarded by three warships. Ahmose kept to his cabin on the deck, looking at the distant horizon with a set face and eyes brimming with sadness and pain. After several days of traveling, little Dabod appeared with its scattered huts and the fleet moored on its shore as day ended. The king and his guard disembarked in their handsome clothes, attracting all eyes and bringing hurrying to them a throng of Nubians, who went before them to the house of the governor, Ra'um. News spread in the city that a great envoy from Pharaoh had arrived to visit the family of Seqenenra. The news reached the governor's house before the king and as he approached he found the governor and the royal family in the courtyard of the palace, waiting. As the king went up to them astonishment and joy silenced their tongues. Ra'um went down on his knees and all let out a cry of joy and happiness and hurried to him. The young queen Nefertari was the first to reach him and she kissed his cheeks and his brow. Then he looked and he saw his mother Queen Setkimus reaching out her arms and he clasped her to his breast and gave her his cheeks to kiss tenderly. His grandmother Queen Ahotep was waiting her turn and he went up to her and kissed her hands and her brow. Finally, he saw the last, and the best, of the people—Tetisheri, whom white hair had crowned and whose cheeks were withered with age. His heart beat fast and he took her in his arms, saying, "Mother, and mother of all!"

She kissed him with her thin lips and said, as she raised her eyes to him, "Let me look on the living image of Seqenenra."

Ahmose said, "I chose, Mother, to be the messenger who would bring you the good news of the great triumph. Know,

Mother, that our valiant army has won outright victory and defeated Apophis and his people, driving them into the desert from whence they came and liberating the whole of Egypt from slavery. Thus Amun's promise is fulfilled and the souls of Seqenenra and Kamose rejoice."

Tetisheri's face lit up, her tired eyes beamed, and she said joyfully, "Today our captivity is ended and we shall return to Thebes. I shall find it as I left it, the city of glory and sovereignty, and I shall find my grandson on the throne of Seqenenra, continuing the glorious life of Amenhotep that was cut short."

Lady Ray, the queen's lady-in-waiting, arrived, carrying the crown prince in her arms. Bowing to the king, she said, "My lord, kiss your little son, Crown Prince Amenhotep."

His eyes softened and an outpouring of tenderness overcame him. He took the little one in his arms and brought him close to his mouth till his longing lips touched him and Amenhotep smiled at his father and paddled at him with his two little hands.

Then the royal family entered the house, filled with joy and tranquility, and spent the evening on their own, talking and remembering the days that had passed.

32

The soldiers loaded the family's possessions onto the royal vessel. Then the king and his clan transferred to that and came out to bid farewell to Governor Ra'um, the members of his government, and all the people of Dabod. Before the ship raised its anchors, Ahmose summoned Ra'um and told him in his men's hearing, "Honest Governor, I commend Nubia and the people of Nubia to you, for Nubia was our place of refuge when we had no other place to go, our country when we had no country, our shelter when our supporters were few and our friends were dead, and the depot for our arms and our soldiers when the call to struggle came. Do not forget what it did, and from this day on let us not deny to southern Egypt anything that we desire for ourselves and let us shield it from whatever we would not wish for ourselves."

Then the ship set sail with the guard's ships behind it, making its way toward the north, bearing men and women whose hearts yearned for Egypt and its people. After a short journey, the ship reached Egypt's borders and received a wonderful welcome, the men of the south coming out to them in Governor Shaw's ship, the boats of the cheering and singing locals all around them. Shaw climbed onto the deck with the priests of Biga, Bilaq, and Sayin, the headmen of the villages, and the elders of the cities. They prostrated themselves to the king and listened to his counsels. Then the ship moved on toward the north, the people welcoming it from the shores, boats surrounding it, and the governors, judges, headmen, and notables climbing on board at every city. The ship continued to hasten north until the darkness of dawn parted one day to reveal, on the distant horizon, the high walls of Thebes, its huge gates, its immortal splendor. The family hurried from their chambers to the front of the ship, their eyes hanging on the horizon, affection and passionate attachment gleaming in their looks and their eyes brimming over with tears of thanks, as their lips muttered quietly, "Thebes! Thebes!" Queen Ahotep said in a trembling voice, "Dear God! I did not imagine that my eyes would ever again fall on those walls."

The ship started to approach the southern part of Thebes with a favorable wind until they were able to make out companies of soldiers and leading townspeople waiting on the shore. Ahmose realized that Thebes was extending its first greetings to its deliverer. He returned to his cabin on the deck followed by his family and sat on the throne with them around him. The soldiers gave a military salute to the royal ship and the great men of Thebes ascended to its deck, led by Prime Minister Hur, the commanders Mheb and Ahmose Ebana, the Grand Chamberlain Seneb, and Tuti-Amun, governor of Thebes. Then came an aged priest, his head blazing with white hairs, leaning on his staff and walking with unhurried steps, his back bent. All prostrated themselves to Pharaoh, and Hur said to him, "My Lord, Liberator of Egypt, Deliverer of Thebes and Destroyer of the Herdsmen, Pharaoh of Egypt, Lord of the South and the North: all of Thebes is in the markets waiting with longing and impatience the coming of Ahmose son of Kamose son of Seqenenra and his glorious family, so that they may extend to them all the greetings all wish to extend."

Ahmose smiled and said, "The Lord grant you life, loyal men, and greetings to Thebes, my beginning and my end!"

Hur indicated the venerable priest, saying, "My lord, permit me to present to Your Majesty, Nofer-Amun, chief priest of the Temple of Amun."

Ahmose looked at him with interest and extended his hand to him, smiling and saying gently, "It pleases me to see you, Chief Priest."

The priest kissed his hand and said, "My Lord, Pharaoh of Egypt and son of Amun, renewer of the life of Egypt and reviver of the path of its greatest kings: I had promised, my lord, that I would not leave my room so long as there was in Egypt a single one of the accursed Herdsmen who humiliated Thebes and killed its glorious master. I neglected myself, the hair of my head and body grew long, and I renounced the world, taking only morsels of food to still my hunger and sips of pure water so that I might share with our people in the filth and hunger that they suffered. So I remained, until God ordained to Egypt His son Ahmose. He campaigned righteously against our enemy, scattered him, and drove him from the country. Then I excused myself and released myself from my confinement, so that I might receive the glorious king and pray for him."

The king smiled at him. The priest requested permission to greet the family, which the king granted him, and he went to Tetisheri and greeted her, then turned to Queen Ahotep, to whom he had been close during the reign of Seqenenra, then kissed Setkimus and Nefertari. Then Hur said to his master, "My lord, Thebes is waiting for her master and the army is drawn up along the roads, but the chief priest of Amun has a request."

"And what is the request of our chief priest?"

The priest said respectfully, "That our lord be kind enough to visit the temple of Amun before going to the royal palace."

Ahmose said, smiling, "What a profitable and auspicious request to fulfill!"

33

Ahmose left the ship followed by his queens and the great men of his kingdom. The officers and soldiers who had fought with him from the first day greeted him and the king returned their salute. He climbed into a beautiful royal litter, the queens got into theirs, the litters were raised, and a battalion of the royal guard preceded them, with the chariots of the entourage following and, behind them, another battalion of the royal guard. The royal procession made its way toward the central southern gate of Thebes, which was decorated with flags and flowers, the doughty soldiers who had breached these same walls only yesterday drawn up on either side.

The royal litter passed through the gate of the city between two rows of bristling lances, after the guard of the walls had blown their bugles, and flowers and sweet-scented herbs fell on them as they entered. Ahmose looked around him and saw a scene amazing enough to startle the most composed soul. He saw all the people of Egypt at a single glance. He saw bodies covering the streets, the walls, and the houses; nay more, he saw souls purified by worship, love, and ardor. The air rang with the cheers rising from their hearts, the people enthralled by the sight of the Sacred Mother in the dignity of her old age and the venerability of her grandeur, and of her valiant great-grandson in the flower of his strength and youth. The procession moved as though plowing through a bottomless, billowing sea, souls and eyes hanging on it. It took several hours to cover the distance to the temple of Amun.

At the door of the temple, the king was received by the priests, who prayed for him at length and walked in front of him to the Hall of the Columns, where offerings were made on the altar. The priests chanted the Lord's hymn with sweet, melodious voices that continued resounding in their hearts long after. Then the chief priest said to the king, "My lord, permit me to enter the Holy of Holies, to make ready certain precious things that concern Your Majesty."

The king granted him permission and the man departed with a troupe of priests. They were gone for a short time and then the priest appeared once more, followed by the other priests carrying a coffin, a throne, and a golden chest. All these they placed in front of the royal family with respect and reverence and Nofer-Amun, advancing until he stood before Ahmose, said, in a magical, penetrating voice, "My lord, these things that I place before you for your inspection are the most precious relics of the Sacred Kingdom. Valiant Commander Pepi, of immortal memory, put them in my safekeeping twelve years ago, so that they might be out of reach of the enemy's greedy hands. The coffin is that of the martyred king Seqenenra and preserves his embalmed body, whose shrouds enfold grievous wounds, each one of which records an immortal page of bravery and sacrifice. The throne is his glorious throne, which fulfilled its rightful duty when he announced from it Thebes' word of defiance, choosing the sufferings of the struggle and its terrors over silence under a humiliating peace. This golden chest contains the double crown of Egypt, the crown of Timayus, last of our kings to rule a united Egypt. I gave it to Seqenenra as he left to fight Apophis. He plunged into the thick of the battle with it on his noble head and everyone in the valley knows well how he defended it. These things, my lord, constitute the sacred trust left by Commander Pepi and I praise the Lord that He extended my life so that I could hand them back to their owners, may they ever live in glory, and glory in them!"

The eyes of all turned to the royal coffin. Then all, with the royal family at their head, prostrated themselves and made humble prayer.

The king and his family approached the coffin and surrounded it. Silence enveloped them all but the coffin spoke to their hearts and innermost souls. Tetisheri, for the first time, felt weary. She supported herself on the king's arm, her tears hiding the beloved coffin from her eyes. Hur, resolved to staunch the Sacred Mother's tears and still the sufferings of her heart, said to Nofer-Amun, "Chief Priest, keep this coffin in the Holy of Holies until it may be placed in its grave with solemn ceremony befitting its owner's standing."

The priest took his master's permission to order his men to remove the coffin to the sanctuary of the Divine Lord. Then the priest opened the chest, took out the double crown of Egypt, reverently approached Ahmose, and crowned with it his curly hair. The people, seeing what the priest had done, all cheered, "Long live the pharaoh of Egypt!"

Nofer-Amun invited the king and queens to visit the sacred sanctuary and they proceeded there, Tetisheri still leaning on Ahmose's arm. They crossed the sacred threshold that separates this world from the next, prostrated themselves to the Divine Lord, kissed the curtains that hung before his statue, and prayed a prayer of thanks and praise for His preparing their success and restoring them in triumph to the motherland.

The king then left and went to his litter, as did the queens. The throne was loaded onto a large carriage and the procession resumed its progress to the palace between crowds that cheered and prayed, exulting and acclaiming the greatness of God, waving branches and scattering flowers. They reached the old palace toward the end of the afternoon. Tetisheri had been much affected. Her heart was beating hard and her breathing was irregular, so she was taken in her litter to the royal wing, where the queens and the king joined her and sat anxiously in front of her. However, she recovered her composure, and, by the strength of her will and her faith, she once more sat upright and looked tenderly into the beloved faces, saying in a weak voice, "Please excuse me, children. For the first time, my heart has betrayed me. How much has it borne and how patient it has been! Let me kiss you all, for when you are as old as I, the achievement of one's hopes brings on the end."

34

Evening came and night descended but Thebes knew nothing of sleep and stayed awake in revelry, the torches shimmering in the streets and suburbs, while the people gathered in its squares to chant and cheer and the houses rang with music and song. That same night, Ahmose did not sleep despite his exhaustion. The bed irked him, so he went out onto the balcony overlooking the vast garden and sat there on a luxurious divan in the light of a dim lamp. His soul wandered in the oppressive darkness, the tips of his fingers playing affectionately and tenderly with a gold chain, at which, from time to time, he gazed, as though his very thoughts and dreams emanated from it.

The young queen Nefertari joined him unexpectedly, excitement having driven slumber from her eyes. She thought that her husband was as happy as she and sat beside him full of gaiety and happiness. Smiling, the king turned toward her and her eyes fell on the chain in his hand. She took it in amazement and said, "Is this a necklace? How lovely! But it's broken."

Gathering his thoughts, he said, "Yes. It has lost its heart."

"What a pity! Where did it lose it?"

He replied, "I know only that it was lost against my will."

She looked at him affectionately and asked, "Were you going to give it to me?"

He replied, "I have put aside for you something more precious and more beautiful than that."

She said, "Why, then, do you grieve for it?"

Making an effort to speak naturally and calmly, he said, "It reminds me of the days of the first struggle, when I set off to seek Thebes disguised in the clothes of a trader and calling myself Isfinis. It was one of the things I offered people for sale. What a lovely memory! Nefertari, I want you to call me Isfinis, for it's a name I love and I love those who love it."

The king turned his face to one side to hide the emotion and yearning that were written on it. The queen smiled with pleasure and, happening to look ahead, saw the slowly moving light of a lamp in the distance. Pointing, she said, "Look at that lamp!"

Ahmose looked in the direction in which she was pointing. Then he said, "It's a lamp in a boat floating close to the garden."

The boatman seemed to want to draw close to the palace garden and let its newly arrived inhabitants hear the beauty of his voice, as though he would greet them on his own after all Thebes had greeted them together. Raising his voice, he sang in the silence of the night, his notes echoed by a reed pipe:

How many long years I lay in my room,
Suffering the pain of a grievous ill!
Family and neighbors, doctors, quacks,
All came, but the sickness confounded my physicians' skill.

Then you arrived, my love, and your charms surpassed their
  cures and spells—
For you alone it is who knows what makes me ill.

His voice was beautiful and captivating to the ear, so Ahmose and Nefertari fell silent, the queen gazing at the light of
the lamp with sympathy and tenderness, while the king looked
at the ground between his feet with half-shut eyes, the memories keening in his heart.